Lying To Love You

A Billionaire Romance

Nicola Jane

Copyright © 2019 by Nicola Jane – original version (Named Heart of Sin)

Copyright © 2023 by Nicola Jane.

All rights reserved.

No portion of this book may be reproduced in any form without written permission from the publisher or author, except as permitted by U.K. copyright law.

Meet the Team

Editor: Rebecca Vazquez – Dark Syde Books
Cover Design: Wingfield Designs
Formatting: Nicola Miller

Disclaimer:

This book is a work of fiction. The names, characters, places, and incidents are all products of the author's imagination and are not to be construed as real. Any similarities are entirely coincidental.

Spelling Note:

NICOLA JANE

Please note, this author resides in the United Kingdom and is using British English. Therefore, some words may be viewed as incorrect or spelled incorrectly, however, they are not.

Acknowledgements

This book is so out of my comfort zone and nothing like I've written before. If you're a regular reader of my work, thank you for sticking with me and exploring this side of my mind. If you're new to my books, welcome. I hope you enjoy.

Social Media

I love to hear from my readers and if you'd like to get in touch, you can find me here . . .

My Facebook Page

My Facebook Readers Group

Bookbub

Instagram

Goodreads

Amazon

Or, Linktr.ee, where you'll find all of the above plus my website.

https://linktr.ee/NicolaJaneUK

Contents

Playlist	IX
Chapter One	1
Chapter Two	34
Chapter Three	63
Chapter Four	93
Chapter Five	121
Chapter Six	150
Chapter Seven	176
Chapter Eight	197
Chapter Nine	235
Chapter Ten	259

Chapter Eleven	286
Chapter Twelve	308
Chapter Thirteen	330
Chapter Fourteen	356
Chapter Fifteen	377
Chapter Sixteen	407
Chapter Seventeen	430
Chapter Eighteen	461
Chapter Nineteen	487
Chapter Twenty	512
Chapter Twenty-One	530
1. A note from me to you	539
2. Popular books by Nicola Jane	541

Playlist

https://open.spotify.com/playlist/2EnKCY5InXhUQV0v5I8jDw?si=861ce5126ca24b7b

Red Flags – Mimi Webb
S & M – Rihanna
Womanizer – Britney Spears
Toxic – Britney Spears
Promiscuous – Nelly Furtado ft. Timbaland
Dangerous – Kardinal Offishall ft. Akon
Sweet Dreams – Beyoncé
Love the Way You Lie (Part II) – Rihanna ft. Eminem
Sweet Lies – Nathan Dawe ft. Talia Mar

24/5 – Mimi Webb
Without Me – Halsey
I Knew You Were Trouble – Taylor Swift
Good Without – Mimi Webb
What We Had – Sody
Out Of Reach – Gabrielle
Real Girl – Mutya Buena
Should I Stay – Gabrielle
Is it Just Me? – Emily Burns ft. JP Cooper
Glimpse of Us – Joji

Chapter One

Alivia

I hate being late. It makes me feel uneasy, and the day always seems to go wrong whenever I have to rush first thing. Luckily, I made up for sleeping in after my alarm by skipping breakfast and rushing my shower. It's so important that everything runs smoothly today.

I pause at the large glass door and take a deep breath, holding it for a second before slowly releasing it and then composing myself. I pull the heavy door and step inside. My heels click against the white marble flooring and the sound echoes around the vast reception area.

As I approach the glass desk, the receptionist looks up. Her perfect, flawless makeup makes me stare in awe. She is immaculate, with not a single crease in her bright white shirt. "Welcome to Cossacks. How can I help?" she asks clearly with a wide smile.

"I have an interview with," I pause, pulling the letter from my pocket and opening it, "Ms. Bradley at Glamour Cosmetics."

"Take the elevator to the second floor and report to the office there," she says, pointing a well-manicured nail in the direction of the elevators.

I follow her directions, and when the elevator opens, I step out onto more marble. This receptionist looks more relaxed, and she gives me a friendly smile. "Good morning. Are you here to see Ms. Bradley?" she asks, and I nod. "Please take a seat. She's with her son at the moment but shouldn't be too long."

I take a seat on a black leather couch and pull at the hem of my short grey dress. I used the last of my money to get this dress and I'm praying it gets me the job. I hear yelling from inside the office and I look at the receptionist, who rolls her eyes. "They always fight like that," she explains.

The office door swings open and a suited man walks out. His blue eyes fix on me, and I find myself holding in a breath. He's gorgeous, and I can't help but stare. His shirt pulls tight over his muscles as he moves, and I can see tattoos through the cotton material.

"I haven't finished yet, Vass, come back here," shouts a female from inside the office.

"Your nine o'clock has arrived," he shouts back, pushing the button for the elevator. It opens and I watch him step in. He turns to face me, and we lock eyes before he smirks, winking as the doors slide closed. I release my breath and try to gain control of the butterflies now fluttering in the pit of my stomach.

"Gorgeous, isn't he?" The receptionist sighs dreamily. I glance at her and nod. "He's the best fuck I've ever had," she whispers, and I raise my eyebrows. "We aren't together or anything. Vass is a playboy of epic proportions. I was lucky to get one night with him," she explains.

"Thanks for sharing," I mutter, because, honestly, what else is there to say?

"Ms. Caldwell, please come in. Sorry to have kept you waiting." I look up towards the office to find an older lady with a kind smile. I stand, straightening my dress, and follow her inside the office. It's immaculate. Everything inside is so shiny and white, it's almost clinical.

"I'm Jenifer, the CEO of Glamor Cosmetics. Do you use our products?" she asks, pulling out a blue file and placing it on her desk.

"Honestly, no," I say, and she glances up at me with an amused expression. "I use very minimal makeup, but I know all about your products and I've researched the company heavily."

"Really? Tell me something you've learnt," she says, pinning all her attention on me.

"That you started off selling products from home for a small company. You loved it so much that you trained in advertising and became top of your sales leader board within that company. They asked you to take on a permanent role, and once you gained the experience and knowledge that you needed, you went out on your own and began creating products under the Glamour name. You aim your products mainly at high-end stores because you use the best ingredients to give maximum results, so they're expensive but worthy of the price. The Glamour lipstick is your bestselling product to date, especially shade number eight, which is the most popular summer colour to wear this year and was featured in the London Fashion Show on several models."

Jenifer leans back in her seat and smiles. "You have done your homework. I'm impressed."

"Thank you. I really want this position. It's my dream job, and I'll work so hard for you. I came top of my class in marketing and research, and I have some amazing ideas."

"Your CV was pretty impressive, and I have no doubt that you can do this job and go far within this company." She pauses and looks at the file, then closes it and leans forward. "The thing is, something else has come up, and speaking with you makes me think you would be the ideal candidate to help me out."

"I'm listening," I say.

"How about I offer you almost double the pay of this position, a guaranteed office, a company car, and the promise of a career in my company afterwards, if you can pull this off?"

I laugh. "Who would turn that down? I'm in," I say.

"You might want to hear what it is first," she mutters. "My son was here this morning. His business is struggling at the moment, and due to the nature of the business, it needs special marketing, appealing directly to a certain clientele."

I nod enthusiastically. How hard can it be? And it'll give me a chance to impress Jenifer with my skills and knowledge. She'll be offering me management roles by the time I'm done. "Okay, what's his business?" I ask.

"Maybe it would be better to show you first?" she suggests.

"Sure, whatever you think."

Half an hour later, the car stops outside a set of black metal gates. The driver presses a button on a key fob and the gates slowly open. As the car crunches along the gravel driveway, a large, stately-looking home comes in to view.

It takes my breath away with its beauty. There are large pillars either side of a black double door. The steps leading up to the door are adorned with large pots overflowing with bright, beautiful flowers. There's a water feature set in front of the building with water cascading out of the centrepiece and trickling into the base.

"Wow, this is amazing," I gasp, already picturing the photos for my marketing campaign.

"This is The Luxe," Jenifer explains as she exits the car.

"I've heard that name before," I mutter, trying to remember where.

The driver opens my door, and I step out, my heels unsteady on the white stones. I follow Jenifer up the steps, and the door swings open without us having to knock. A large man in a black suit greets her warmly and gives me a nod.

"Maxim, is it busy today?" she asks.

"Yes, ma'am," he replies in a deep voice.

"Tell Vass I'm here, please," she says politely, and he gives a nod and wanders off in the direction of the winding staircase.

Jenifer leads the way through a door to the right. It opens out into a large bar area with low-hanging chandeliers and seating booths running along the walls. There are smaller tables running down the centre of the room.

We each take a stool at the bar, and a Hispanic-looking man places glass bottles of water in front of us. "Nice to see you, Ms. Bradley," he says in broken English. She gives him a warm smile in greeting, and he goes about serving other customers.

"Mother, what can I do for you? Haven't you had enough of me today?" The man I saw leaving her office earlier sidles up beside Jenifer and kisses her cheek.

"Yes, I have, Vass, but I want you to meet someone," she says, turning to me. "This is Alivia Caldwell. She's in marketing, and she is the answer to your problem."

Vass eyes me suspiciously. "Mother, we discussed this already. I'll sort it out, just give me time."

"Vass, you don't have time. It ran out. I'm paying Alivia a very good wage, and you'll accept her help. It'll solve all your problems, so that I can sleep easier," she says firmly, glaring at him.

Vass glances at me again, and his expression tells me he's not at all happy with the arrangement. "Do you know anything about gentlemen's clubs?" he asks.

The question takes me by surprise, and I stutter. "I . . . erm . . . well, no, I guess not."

"So, how are you going to be of any use to me here?" he asks.

"Vass, this isn't up for discussion. I said I was going to intervene had you not sorted anything by today and you haven't, so accept this is happening. Show Alivia to her office and get her set up. After a bit of research, I know she'll be perfect," says Jenifer sharply.

She stands abruptly. "Good luck, Alivia. If Vass gives you any problems, reach out to me." She hands me a business card, and Vass rolls his eyes. "I'll check in with you later, Vass. Play nice." And then, she swans off, leaving us alone. I bite my lower lip and look around the lavish room. I have no clue about gentlemen's clubs, but I know I can do this. I'm skilled, and with some research, I'll boss this.

"Right. I guess I should show you to the office then," says Vass, breaking the awkward silence. "This way."

I stand and follow him towards the staircase, wishing I hadn't worn heels today. They're squeezing my feet painfully, and each step is a reminder that I hate heels. We stop outside a door at the top of the stairs, and Vass opens it. I step inside, gasping as I take in the floor-to-ceiling bookshelf that is bursting with books. I love reading.

There are two desks, one at the back of the room under the large window and another to the side of it. "This is your office space. My secretary is at this desk. She's tied up at the moment, but you'll meet her soon. You can take that desk," he says, pointing to the one under the window. "I'm through here," he adds, pointing to a conjoining door. "But please knock or buzz me on the phone before you come in. Sometimes, I'm busy. Do you like sex, Alivia?" he asks, and I almost choke on my own saliva.

I cough. "Sorry, what?"

"You don't look like the type to let herself go. I bet you've been in a relationship since you were fourteen, lost your virginity to the guy, and now, you have a house and a pet dog and a boring, vanilla sex life where you fake an orgasm just so he gets off and lets you sleep."

He's almost correct, only the guy he's talking about dumped me for my friend just four weeks ago. "If you don't mind, I have some research to do," I mutter, heading for the desk.

He gives a small laugh before going into his office, returning minutes later with a box containing a new laptop. "Do your research and then come and find me. I'll show you around."

I take it and sigh in relief when he returns to his office, closing the door. I get he's unhappy about his mother stepping in and hiring me, but I have a job to do, and no amount of weird questions will disarm me enough to run out of here and give up my dream.

I spend the next hour researching the club. There isn't an awful lot in the media about The Luxe, apart from an opening night which Vass held when he took over the running of the club from his father. There are a lot of pictures of Vass, though, and in each one, he has a different woman on his arm. It seems he's quite the celebrity and has a bad boy reputation of being London's hottest bachelor. I laugh to myself, flicking through the pictures while wondering why women hook up with him if he's such a playboy. I jot down some ideas to get this club on the map and decide to go and see Vass for that tour.

I'm looking down at my notes as I push through the conjoining door, and when I glance up, Vass is glaring at me with what I can only describe as pure anger. Glancing to his left, I can see why. There's a short-haired blonde girl kneeling on the floor. It's odd enough that she's kneeling, but the fact that she's naked with her arms tied behind her back makes it so much worse. I press my lips together, my eyes widening in shock, and then I take a step back through the door and close it. I stand still for what feels like forever, and then I let out a long breath, giving my brain time to process what I just saw.

I'm still standing in the middle of the office when the conjoining door flies open and Vass storms in. He stops inches from me and points a finger in my face. "What did I say about knocking?" he yells.

"I'm so sorry, I completely forgot. I was so busy thinking of ideas that—" He cuts me off by placing a hand up in my face.

"I'm not interested in your excuses. If you can't follow simple instructions like knocking on my office door, then what use will you be to me?" he shouts.

Frankly, I'm quite offended by his slight overreaction. I take a step back. "I forgot. It won't happen again. You don't need to use that tone."

Vass places his hands on his hips and takes a deep breath before releasing it slowly, like he's trying to calm himself. "You'll need to sign a non-disclosure form before I show you around. Follow me."

We go back into his office, and I'm happy to see the girl is no longer there. He shoves a piece of paper across the desk, and I glance over it. It's a standard form about not talking to the media and such about what goes on at The Luxe, and so I scribble my signature across the bottom. Vass snatches it back and shoves it in his top drawer. "Let's get one thing straight. I don't want you working for me. This is completely down to my mother, who seems to think she has all the answers. You won't last two minutes here. I can guarantee that after I show you around, you'll run a mile. You have to be very open-minded."

"Or desperate," I mutter to myself, but he catches it, raising a brow.

"Anyway," he sighs, choosing to ignore my comment. "Let's get this over with, so I can get on with my day."

I follow Vass back out of the office and down the marble staircase. We walk through the entrance hall, where the reception desk is situated. A glammed-up girl is filing her nails and chewing gum. It irks me, but she flutters her eyelashes at Vass, and he winks. It's obvious he's employed her purely because she's gorgeous.

We go back into the bar area where I sat earlier with Jenifer. "Carlos," says Vass, leaning on the bar, "this is Alivia, my new marketing girl."

I frown at the demeaning introduction but shake the bartender's hand anyway. "Nice to meet you again, Carlos," I say politely.

Vass has already begun to walk off, so I follow quickly, my heels pinching with each step. He opens a set of large, white double doors which take us into another room. There's a stage at the front which is currently unoccupied and tables spread evenly throughout. I again notice the booths around the edge of the room, each with a large, deep dish in the middle where I assume ice and bottles are kept.

"This room is for the evening entertainment. We have shows lined up most nights. They vary, but I'll get the details to you. The booths are for privacy, and they cost extra to rent on top of the club membership fee," says Vass, continuing his walk through the room. "And in here," he says, pushing open another set of double doors, "is where people come when they've seen enough of the show."

The room in front of me is huge. Beds are set up throughout, and there are hooks on the walls and large wooden contraptions with handcuffs on chains. There's even a large cage hanging from the ceiling. I almost gulp in shock, but I realise Vass is watching me. He wants me to run. Instead, I smile and give a curt nod, indicating that he can continue.

"Couples, groups, whoever wants to join can do so in this room. It's a free-for-all in here," he says. "For privacy, there are rooms available, but this room is very popular."

Oh god, how I want to run. This isn't what I pictured when he said a gentlemen's club. I was thinking of the clubs my grandpa used to go to on Sunday afternoons while Gran cooked his lunch. The Legion was his favourite watering hole, and I know there were no rooms for kinky fuckery.

"Fantastic. I'm getting some great ideas," I say, forcing a smile. He smirks. "I mean about advertising." I clarify with a scowl, and he laughs.

"Stick around in the evenings and you'll get all kinds of ideas." He grins. "You'll be able to spice up that vanilla sex life."

"I don't have a vanilla sex life. Will you stop analysing me?" I huff, folding my arms and following him out of the room.

We go back through the bar and reception area, where he unlocks a set of black double doors. They lead us into a passageway, the walls and carpeted floor decorated in deep red. There are gold light fittings running along the walls, giving the passage a dim light. There are doors on both sides, and Vass opens the first one. "All these rooms are pretty much the same," he explains, stepping inside. There are comfortable chairs in the small room, all facing a mirror mounted on the wall. Vass pushes a button and the mirror turns into a glass window looking into another room. There's a bed inside and a table with various sex toys laid out neatly.

Vass smirks at me, noticing the blush that creeps up on my cheeks. "People like to watch. They come here and get a private showing from whoever feels like being watched. That could be a couple having sex, it could be a male or female masturbating, anything goes really."

I nod. "Right, excellent," I say with another forced smile.

"Do you like to watch?" he asks.

"That isn't appropriate," I mutter, stepping from the room. Standing so close to him when he's asking these personal questions has me wanting to run again.

"So, you like to be watched?" he presses.

"No, I didn't say that. I don't . . . oh Jesus, please just stop," I huff.

He grins. "You can't be a prude when you work here, Liv."

"My name is Alivia," I snap.

I follow him farther down the passageway to a door at the end. "These rooms are different," he says, opening the door. There's a comfy chair again and a television screen playing out a porn movie. The woman is screaming at the top of her lungs and it flusters me for a second, so I step out of the room.

"I get the picture," I mutter, marching back along the passage and out through the black double doors. Vass is hot on my heels.

"I'll show you the private rooms." *It's like a never-ending nightmare.*

We go back upstairs, and I take this time to gather my thoughts and remind myself that I need this job. He opens a white door and waits for me to step inside. The room is gorgeous, and it makes me gasp aloud. Vass steps in behind me and closes the door. "You like?" he asks, and I nod, staring in awe at the lavish furnishings that adorn the room. There're various shades of white and gold, and the biggest four-poster bed I've ever seen in my life. Everything about this room screams money. "We spent over a million trying to get the rooms right," he says.

"It's amazing," I mutter. "How much does it cost to rent a room like this?"

"Well, the club has memberships, and rooms depend on the type of membership you choose. This room would come under the gold membership. Our platinum rooms are similar to this, but they have large televisions and toys included, along with bathrobes, a spa bath, and a walk-in shower for two."

I make my way over to the floor-to-ceiling window and look out over the fields that run from the back of The Luxe. "It's worth paying the membership just for this room," I joke.

"Lay on the bed," he suggests. "It's amazing."

"I'll take your word for it," I say with an uncomfortable laugh.

"No, honestly, try it out. We went all over the world to get the best mattresses made with the right material and the perfect springs," he insists, gently leading me back towards the bed. I lower down and sit on the edge. He's right, it feels like the perfect kind of mattress, not too firm but not too bouncy.

I lay back and groan. "Wow, this is so comfy." My eyes close in pleasure. The last time I laid on a bed this comfy was . . . well, never. Vass sits next to me, and I open one eye.

"Your feet hurt," he states.

I frown. How does he even know that? In fact, how is he reading me so well? First, the crap sex life, and now, the feet. Before I can answer, he's running his hand down my leg and raising my foot. He flicks off my heel and my eyes almost bug out of my head. "What are you doing?" I squeak.

Vass grips my sore foot and squeezes gently, causing another groan to escape my lips. "Easing the pain," he says, rubbing and massaging the ache.

My brain is screaming at me to sit up and tell Vass to shove his foot rub up his cocky arse, but other parts of my body are reacting in a way I have never experienced before, which keeps me laying here while my new boss massages my foot.

Vass

My mother is the most infuriating woman I know. How dare she push this woman my way in the hope it appeases my grandmother long enough for her to sign the business over? Alivia doesn't fit here. I can smell her fear a mile off, and her innocent eyes have already been exposed to way more than she's ever seen before. I could tell she wanted to run when I showed her around, and when she saw the porn film, she about broke her neck to get out of the room.

I glance at Alivia's face, now relaxed and almost blissful. I find myself wondering if this is the face she'll pull after I've fucked her. If she keeps groaning like that, I may find out sooner than I think.

She opens her eyes and suddenly sits up. I wondered when her brain would kick into gear and tell her to wake the fuck up. "Was that good?" I ask with a wicked smile, and she rolls her eyes in a defiant show of courage. I've never wanted to spank a woman as much as I do right now when she rolls her eyes like that.

"Shall we go over my ideas now?" she asks, standing and pushing her feet back into the heels.

We get back to her office and Bianca, my secretary, is sitting at her desk. She blushes when she sees Alivia, knowing that the last time they saw each other, Bianca was on my office floor, naked and bound. Alivia's eyes widen and she looks between me and Bianca. "This is my secretary, Bianca," I say with a grin.

"Of course, it is." Alivia sighs, marching over to her desk and grabbing a notepad. I wink at Bianca and then lead Alivia into my office. Taking a seat behind the expensive oak desk, I rest my elbows on it and lean forward as Alivia opens her notepad.

"So, I was thinking we could start by getting in a photographer. I know a few good ones who will do this place justice. We can get a brochure up and running that we can market out to large companies. In the daytime, when the place is quiet, maybe we could consider opening up for business meetings. An exclusive club like this would be an ideal place for local businesses. There's a golf course just up the road, so we could target the clients there."

I watch her beautiful mouth move. She's excited and loves talking business. Her green eyes are sparkling, and her long dark lashes flutter as she chatters away. "I'd like access to your current client list. If I can research some of those, I'll be able to see what kind of clientele currently use The Luxe, and then I'll get a feel for who we need to target," she continues, oblivious to the way she has me hypnotised.

"How many sexual partners have you had?" I suddenly blurt out, and I inwardly hit myself. What is wrong with me today? The need to see her blush is spurring me on.

She gives me a stony stare. "Mr. Bradley, I don't appreciate the way you keep prying into my personal life. There are laws these days, and you're crossing all boundaries."

"Mr. Fraser," I correct her, and she gives me a confused look. "You said my name wrong. My mother is Bradley. She changed it after my father left her, but my surname is Fraser," I explain.

"Whatever," she huffs. "Why the interest in my personal life anyway?"

I shrug. I don't even know the answer, to be honest. At first, I was just trying to embarrass her so she would realise this position wasn't for her. But then I liked the blush on her cheeks, and now, well, now I just want to know. "I like to get to know my employees," I say.

"Yes, I noticed. You'll be asking me to kneel on your office floor naked next," she says, and I throw my head back and laugh. I like her frosty attitude and dry jokes.

"No, those moments are for special employees, like Bianca."

"I'd say lucky Bianca, but I don't feel she's lucky at all."

"I like your ideas. Get some photos and we'll look at brochures," I say, leaning back in my leather chair. Maybe she'll bring in new business. It can't hurt to have her think that's the reason she's here.

My office phone buzzes. "Yes," I answer.

"Mr. Fraser, I have your mother on the line," says Bianca.

"Okay, put her through." Once the call is connected, I place my mother on hold and turn to Alivia. "Thanks, Alivia," I say, dismissing her. I wait until she's gone back to her desk and reconnect the call. "Mother, always interrupting my day." I sigh.

"Oh, Vass, do stop pretending you hate me. How is it working out with Alivia?"

"Fine," I mutter. "She didn't run, if that's what you're asking me."

"Fantastic. I knew you'd like her," she says enthusiastically.

"Mother, I didn't say that. Stop meddling. I mean, she's good at the marketing, and it's obvious she wants to please, but I'm not so sure about the other thing. I'll sort it myself."

"Vass, you're out of time. Speak to the girl and get her on side. I've done a little digging, and she needs the money. There's nothing in her bank account, her rent is overdue . . . she ticks all the boxes."

"Stop meddling," I repeat, more firmly this time, before disconnecting the call.

Drumming my fingers on the desk, I need a distraction to take my mind off the bigger stuff and a certain brunette. I could fuck Bianca. So far, I've managed to control myself with that girl, strictly playing. If I go all the way, I'll have to get rid of her, and I can't be bothered to advertise the position and hold interviews.

I head down to the bar and find Mr. Clayton Hague is there with his wife. She makes a beeline for me and runs her hand along the lapel of my suit jacket. "Darling, it's so good to see you," she coos with a wide smile that shows off her perfect white teeth.

"Kathryn, how are you, and Clayton, of course?" I ask, glancing between the pair.

"We have the afternoon off from the office and thought we'd come in and see who was around," says Clayton.

"You're a bit early. The real games don't start until after seven today," I say, taking a water with lemon from Carlos.

"Are you free?" asks Kathryn, glancing at her husband for consent. He gives a nod, and I ponder the offer. I do need to burn off this stress, but I've avoided Kathryn because she gets a little too attached and what begins as a threesome always ends with her trying to push her husband out. She did the same to Alex last month.

"I have meetings all afternoon, but maybe another time," I suggest, and she pouts. "Deano is around here somewhere today. Check the main room," I add, taking my water and heading back towards the reception area.

Amy, the new receptionist, looks up at me and her face lights up. I hate that she chews gum at the desk and pays little attention to the job she's hired to do. I turn to Maxim, "Max, can you watch the front desk? I need a word with Amy," I say, and he gives a knowing nod. Amy stands in delight and takes my hand without hesitation. I can afford to lose Amy. She's terrible at the job, which is probably one of the reasons I hired her.

Chapter Two

Alivia

I'm sipping the coffee that Bianca made me while gawping at her in astonishment. "So, you're happy with that?" I ask, and she nods. "How did you even know you liked that kind of thing?"

"I didn't until I started working here. I swear, don't knock it until you've tried it," she tells me with a smile.

"I'm not brave enough. After recent events, I can quite happily live without men and sex for the rest of my life." I sigh.

"Messy break-up?" she guesses, and I nod.

"Move to Tower Hamlets, he said. We'll be happy, he said. And then I caught him in bed with my friend."

"No way," gasps Bianca. "What the hell?"

"I know, shocker," I mutter. "So, now, I have a crappy apartment in the worst area ever, and my landlord is the biggest sleazebag in the world. He offered to sleep with me to pay the rent." I shudder at the memory.

"Oh my god, did you?" she asks.

"God, no. He's about fifty years old and smells almost as bad as his apartment block."

Bianca laughs. "Well, this job pays well, so it's worth sticking around. I get bonuses and a clothing allowance. It's the best place I've worked, and the boss is a bonus all by himself."

"Doesn't he worry that employees will have him up on a harassment charge?" I ask.

"No, we sign a contract of consent. He isn't stupid, just a sex addict," she says. "And who in their right mind would turn him down? The guy is a god."

"Well, personally, I think you're crazy, but to each their own, I guess."

I watch the rain drizzle down the office window. Damn this weather—one minute, it's sunny, and the next, it's raining. I have no jacket and no money for a taxi, and thanks to Ms. Bradley, I'm stuck here, miles from my apartment. The office door opens, and Vass practically falls through it, fastening up his trousers. I raise an eyebrow, as he hasn't noticed me sitting here. Bianca left over an hour ago.

He looks up and freezes when he sees me. "What are you still doing here? Your hours are nine to five, and it's now," he looks at his expensive watch, "after six."

"It's raining," I say as a way of explanation.

"Then get a cab," he suggests. *If only it was that easy.*

"I didn't expect to be out this way today. My interview was with Glamour Cosmetics. This was totally out of the blue, so I didn't bring my purse," I say with a shrug.

"What were you planning on doing to get home, walking?" I nod, and he looks at me like I'm crazy. "The Luxe is miles away," he states, "and your feet already hurt from your stupid choice in footwear." He sighs heavily. "I'll take you."

"No, it's fine. I'll walk just as soon as this rain slows," I argue. I hate to put anyone out, especially him.

"Alivia, I'll take you," he snaps. "Get your stuff together."

I pick up my bag and follow him down the stairs. The receptionist is putting things into a box and snivelling. Another woman is consoling her, and when she sees Vass, she glares at him. He gives her a wink but continues on out the door with me following.

He presses his key fob towards a black Bentley SUV. He opens the passenger door, and I climb inside, impressed by the cream leather interior. The car is immaculate, which indicates that he doesn't have kids. I laugh at the thought of Vass having children with sticky fingers touching this interior.

He gets into the driver's seat. "Put your address into this," he says, handing me his satnav. The thought of him seeing my ugly little apartment in Tower Hamlets has me lying and putting in a nearby address. There's a posh apartment block overlooking the River Thames which is just five minutes away from my actual address.

I hand it back to him, and he glances at it and then at me. "You live in that new building?" he queries, and I nod. "Wow. I looked at those apartments when they were building them. Some were going for half a mill."

I shrug and stare out the window straight ahead. *Why the hell did I pick something so unbelievable?* Vass starts the engine and drives away from The Luxe. "What happened with the receptionist?" I ask. "She looked upset."

Vass slows near the gates, and while he waits patiently for them to open, he presses a button to lower his window. The gatehouse keeper comes from his little hut. "Guy, I'm expecting Ms. Collinsworth in half an hour. Can you tell her I've had to attend a last-minute meeting and I shouldn't keep her waiting too long? Have Maxim show her straight up to my room," he instructs. The man tips his cap and goes back into his hut.

"Sorry, I really don't mind walking if I'm keeping you from things," I mutter, hating that I'm an inconvenience.

He drives out the gates and follows the satnav left onto a quiet country lane. "The receptionist was chewing gum and filing her nails as we walked past her earlier today. Is that acceptable?" he asks.

"I noticed," I admit. "I wondered if she'd been hired just to sit and look pretty," I add with a smile.

"Nobody sits and looks pretty in The Luxe. Everyone has to pull their weight and work hard. Anyway, she was fired. You aren't keeping me from anything that can't wait. Annalise will understand," he says. "What do you plan on doing for the rest of the evening?"

Slobbing in my pyjamas and avoiding my sex-pest landlord, I think to myself. "Not much. I might head down to the gym for an hour."

"Is that safe, to go out alone this late?" he asks.

"Who said I'm going alone?"

"I just assumed. Is your vanilla boyfriend going?"

"I have no idea if Daniel still goes to the gym. When he was with me, he went every night, but I think back now and realise that was code for fucking around."

Vass looks at me and then turns his eyes back to the road. "Sorry, I didn't realise."

"Don't be, it isn't your fault."

"Were you together long?" he asks.

"Yeah, we had a house together. I met him when I was at school, and then we met up at a school reunion a few years later and hit it off. We were together for almost four years," I say.

"Have you been single long?"

"Four weeks," I mutter, and he glances at me again.

"Things are still raw?"

I shrug. "Not really. I've turned the love into hate and now it feels so much better," I say, leaving out the fact that Daniel cheated with Becca, my friend, and that we were really close. I'd met her through work. I was head of marketing, and when I hired her as a trainee, we became good friends.

We drive the rest of the way in silence. Vass stops the car directly outside the Riverside Development and turns to me. "Have a good evening. Should I send a car to collect you in the morning?"

"No, I'll get there. It's not a problem."

"Alivia, I'll send a car. You can't pay for a taxicab every day, it'll cost a fortune. My mother didn't think of that, did she?" he asks, and I shake my head with a smile.

"Thanks, Mr. Fraser," I say.

He gives a slight nod. "Vass . . . call me Vass." And then he adds, "Half past eight, tomorrow."

I get out, noting he doesn't drive off right away, so I turn awkwardly and wave, hoping he'll take the hint. He doesn't budge, and so I turn to the glass building. It looks rather intimidating this close. I can see a doorman on the other side of the door, chatting to another man sitting behind a desk. I glance back, and Vass is still waiting, so I take a deep breath and push the door, going inside.

Both men turn to me, and I smile and give a small wave. Vass is still watching, so I take another few steps. The men share an inquisitive look. "Can we help you?" asks one of them.

"I live at the back of here, near the college. My new boss out there in the nice car, he doesn't know that. I didn't want to show him where I live, so I gave this address, but now he's watching me, so I had to come inside," I explain, feeling foolish. Both men laugh.

"Go through those doors just over there. He'll think you've taken the stairs," says the one behind the desk.

"Thank you so much. Let me know when he's gone," I say, heading for the door.

A minute later, the guy pops his head around the door. "You're clear," he says, and I follow him out.

"I'm Alivia."

"Berny and Clive," says the doorman. "If he comes back, what should we tell him?"

"He won't be back. It was a one-off because of the rain," I say. "Thanks again for your help," I add, heading back out into the rain.

It takes me five minutes to walk home. I let myself in through the front door and then head up the first flight of stairs to my apartment. Keith is already standing outside my door. His white vest is stained and dirty, and his grey hair hangs limply over his forehead, looking greasy. "Did you get the job?" he asks, moving to the side so I can unlock my door.

I sigh. "Yes. I'll have your money by the end of the month."

He grabs my wrist. I look down at where he touches me and an involuntary shiver runs down my spine. His nails are too long and dirty. "That's not good enough, I'm afraid. I need it by tomorrow," he states.

"It's a new job. I can't ask for an advance when I've been there one day," I snap.

"Then you'd better find a way to pay. It's not like I haven't given you any options. I've been very understanding and accommodating."

I pull my wrist from his grasp and head inside my apartment, slamming the door in his weaselly face. It's times like this when I hate Daniel. I should be in my house with my old job, which I loved, by the way, but instead, I'm stuck here with a creepy landlord and a job in a sex dungeon. To add to my anxiety about the whole situation, my parents don't know about me and Daniel yet. I don't want to upset them, and they'll worry, especially when I tell them I left my job. I worked hard to help Daniel market his company brand, and the company was growing. People always wanted to buy or rent houses, so we both decided it was time to hire a trainee, and so I hired Becca. She was fresh out of college and eager to learn, and we both really liked her. I shake my head as images of Becca snuggled up in my bed with Daniel flash through my mind.

I jump in the shower and let the water wash the images away, but when they're replaced with ones of Vass and his gorgeous body, I switch the shower to cold. I need to think of ways to come up with rent before tomorrow, not how hot my boss is.

I finish quickly and head to the kitchen, placing my meal for one in the microwave. Turning on my television, I flick through the channels until I settle on an old sitcom. My mobile vibrates across the small table by the sofa, and I reach for it, accepting the call and placing it to my ear. "Hi, Mum, how's things?"

"Hey, Liv. Things are good this end. What about your end?"

"Same old, work, sleep, repeat. How's Dad?"

"Watching football. You'd think he'd get sick of the team losing. Are you coming home this weekend?" she asks hopefully. "We miss you and Dan."

I close my eyes as pain squeezes my heart. My parents adored Daniel, so this will hit them hard. "I don't know what our plans are yet. I'll text you on Friday," I say. She accepts that, and after a few more minutes of catching up, we say our goodbyes and I go and retrieve my pathetic excuse for a meal from the microwave oven and watch the sitcom, feeling the loneliness wrap around me.

I can hear an annoying buzzing. Opening one eye, I realise it's light outside, and then I throw the covers off and sit up, grabbing my phone in a panic. I have fifteen minutes to get dressed and get back to the Riverside for the car that Vass is sending to collect me. I rush around the apartment with my toothbrush in my mouth while I pull on a striped fitted dress. Looking in the mirror, I run my fingers through my hair. That will have to do, even though the waves look a little crazy. I squirt a dot of tinted moisturiser into the palm of my hand and rub it into my face, hoping it will cover the 'just out of bed' look.

I snatch my phone from the bedside table and grab my handbag as I leave the apartment, crashing straight into Keith. I'm pretty sure he stands outside my apartment and listens at the door. "Don't forget, today I need the—"

"Yes, Keith, I know," I snap before he can finish.

I run all the way to the Riverside, and as I round the corner, I spot a black SUV. Vass is leaning against it, his arms folded across his chest. His shades cover his gorgeous blue eyes and his suit jacket pulls tight against the strain of his muscly arms. He spots me before I can step back out of sight, and his smirk tells me he knows my game.

"Good morning, Liv," he says, pushing his sunglasses up on his head.

"It's Alivia, Vass. Sorry, I had to pop to the shop before work," I lie.

"Whatever you say. Get in."

I climb into the SUV and fasten my seat belt, ignoring the fact that Vass is watching me. He gets in, still smirking knowingly. "What did you need from the shop?"

"Stamps," I blurt out, and Vass laughs.

"I know you don't live in that building, Liv," he confesses.

I glare at him. "Of course, I do. What are you talking about?"

He looks back at the building and then to me. "Okay, prove it. Take me up to your apartment."

"I'm not showing you my apartment. Besides, we need to get to work."

"I'm the boss, I can be late." I watch in horror as Vass steps back out of the SUV and then turns back to me. "Come on."

"Look, Vass, let's forget that and get to work. I have a lot to do today." I groan as he begins to walk towards the building, and I begrudgingly get out of the SUV. "Okay, just stop. You win, okay, I don't live here."

He turns to me with a smug smile. "Don't you think I check out my employees? I knew you didn't live here last night."

"So, you let me lie and then walk the rest of the way home in the rain," I huff, getting back into the SUV.

He follows, clipping his seatbelt into place while laughing. When he drives out of the carpark, he turns right instead of left. "Where are you going?" I ask. "It's that way."

"I want to see why you were hiding your real apartment."

"You really don't. It's an awful place to live, with a terrible landlord." I sit upright, wiping my sweaty hands over my dress, and staring wide eyed at his relaxed face. Vass doesn't seem to feel my panic and drives us back to my apartment. I give him a defeated look as he steps from the car and pray silently that Keith isn't around.

Vass

I see the apprehension on Alivia's face. She doesn't want me here, and I don't understand why. Is she ashamed of where she lives? It doesn't look great from the outside, but I'm not the kind of person to judge, and she needs to know that.

Alivia trudges up the steps leading to the building and pushes her key into the lock. It opens and an elderly man stands in the entranceway sniggering at her. I don't like the vibes this man gives off, and I notice the way Liv's shoulders tense up. He makes her uncomfortable. "You got it already? What did you do, sell your body?" He grins.

"I forgot something," she mutters, pushing past him. He doesn't make it easy for her to get past and she's forced to brush against him. I flex my fingers before clenching my fists. I don't like the way he leers at her. His eyes fall to me, they're full of suspicion but he steps out of my way and I follow her.

We get to her door, and she opens it. I'm pleasantly surprised. The décor is fresh and clean, and her furnishings are pretty and girly. Once inside, she turns to me. "See, nothing exciting."

"What was he talking about downstairs?" I ask.

She fidgets with her bag. "Ignore him. I told you, he's weird."

"He's your landlord?"

"Yeah, Creepy Keith is his nickname," she says with a small, sad smile.

"You owe him rent?" I ask, and she shakes her head.

"Look, are we going to the office or not?" I follow Liv out and back downstairs, where creepy Keith is still waiting in the entrance hall.

"Don't forget the rent," he barks as we head out. I turn back to him, fixing him with a steely glare.

"How much does she owe?" I snap, and he looks to Alivia, who shakes her head at him. "Ignore her. How much?"

"Six hundred and fifty," he replies.

"Jesus, for this shithole?" I mutter, pulling out my wallet and counting out the notes. I hand him a bundle of fifties, and he frowns at me. "You don't take fifties?" He nods with a crooked smile that shows off his stained teeth, holding out his greedy hand.

I shake my head in disgust and guide Liv from the building and back to my car.

When we get in the car, I turn to her. "Liv, you can't stay there. The guy's a creep."

"He's okay. You get used to him. You shouldn't have paid the rent. I was sorting it. I can't pay you back until I get paid."

"Don't worry about that. I wouldn't put it past him to offer you another way of paying. He was undressing you with his eyes," I say with a shudder. The look she gives me tells me I'm right. "Jesus Christ, you can't stay here."

"He won't bother me now until next month, and I should be able to pay him then," she says. My mother's words ring in my ear. Maybe Alivia would go for the deal.

Once we get to The Luxe, Alivia goes straight to her office. Bianca is already waiting in mine with a coffee and bagel. "Good morning, Sir," she says with a smirk. I slap her arse as I pass her, and she gasps.

"How's the new girl working out?" I ask.

"I like her. She's nice, and she has some great ideas," Bianca replies.

There's a knock on the office door and Bianca opens it. Clarisse doesn't wait for an invite, she just marches in without acknowledging Bianca, which annoys me. I give Bianca a nod, dismissing her, and she closes the door quietly.

"How dare you fuck the receptionist and then sack her? Do you know how hard it's getting for me to dodge your bullets?" yells Clarisse.

I lean back in my chair and give her a cocky smile. "Good morning, Clarisse."

"Don't 'good morning' me, Vass. She was so upset, I ended up paying her two months wages with the promise of a glowing reference. I don't want to give her a glowing reference because she was fucking shit at the job," she shouts.

"That's exactly why I sacked her," I said. "You're the office manager. You should have sacked her ages ago." I'm pushing my luck, and Clarisse looks fit to burst.

"Fuck you, Vass. Who did you leave with?"

"My new marketing manager," I reply, wiggling my eyebrows.

"Oh joy, another woman for you to fuck and chuck," she groans. "How old is this one?"

"Actually, she's Jenifer's idea. She went for an interview for the position at Glamour Cosmetics. Jenifer saw something in her and brought her here. She thinks Alivia is the one. She's twenty-three," I tell her.

"Really? Well, that's a turn up. Although your Mum did warn you that she'd find someone if you didn't. Twenty-three is a little young, though. Will she go for your thirty-year-old arse?"

"I'm only seven years older, and I've had younger." I grin. Clarisse sighs, sitting down in the chair opposite my desk. "You know, this would all go away if you'd just agree to do it."

"Your grandmother knows I'm not into you like that, Vass," she says with a laugh.

"You could pretend. You used to love my cock," I mutter, and she laughs harder.

"Like I've said a million times, you're the reason I prefer women."

There's a knock on the conjoining door and Clarisse jumps up to open it, delight in her eyes. She steps back, allowing Liv to come in, and once Liv's back is to her, she gives me the thumbs up. "Sorry, I just wanted to run some things by you," Liv says politely, and Clarisse grips her heart in a mocking gesture.

"I'm free. Ignore Clarisse, she isn't important," I drawl, scowling in her direction.

Alivia looks at Clarisse and smiles. "Actually, I'm quite a big deal around here," says Clarisse.

"I'm the one who soothes the broken hearts you leave behind."

"Go and bug someone else, I have work to do." I sigh, and she blows me a kiss before leaving the room. "Sorry about that. You'll get used to her. She's the office manager," I say to Liv.

"She seems nice. You're good friends?" she observes, and I nod. Our mothers were best friends, so we naturally became close because our parents were always together. We tried being together in a relationship, but it didn't work. We were better at being friends, and then as Clarisse got older, she admitted that she was bisexual. We still hook up occasionally—if I have a willing girl wanting a threesome, Clarisse will always oblige.

We spend the next hour going over ideas and decide to arrange a meeting with the board. This is an ideal opportunity to introduce my grandmother to Alivia, not that I've decided if I'm going ahead with what my mother wants, but it wouldn't hurt to introduce her. I email the board members and schedule the meeting for Friday morning. Then I call my mother and tell her that Alivia has returned for a second day, meaning I haven't managed to scare her away. "Did you offer Alivia a company car?" I ask.

"Yes. I had to sway her to take you on somehow," she replies. "I've spoken to Callum and an order has been put in for a Mini Cooper, I believe."

"Cancel that. I'll sort the car," I say. The line goes quiet, and I know her brain is going overtime wondering why I'm offering to sort the car. I couldn't give her an answer even if she asked me, but something inside makes me want to look after Liv and I hate the thought of her driving in our standard Mini Coopers that we offer other staff. No, Liv is different and she deserves better.

I look into the brown paper bag that Bianca dropped in for my lunch. The chicken salad sub doesn't look too appetising today. I pop my head into their office, where both Bianca and Alivia are tapping away on their laptops. "Liv," I say, and she glances up.

"Alivia," she corrects me, and I smile.

"Alivia, have you had lunch?" I ask. She shakes her head. "Great, follow me." I know she probably doesn't have the money for her lunch, and I could use the company.

We head out to my SUV. "Where are we going?" she asks. From the little time I've known her, I'm pretty sure she wouldn't want a pity lunch, so I tell a white lie.

"A lunch meeting with a company that makes fantastic brochures. I thought I could introduce you." She seems to buy this because she gets into the car without another comment.

Ten minutes later, I stop outside my favourite Italian restaurant. I often eat here, so the owners know me well. Alivia glances at me. "I thought you meant a sandwich somewhere."

Once inside, Giovanni greets me with so much enthusiasm, even Liv raises her brow in gest. "Come, come," he says, guiding us to a table for two.

Liv shakes her head. "Oh, we have someone joining us," she says, and Giovanni looks to me for direction.

I wave my mobile phone in the air. "I just got a cancellation text, but we're here now, so we should eat," I say. Alivia scowls at me, lowering herself into the chair that Giovanni pulls out for her.

"Why do I feel like I've been tricked into lunch with you?" she asks warily.

"You know, you should be thankful. I have women lining up for a date with me," I say, with a cocky grin.

She opens the menu that Giovanni hands to her. "This is not a date," she says firmly. "And, yes, I've read about the most eligible bachelor in London. It must be hard for you batting these women away, you poor man."

I grin wider. "You have no idea, Liv."

"Alivia," she corrects, and I nod.

The waiter approaches us with a glass bottle of spring water. He places two glasses in front of us with a slice of lemon in each and pours us each a glass. "Would you like wine or anything else?" I ask Alivia, and she shakes her head.

As predicted, Alivia tries to order the cheapest thing on the menu, a green salad. I refuse to feed her rabbit food and order her a spaghetti carbonara because it's the best thing I've ever tasted, and I'm certain she needs the carbs.

Chapter Three

Alivia

My stomach growls from the amazing smells of the Italian food. A plate of garlic bread and olives is placed in front of us while we wait for our lunch. "Go ahead, eat something," insists Vass.

I pop an olive into my mouth just to keep him quiet. "So," I start, "why would you invite me out to a fake business meeting when you have fangirls wanting to date you?"

"I didn't want to eat lunch alone. I've seen Bianca naked, so lunch would give her false hope that I was interested in something more. Fangirls only want one thing, and you look like you need a good meal inside you."

"Bianca's a nice girl. Why wouldn't you want to date her?" I ask.

"I don't date," he says simply.

"What, like ever?" I ask, not quite believing that someone as gorgeous as Vass never dates, especially when he clearly gets a lot of attention.

He shrugs. "It's too complicated, especially when you have a business like The Luxe."

"I'm sure there are women out there who would accept it," I say.

He laughs. "Find me one and I'll consider dating her. She doesn't just have to accept The Luxe—it comes with all kinds of demands. I'm not a normal, vanilla kind of guy," he says with that bad boy glint in his eye.

I feel myself blushing. I want to know more, but I'm too shy to ask a man I barely know about his sex life. He intrigues me, though, and so I bait him. "I don't think it would bother me. It's clearly a great money maker. I guess the unsociable hours might be an issue if you spend lots of late nights there, but if you made time to fit me in, I wouldn't complain," I say. Realising what I've said sounds like a total come-on, I freeze mid-olive popping. "Oh god, I wasn't coming on to you then. I mean, I just meant . . ." I give up, not able to backtrack out of that.

"I know what you meant, relax," he assures me. "Girls think they can handle it, they start off with your mindset, and the money helps, but I can't give up the lifestyle. I like the sex too much."

"Oh." I gasp, finally realising that he means he takes part in the evening activities. "That is a lot to ask of someone," I add with an awkward laugh.

Our meal arrives and my mouth waters as the spaghetti is placed in front of me. It smells so amazing. I don't remember the last time I had a cooked meal in a restaurant. Daniel was always too busy to go out to eat, although it turns out he went out quite a lot with Becca. "So, this landlord," begins Vass, and I roll my eyes.

"Don't worry about it. I can handle creepy Keith."

"Do you need a wage advance?"

"No, you already kind of gave me one today by paying the rent. You've been so kind, and I really appreciate it, but I'll be okay," I insist.

"Can your parents help you out?" he suggests.

"They would, but they don't live nearby, and I haven't been totally honest with them," I admit.

"About creepy Keith?"

"No, about everything. I moved to Tower Hamlets with Daniel to help start his property business. My parents love him so much and it will break their hearts when I tell them we're no longer together. I want to get back on my feet, so they can see I'm doing okay," I explain.

"I get that. Well, you're halfway there now you have a job. Why did you leave the last job?" he asks.

I feel like I'm coming across as such a sad case, but there's no way out of the explanation. Vass will need to contact Daniel for my reference anyway, and when he sees the position I had there, he'll wonder why I went for an interview at a cosmetics firm, even if it is a well-known brand. "It was Daniel's company. When I took the job, it was only supposed to be short-term, just while he got up and running. I ended up staying."

"I guess it would have been awkward to stay after he cheated on you."

"A little. The fact that his girlfriend also works there and has now stepped into my position was even more awkward," I add with a weak smile.

"Ouch," says Vass.

"Have you ever been cheated on?" I ask, taking another mouthful of the delicious creamy spaghetti.

Vass raises his brow and grins. "No, Liv, I don't stick around to be cheated on."

"It's Alivia, and, yes, the receptionist at your mother's firm mentioned you're a 'hit 'em and leave 'em' kinda guy."

He laughs. "Usually, although there are exceptions."

"Anyone ever turn you down?" I ask, placing my fork down.

"No," he says with another cocky grin, and I shake my head. I can believe that no one has ever turned him down. The way his eyes flash with a devilish glint is enough to have any woman fall to her knees, but topped off with that hot body and those strong arms . . . the man's a god.

"Don't you ever get bored?"

"Of sex on tap and no nagging wife?" He shakes his head. "It's the best life ever."

Once back at the office, Bianca practically pounces on me. "So, what did he want? Where did you go?" she asks eagerly.

I place my bag down and take my seat. "Just for lunch. The meeting was a no-show, so we just had something to eat and came back here."

She eyes me suspiciously. "Why?"

"Because it was lunchtime and neither of us had eaten."

"Vass never takes people out to lunch. It doesn't make sense."

I shrug. The last thing I want to do is piss off Bianca, as she's been really nice to me. "It was very awkward. He didn't talk much," I lie.

Vass comes into the office, watches me for a second, and then turns to Bianca, "Ready?" he asks, and she nods eagerly, standing from her chair.

"Can you take messages if anyone calls?" Bianca directs me, and I give a nod. Vass is back to watching me with an intensity that wasn't there over lunch.

"We'll be unavailable for around an hour," he says, and then he takes Bianca's hand and leads her from the office. I stare after them. It sounds silly, but I have an ache in my chest. I want to know where they're going and what they're doing. Instead, I busy myself with work. I have no right to think about Vass in that way--he's my boss and a self-confessed manwhore.

It's been over an hour and they still haven't returned. I feel fidgety and decide I need to walk. I do my best thinking when I'm walking, plus the photographer is coming tomorrow and I could do with looking around again to see which areas I want to photograph.

I head downstairs, where the office manager, Clarisse, is on the front desk chatting to an older couple. They have an air about them that screams rich. She catches my eye and smiles, and then I overhear her tell the couple that Vass is in the main room training a new girl. I bite on my lower lip. It's almost like a compulsion—I have to see what they're doing. Besides, I reason, it's not being nosey if I'm looking for photo opportunities.

No one pays much attention to me as I pass through the bar area and head for the large, white double doors. I pause for a second and look around. I catch Clarisse watching me from the bar doorway, a smile tugging on her lips. She isn't telling me no, so I quietly push one of the doors and slip inside.

I stay by the doors. The lights are low and the room looks mysterious, and my eyes are drawn to the stage at the front of the room. Bianca is on some kind of cross, completely naked and tied by her wrists and legs. Vass is standing in front of her, his back is to me. His stance is tall and guarded, like a predator. He's removed his shirt, and I watch in awe as his muscles bunch together with every little movement. He raises some kind of whip and runs it over Bianca's stomach. She whimpers, and he cracks it against her skin. "What did I say about making noise?" he roars.

"Sorry, Sir," replies Bianca meekly.

He presses the whip between her legs, and Bianca presses her lips together. I assume she's trying to keep quiet. He begins to rub her vigorously, and she throws her head back with pleasure.

I feel like I'm intruding being here, and I'm not sure how either of them would react if they saw me. I slip back out the doors and into the bar.

Leaning back against the door, I take a deep breath. "Hot, isn't he, when he's all riled up like that?" asks Clarisse, and I jump in fright. I didn't see her waiting there. "He has so much control over himself, and I find that a bigger turn-on than actually fucking him."

"Oh, you and he are . . ." I begin, but she laughs and shakes her head.

"God, no, he wishes," she says and then saunters off towards the bar.

I get back into the office and let out a long sigh. I've never watched anyone being intimate before, unless you count the time that Daniel talked me into watching a porn film with him, which didn't go too well because I spent the entire time giggling at the stupid faces they pulled and the unbelievably fake orgasms they were acting out. But, oddly enough, seeing Vass like that gave me all the feels. I shake my head, silently screaming at myself to get a grip. I'm on day two of a job I desperately need, and having dirty sex with Vass Fraser can never happen.

I check my emails and do more research on The Luxe. I go through the pictures of Vass that are all over the internet, and now that he's given me his real surname, a lot more come up in my search. Clarisse appears in a few of them, and I click on one featured in London's Times newspaper. It's dated last month.

'Hot bachelor Vass Fraser was spotted at the invite-only opening of Las Deux this evening. It's said to have an exclusive guest list of over four hundred hot celebs, some of whom are attending this evening's event. Mr. Fraser declined to comment on whether he and Ms. Clarisse Underwood (pictured) are dating, but our own body language expert says the signs are definitely there. This is the sixth time they have been snapped together in the last three months. We're putting our money on Vass being off the dating market very soon. Sorry, ladies.'

I lean back in my chair. Vass didn't correct me when I asked if they were good friends, and

Clarisse didn't seem bothered that he was in a room with a naked woman. He did point out that some women were an exception to his 'bag 'em and bin 'em' rule. My thoughts are interrupted when Vass returns. He looks cool and calm as he pins me with his intense stare again. This time, I look away, turning my attention to the computer screen.

"Are you okay?" he asks.

I look back to him and smile. "Yes, of course. Are you?"

He nods. "Bianca will be back shortly. Any messages?"

I rip off the top page of my notepad and hold it out to him. "Nothing urgent. Ms. Collinsworth asked that you call her back about this evening's dinner arrangements."

He glances down at the paper and gives a nod before disappearing into his office. Bianca returns minutes later. Her cheeks are rosy, and she looks fresh out the shower. "Sorry, time ran away. Everything okay while I was gone?" she asks.

"Yeah, I passed the messages to Vass. Nothing urgent." I avoid looking at her face, feeling embarrassed now that I saw her naked.

We work for another hour in silence and then I finally look up. "Bianca, is Vass dating Clarisse?" I ask.

She pauses her work and looks up at me. "No, they're old friends. Why?"

"I was researching the company and got side-tracked with newspaper articles. Just gossip rags," I mutter, waving my hand dismissively.

"She spends a lot of time here, and I think they hook up on certain things," she says with a shrug.

"Like what?"

"Well, yah know, group sex and threesomes. Clarisse is bisexual and she's happy to share Vass with another woman."

"Wow, that's weird, isn't it?"

"Not really. Vass doesn't do relationships, and Clarisse knows that better than anyone." The door opens and a tall, suited man comes in. He's good-looking, and Bianca instantly glows when she sees him.

"Hey, gorgeous, you okay?" he asks, swooping down and kissing her on the cheek.

She smiles. "I'm great, thanks to you, Alex," she says.

"Glad I arrived when I did. Always love to finish a job." He winks, and Bianca blushes and grins.

"This is Alivia," she introduces. "She's going to be looking after the marketing side of things here."

Alex approaches, holding out his hand. I take it, and he gently pulls me to stand, letting his eyes run up my body. I'd usually be outraged at this type of behaviour, but instead, I find myself blushing. Something about the men in this place turns me into a quivering wreck. "You are gorgeous," he states sincerely. "Please tell me you're single."

"Alex, stop chatting up the staff and get in here," Vass shouts, making me jump in fright. He's standing in the conjoining doorway glaring at the two of us. His heated stare has me taking my seat quickly and fidgeting with my fingers like a schoolgirl caught kissing behind the bike sheds.

"You kept Liv a secret, didn't you?" Alex smirks, shoving his hands into his trouser pockets and not budging from my side.

"It's Alivia," snaps Vass, and my eyes meet his. It sounds sexy when he says my name like that.

"Touchy. You don't normally mind me chatting up the staff. In fact, just an hour or so ago, I was fu—"

"Get in here," snaps Vass, stomping back through to his office before he can finish.

Alex follows after him at a slower pace. "Whoops. Someone needs to release that anger," he says quietly, so only we can hear him.

Once the door closes, Bianca turns to me. "Okay, total truth, Vass or Alex?"

"Both," I say with a grin.

"At the same time," adds Bianca, and we burst into a fit of laughter. "Alex is Vass's best friend."

"Was he the reason you were gone over an hour before?" I ask. The words they exchanged made me think they've hooked up.

"My god, the man is a machine. There is no end to his talents, and when I say big, I mean huge." She giggles, placing her hands a good space apart to indicate Alex's size.

"And Vass?" I query, the words slipping out my mouth before I can stop them, I resist the urge to slap my hand over my mouth.

"Never seen it, let alone touched it." She pouts. "He doesn't let me touch him at all."

"Oh, I assumed when I saw you on his floor yesterday that you were, well, yah know."

"No, we just play. He's teaching me some stuff, so I can partner up with a member of The Luxe."

"Sounds fun," I say with a frown. I'm not sure how much he can teach her if he hasn't had sex with her and she isn't allowed to touch him.

It's five o'clock exactly when Vass comes back into our office. "Let's go, Liv," he says, holding up his car keys.

"It's Alivia, and I can walk this evening. Look," I say, pointing outside, "no rain."

"I'll take you. No arguments."

He stops the SUV outside my apartment building and asks, "Shall I walk you inside?"

"No, I'm good."

"What are you doing tonight?"

I shrug. "Maybe the gym. I don't know. What's your obsession with what I do after work?"

"I just want to know what you do all alone in that little apartment all night," he says with a shrug.

Getting out of the SUV, I turn back to him with a daring smile. "I walk around naked." I slam the door and head up the steps quickly, Vass's shocked expression making me smile all the way up to my door.

I chuck the meal for one back into the freezer and sigh. It looks so unappetising since the amazing carbonara I had for lunch. There's a light tap on the door and I groan, I can't face creepy Keith this evening.

"You got your rent, so what the hell do you want now?" I yell, making my way to the door. I pull it open and press my lips closed when I see Vass leaning against the frame in shorts and a vest.

"What are you doing here, and what are you wearing?" I ask with a laugh. I'm used to seeing him in a shirt and tie.

"You aren't naked," he states.

I smile wider and bite on my lower lip. "You caught me at a bad time. I can't cook naked."

"In that case, get your gym gear on. We're going for a workout." The last thing I feel like doing is going to the gym, and my expression tells him that. "We can either go to the gym or sit in your apartment naked together."

Within five minutes, I'm in my gym gear. When I step into the living room, Vass is holding a photo of me and Daniel. He glances at me. "Why do you keep a photo of him?"

I feel my face turn crimson at being caught out. "I loved him," I say simply, and he frowns and places it back on the shelf.

"You don't like to wear many clothes to the gym?" he asks, eyeing my short shorts and cropped top. I look down at my get-up.

"Should I change?" I ask.

"Hell no. I want to see that arse on the running machine. Just make sure I get the machine behind you," he jokes, and I swat his arm.

We decide on my gym, seeing as it's a five-minute walk from my place. We take a steady jog so that we're warmed up and ready to work out. It's been at least three weeks since I came to the gym, and I'm dreading it. I sign us both in at the reception desk, putting Vass down as my guest, and then we head up to the second floor. It's fairly quiet for a Tuesday, which is good because it means we won't have to wait for equipment.

I push the glass door and freeze, causing Vass to run into the back of me, jolting me forward so I almost fall flat on my face. Saved by strong arms catching me, I slowly look up into the eyes of Daniel.

"Careful . . ." he starts but realises it's me and stops. "Liv," he mutters. We stay like that for a few seconds, his arms around my waist as we look into each other's eyes. There's still that pull between us. Vass steps forward and takes my arm, gently pulling me back to his side.

"Are you okay?" Vass asks, and I nod, not taking my eyes from Daniel. It's been four weeks since I last saw him, and the pain doesn't seem to hurt so much now.

Vass

I recognise Daniel from the photograph I was just examining in Liv's apartment. She's still staring at him, and I can see in his eyes that he's checking her out. The fact he knows her body and has seen her completely naked and vulnerable has me clenching my fists with agitation. I instantly hate this guy and the way he's looking at her.

"Liv, how are you?" he asks.

"I'm good," she replies politely. "You?" Daniel nods and his eyes flash to me for a second, prompting Liv to also look at me. "Sorry, this is Vass, my—" I cut her off, leaning forward to shake Daniel's hand.

I grip it firm and smile. "Her boyfriend."

"Oh, I didn't know you'd met someone," he says, looking at Liv like he's annoyed. I feel Liv's eyes burn into the side of my head, but I don't look at her. This guy needs to know she's moved on so he doesn't try and worm his way back into her bed . . . and I can tell he wants to.

"Should she have announced it?" I ask. He doesn't get a chance to answer before a bouncy blonde runs over to us. She freezes when she sees Liv and grips onto Daniel's arm like she's worried Liv will snatch him from her. Liv's face morphs into one of anger, so I take her hand and give it a small squeeze, letting her know I'm right here for her.

"Alivia, I didn't expect to see you here," she says in a squeaky, annoying voice. She looks at me and her face breaks into a smile. "Oh my god, you're Vass Fraser." I give a nod and a tight smile.

"Was I supposed to change my gym as well as my job and home?" asks Liv coldly. Daniel and the girl exchange a wary look.

"I'm glad I bumped into you actually, Liv," says Daniel. It's on the tip of my tongue to correct him, but I refrain. I wonder why she doesn't correct him like she does me, and I ignore the feeling that gives me.

"Shall I leave you to talk?" I ask her, but she shakes her head, squeezing my hand.

"No, whatever he needs to say can be in front of you."

"Oh my god, are you two together?" shrieks the girl. I find her irritating, and I wonder why the hell Daniel would leave Alivia for her.

"I'm having trouble with the website and I wondered if you'd come and have a look. There're things I need to add to it and, well, you did all of that, and I can't get it to look as amazing as you did," he says. I want to laugh in this douche's face. Who the hell does he think he is?

"I'm sorry, Daniel, you'll have to get someone in to sort that. I don't work for you anymore, remember," Alivia responds, sounding smug.

"But you set the site up. No one knows how to access it to change it," he says.

"I work for a new company now, so I really don't have the time," she replies firmly.

"Come on, Livvy, not even for me?" he asks with a small, cheesy smile. *God, I want to hit him.*

"Her name is Alivia," I blurt out. Him using pet names in front of me and his new girlfriend is just disrespectful. He glares at me for a second and then goes back to Liv.

"Betty misses you," he says, and the girl glares at him. It's the kind of look that a girl gives her man when he's fucked up big time, and I know she's going to lose her shit when they leave here.

"It was good to see you both. Take care," mutters Liv, pulling at my hand and leading me away.

I watch her cautiously as she chucks her hand towel over the rails of the running machine and jumps on without a word. She starts off slow and then builds it up to a full-on run. It's obvious she needs a minute, so I head towards the bench to lift until she's ready.

Liv stays on the running machine for at least twenty minutes. Her face is glowing and her back glistens with sweat, and I can't deny that it turns me the fuck on. I watch as she fills her water bottle and takes a long drink. Then she pulls her long hair up into some kind of knotted pile on her head and ties it. Other guys around the weights stop and watch her too, and I like that she doesn't even know how beautiful she is.

I work on my biceps, still watching as she looks around the gym to decide where to go next. A short man with oversized muscles approaches her and says something that makes her laugh. I pick a heavier weight, keeping my eyes fixed on them chatting. Her body language is flirty and it instantly pisses me off. The pumped-up meathead pulls out his mobile phone—*who the hell carries a mobile in the gym*—and passes it to Alivia, who taps in what I assume is her number. She laughs again, and I roll my eyes. "Excuse me, would you spot me on the bench?" A blonde is standing in front of me, blocking my view of Liv. I look around her with a frustrated sigh.

"I'm already lifting. Isn't someone else free?" I ask in an annoyed tone, then I freeze. *What the hell am I saying? Why am I watching Liv and getting pissed over her chatting to another guy? This doesn't happen to me, and I certainly never turn my attention away from a gorgeous female.*

Before I can apologise to the blonde, Liv is approaching and the girl has walked away to ask another guy to spot her. "Want to go on the bikes together?" asks Liv, and I nod, following her to the two free bikes.

"You pushed pretty hard on the runner. You feeling better now?" I ask.

Liv shrugs. "It was just a shock seeing him like that. I haven't been to the gym for a while. Maybe I should change to another," she mutters.

"Well, you shouldn't have to, but I know a really good gym near The Luxe. I can get you free membership," I say with a wink. When she looks at me confused, I tell her about the gym owners being members of the club and that they'd offered me free membership because more people would join up knowing I was a member. Ridiculous, really, but it worked.

"Don't you get sick of the constant attention and being recognised?" she asks.

"Sometimes. It pisses me off when the newspapers print lies about me. I never speak to them, so they make shit up, like the story about me and Clarisse being an item."

"I saw some of the gossip columns online. They certainly like to talk about you."

"Who's Betty?" I ask. The question causes that sad look to reappear on her face and I regret asking.

"She's my dog." She sighs. "Silly, really, but I couldn't take her when I left because creepy Keith wouldn't take pets. Not many landlords will, so I had to leave her with Daniel."

"You called your dog Betty?" I ask.

She laughs. "Yeah, I love the old names, they're the best."

"God help your future kids."

We take a steady walk back to her apartment, and I tell her about Alex, mainly because she asked but also because I find myself chatting so easily with her. Everything just flows out of my mouth. She'd make a great therapist.

We stop outside, and she turns to me. "Well, thanks for making me go to the gym, even though I just wanted to slob out on my sofa. I feel much better."

I'm not ready for the night to end, or for us to go our separate ways. She watches as I open the back door of the SUV and pull out my bag. "The night is still young," I say with a grin. "Let's shower and change, then grab some food." Alivia begins to stutter a protest, but I playfully push her towards the steps. "I'm not taking no for an answer."

Chapter Four

Alivia

Keith opens the door before I have a chance to put my key in, his leering face creeping me out. He spots Vass behind me and loses the grin. "Is this your boyfriend?" he asks.

"What the hell's that got to do with you?" asks Vass, clearly irritated by the bumbling old fool. "And do you wait by the door every time she's out, so you can open it when she arrives home?"

"Of course not, and I'm entitled to ask who my tenants bring home. You can't live here, you know. She only pays rent for one person."

Vass rolls his eyes and I cut in before he can reply. "Keith, it's fine, Vass is my boss and he isn't moving in here," I reassure him.

Vass follows me up the stairs to my apartment. "Man, that guy is a pain in the arse and creepy. I'm sure I can find you somewhere better than here," he says. When I left Daniel, I was in a rush to find a place. Getting somewhere in London that's affordable is hard, and then having to furnish it about broke the bank.

"I tried to find a place, Vass. It's hard in London. Everyone wants references from previous landlords or a hefty deposit. This will do until I'm back on my feet. I'll show you where the bathroom is," I say, leading him through to my bedroom. I point to the door that leads to my en suite.

"Nice room," he says with a grin. I'm proud of my cottage-style bedroom. Daniel hated anything cream coloured, especially if it had flowers or anything he classed as girly. When I went shopping for my bedroom, I chose a solid oak bed and a pretty cream cover with a tiny pink flowery pattern, and there's soft pink flowery bunting hanging neatly above the bed with fairy lights entwined in it. I got it all from a local charity shop, saving me a fortune.

"I'm a girly girl," I admit, and he laughs.

"You are that, Liv. You are that."

I don't correct him this time. He's worn me down, and besides, I kind of like it coming from him.

He goes into the bathroom and closes the door. I decide to choose something casual to wear, not wanting to dress up like it's a date or he might think I'm desperate. Casual equals friends having some dinner together. I'm still staring into my wardrobe when the door opens followed by billowing steam. Vass appears wrapped in just a towel, and I almost gasp. Water droplets run down his tanned chest muscles, and his hair is mussed-up like he's run his fingers through it. *Oh, how I want to be those fingers.*

"Are you okay?" he asks, and I nod, not trusting myself to talk. I grab my clothes and a towel and rush past him to the bathroom.

I spend extra time in the shower trying to cool myself off. I need to get a grip. Vass is my boss. I'm still getting over Daniel, and Vass is not the boyfriend type . . . and again, Vass is my boss. I repeat it over and over while I dry myself and dress.

When I step into the kitchen, I regret the casual clothes. Vass is in a light pink shirt that does wonders for his deep blue eyes and black jeans. He looks smart, while I opted for light blue jeans and a cropped jumper that shows off my stomach with the slogan 'winging it' across the front. "Ready?" he asks.

I glance down at my casual wear. "I should change. I thought we were just grabbing a burger or something."

He shrugs. "You look great, and we can eat wherever you like."

"But you're dressed smart, and I look like a slob," I say, turning to go and get changed.

Vass strides towards me and wraps his arm around my waist, lifting me effortlessly off the ground and walking me towards the door. "You look fine, woman. Now, let's go and eat, I'm starving," he says, carrying me out of the apartment.

Vass drives us to another of his favourite restaurants. He tells me they do the best steak here, and that after our workout, we should eat red meat.

A waiter greets Vass in much the same way as the Italian owner at lunchtime. He seats us towards the back of the restaurant and hands us menus.

"Usual to drink, Vass?" he asks, and Vass nods before turning to me.

"What would you like to drink, Liv?"

"The same as you is fine," I say, not wanting to be awkward but also praying he didn't order whisky because it's the one drink I hate.

The waiter returns with a bottle of water and two glasses with a slice of lemon in each. It's the same as what we had at lunch. "Water?" I query. Vass nods and pours it into the two glasses. "Are you a fitness freak?"

"No, but I don't drink alcohol," he says with a shrug.

"A man who owns a sex club and doesn't drink alcohol?" I ask with a smile, and he nods again but doesn't comment further. I feel like I shouldn't push him even though there's obviously a story to tell.

"So, your idea to open up the bar in The Luxe at lunchtime is a hit with Clarisse. She thinks businessmen will love the exclusivity of it," he says.

"I thought Clarisse was the office manager. Does she have a say in how The Luxe is run?"

"No," he replies, "but I like to run things by her. She has a good head on her shoulders, and she's always steered me right in life so far."

"Are you two together?" I ask. "The newspapers seem to think you are."

Vass shakes his head with an annoyed expression. "No. I grew up with Rissa, and she's like a best friend."

"One that you have sex with?" I push, and he frowns.

"Does that bother you?"

I shake my head, my eyes wide like I'm trying to convince him that's not the case, "God, no, why would it?" I ask, "No, I just wondered. There's a spark between you."

"Well, we love each other, just not in that way. Don't you have male friends?" he asks.

"Yeah, of course, but most of my friends live Hackney way, where I lived before here."

"With Daniel?" he asks.

The waiter appears, and Vass orders steak for both of us. It sends a thrill through me that he's taking control as I've never had that in a man before. When the waiter's gone, we return to our conversation. I tell Vass how I first met Daniel in school, how we'd hung around in the same circles but then met up again years later at a reunion. I'm originally from Brighton, and Daniel moved after he left school to Cambridge, so it made sense for both of us to move to London. It was kind of halfway for us to go back and see friends and family, and there were plenty of jobs going in the area.

"And you're not tempted to go back home now you've split up?" Vass asks.

"Yes, very, but I've made a home here. I like London. I have a few friends close by, although most are married or settling down. Plus, my parents don't know about Daniel still, and I'm not ready to tell them."

"Ah, yes, the master plan to get up and running before they realise everything has broken," he says with a smile.

"You might laugh, but my parents are old-fashioned. They believe in marriage and staying faithful. They thought that's where Daniel and I were heading. Mum was convinced he was going to propose this Christmas. Now, I have to tell her he's fucking my understudy."

Vass laughs out loud. "Understudy?" he repeats.

"I trained that bitch up to be amazing, and now, she's replaced me, in my job and in his bed."

"Ouch, what a kick in the teeth."

"You have no idea. I spent months moaning to her as a friend about how Dan was never home and always late or staying out. To think she sat there consoling me when all the time she was with him behind my back."

"What a bitch," he agrees with a wink.

"Yeah, well, she is. No one likes a sneaky cheat. They're welcome to each other."

The waiter brings out our steak and vegetables. Vass is right, the steak is amazing, and I'm too wrapped up in my food orgasm to talk, so we eat in silence, Vass occasionally looking at me and smiling.

After dinner, we get back to my apartment and Vass follows me up the path, insisting on walking me up the steps. As I get to the top, I freeze. "My key," I say, turning to Vass.

"What about it?" he asks.

"Well, you carried me out of the apartment and didn't pick up my keys. I can't get in."

"Tap on the door. That creepy old bastard is probably watching us right now."

I gently tap on the door, but it doesn't open. The downstairs lights of Keith's apartment are all off. "I think he's out or in bed." I wince as the realisation that I'm stuck out here for the night hits me, and I begin to chew on my lower lip. Keith will be so pissed if I wake him, and he already gives me a hard enough time.

"Well, let's go back to The Luxe. You can have one of the rooms for tonight," suggests Vass, and I literally want to kiss him. Not only have I been dying to stay in those luxurious rooms since he showed me around, but it also means I don't have to wake up Keith and cause myself unnecessary misery.

"Are you sure? You're doing way too much for me, and I've only known you a couple of days."

Vass smiles and heads back down the steps to the SUV. "It was my fault for not picking your keys up, so it's the least I can do, and actually, not having you stay there with creepy Keith makes me feel better."

We get back to The Luxe and I'm surprised how busy it is in the evenings. It's almost ten o'clock and there are lots of shiny, expensive cars parked neatly outside. "Is it always this busy?" I ask, following him inside.

"Yes, most of the time. You should see the weekends." It makes me wonder why his mum thought he needed help to get business up.

Inside, the bar is crowded. I'd imagined that in the evenings, the bar would have people half-naked and having sex, but it's nothing like that. The customers are fully dressed in suits and evening dresses, and champagne is flowing, the waitresses walking around the room with trays full of the bubbly liquid. It's almost like a posh charity event, and you wouldn't even know these people are here for anything other than a social gathering.

"Shall we get a drink?" asks Vass, and I nod.

People turn and greet him as we make our way to the bar. Women eye me with distain, clearly unhappy to see their bachelor with an unknown female. Various men shake Vass's hand, and women reach up and kiss his cheek. No wonder he doesn't want to give up this lifestyle—they treat him like a king.

He's automatically handed a water when we reach the bar, then Carlos turns to me and asks, "What would you like?"

"I would love a glass of white wine, if it's no trouble," I say with a smile, and he goes off to pour me a glass.

Vass is already chatting to a couple, and so once I've got my drink, I wander through the room. I don't want to appear like a cling-on and follow Vass around. The double doors to the main room are propped open, and as I approach, I'm faced with a man and woman on stage dancing erotically together. I stop and watch, mesmerised by the music, which is haunting yet alluring. The tables are full, everyone staring intently ahead at the show. I take a step inside, keeping to the back of the room. Nearest to me is a larger man in a tight-fitting suit. Beside him, kneeling at his feet, is a youngish-looking girl in a thong and nothing else. She wears a collar connected to a silk tie which he holds. Occasionally, he strokes her hair, and she rubs her head against his leg, similar to a puppy trying to get its owner's attention.

To the left of me is a booth, and there's moaning coming from that area. I can only imagine what's going on there, but the lights have been turned off above the table, making it difficult to see.

My attention is brought back to the stage when loud moaning fills the room. Another male has joined the pair, and he has his face buried between the woman's legs. I'm drawn to them, unable to look away as she grips his hair between her fingers and throws her head back.

"It's hot, isn't it?" comes Vass's voice, and I let out a squeal. A few heads turn towards us but then go back to watching when they realise there's nothing exciting to see.

"I was being nosy," I mutter.

As Vass leans against the wall, his arm brushes against my own and my skin prickles. "Have you ever watched anything like this?" he asks, and I shake my head. "Liar," he whispers close to my ear. The woman is screaming in pleasure as she shakes violently through an orgasm. "You were watching me and Bianca." I stare at him in shock. *How does he know that?* "I saw you," he adds with a smirk. My face flushes with embarrassment, and I'm glad it's darker in here, so he can't see.

"How does it make you feel?" he asks as I bite on my lower lip. "If you knew how fucking sexy that was, you wouldn't do it around me," he adds, pressing his thumb to my chin and gently tugging to release my lip. It feels like an electric current runs through his finger and races through my skin straight to between my legs, I press my thighs together to ease the ache.

"Vass, where the hell were you?" A woman appears next to Vass, breaking the moment. "I've been waiting for you for over an hour," she hisses.

"Apologies, Annalise, I got caught up." She kisses him gently on the mouth. It's not a lingering kiss, but he still gives me an awkward glance as she pulls away.

"And you are?" she asks, turning to me.

"Alivia Caldwell," I say with a forced smile. I don't like her tone or the way she looks me up and down like she's better than me.

"You realise there's a dress code in The Luxe?" she asks, cocking her eyebrow at my cropped jumper. I glimpse at the black, fitted evening dress that she has on, coupled with black Louis Vuitton stilettos. Her makeup gives her a flawless tone, and there's no denying that she's beautiful.

"Alivia is my guest this evening. I've okayed it," snaps Vass. "Let's go and talk," he adds, taking her by the elbow. "Don't move, I'll be back shortly," he tells me and then guides Annalise away and out of the room.

Vass

I keep hold of Annalise's elbow all the way to the second floor and into my office. She wretches it away once inside and slaps me hard across the face. I take a deep breath to calm myself. "I fucking waited like an idiot, sat on my own in a busy restaurant, and then I come here to find you with some tart who looks half your age," she rages.

I guess comparing the two, Liv does look younger than Annalise, although there's only six years between them. "She's twenty-three," I sigh, "and she isn't a tart but my new employee."

"And you're thirty. Don't you think that's a little old for her? And really, an employee? Is there a difference in your mind? Because you fuck anything and anyone whether they work for you or not."

"I forgot about the reservation. I apologise, but I'm not going to get into an argument over my new marketing girl. We had a meeting that ran over."

"And we have an agreement. I've given you my time, for which some men would be grateful, yet you act like you're doing me the favour. Maybe I won't show up on Saturday. Let's see how your dear grandmother feels when her little black sheep of the family lets her down again."

I bite my inner cheek to stop me saying something I'll later regret. "What can I do to make it up to you?" I ask patiently, and her frown eases to a slight smile.

"First, you can get me a drink. The rest will flow naturally," she mutters.

Annalise takes a step closer and places a well-manicured hand to my cheek, gently rubbing where she slapped me. "Sorry, baby, you make me crazy," she whispers, pressing a kiss to the red mark. I remove her hand, take it in my own to appease her, and then lead her back to the bar.

Alivia is chatting with Alex, and I clench my free hand into a fist. They're laughing as his hand rests on her lower back, and the bare skin to skin contact pisses me off and I narrow my eyes. As we approach, Alex grins at me. "Dude, where the hell have you been? You left Liv unattended in a tank full of sharks."

"Alivia," I say sternly, "is quite capable of looking after herself, Alex. Haven't you got anything to be getting on with?"

He moves his hand from her skin and hooks his arm around her shoulders instead, winking at me. I know he's trying to get a reaction. "I'm getting on with Liv," he says.

"Vass tells me you work in marketing," says Annalise.

Liv nods and takes a sip of Champagne. "Yes. I actually went for a position at Glamour Cosmetics but somehow ended up at The Luxe."

"That makes sense," mutters Annalise, looking up at me. "Your meddling mother as usual."

"You know Jenifer," I say with a tight smile. "Always trying to make me do things her way."

"Well, I trust you told her we have it in hand." I don't miss the way she punctuates the word 'we', like she and I are a thing.

"So, are you spending the night, Annalise?" asks Alex, and I immediately glare at him. I know where he's going with this line of conversation.

"It's becoming a regular occurrence, isn't it?" he adds with a smirk.

Alivia looks down at her Champagne flute and presses her lips together. Alex wants her to think Anna and I are a thing, so he can jump in there. "Are you wanting to join us again?" I ask.

Alex laughs out loud. "Touché, Mr. Fraser."

"When you dogs have finished your pissing contest, I'd like to watch the show," says Annalise coldly.

"Alex will walk you through, and I'll join you shortly. I just need to speak with Alivia," I say.

Annalise makes a show of kissing me on the lips again and then saunters off towards the main room. Alex turns Liv's head towards him and hooks his finger under her chin so that she's looking up to his six-foot frame. "I like you, Liv. When this bastard gets bored of you, which he will, come and find me," he says, placing a quick kiss on her cheek and following after Annalise.

Alivia raises her eyebrows and then takes a large gulp of the Champagne. It makes her cough, so she places the glass down on the bar and then wipes under her eyes. "What was that about?" she asks, staring after Alex.

"He's an idiot, ignore him. Shall I show you to your room for the evening?" I ask.

"You want rid of me?" The question takes me by surprise, and my instant answer is no, I don't want rid of her, and in fact, if Annalise hadn't turned up, then maybe we would still be in the main room watching the show and chatting. But now, Alex has his radar set on her, and I can't spend the night worrying that he's going to end up in her bed.

"Of course not, but Alex will pester you all night, and I feel it's my duty to protect you from him," I say.

"Maybe I don't need protecting." She smiles, and I'm surprised how much her remark riles me. I take her hand and lead her from the bar.

We step into the elevator, and I put the key in the lock to open the top floor. "You may as well spend the night in complete luxury," I say.

The platinum suites are on the top floor. There are four in total, but one of them is my living residence. The elevator opens onto a private floor, and I push in the code for the room next to mine. If she thought the downstairs rooms were nice, she'll be amazed by these. I had Italian designers come in specially to give these rooms a romantic feel. Each room has a different theme, this one being Summer, which I thought Alivia would appreciate since she loves girly décor.

I smile as her face lights up at the sight of the four-poster bed in the centre of the room. The sheer white curtains that surround it are lit up with tiny lights handsewn into the delicate material. "It's so pretty in here," she gasps.

"I thought you'd like it," I say, smiling.

"I don't even want to know what you charge for renting this room," she says, running her fingers over the white marble dresser.

"Some people will pay a huge amount for luxury." I shrug. "There's a bathroom through there and room service is available. Please make use of it as my guest. I'll have some nightwear brought up to you."

I step past Alivia and reach over to open the French doors. There's a small balcony which shows off the London skyline, but it's cold and I doubt she'll want to be out there this evening. She follows me out and rubs her arms. "I bet it's lovely out here when it's a warmer night," she says, and I nod. She nudges me with her arm, and I look down at her and smile. "I really appreciate you keep helping me out, Vass. You're a really great guy," she almost whispers. Our eyes lock for a few seconds before she suddenly rises on her tiptoes and kisses me quick on the cheek. "Thank you," she adds. I give a stiff nod and step back inside, breaking whatever that was between us.

"I'd better get back downstairs."

She nods, a sad expression passing over her face. "Have a good night."

I go to my own room and call Clarisse, who answers on the second ring. "Yes, boss?" she jokes.

"Are you about this evening? I need some nightwear brought to a platinum room."

"I'll get some sent up. Size?" she asks.

"Erm, Alivia-sized," I say with a hopeful laugh.

"Okayyy," she says, dragging out the last syllable.

"What does that mean?" I ask. "Why did you say it like that?"

"Nothing," she says innocently. "Do I send the sort that you like, or what I think Alivia will like?"

"Something she will like," I say, and then add, "Silk, something silk." I clamp my mouth shut because I almost followed that with 'she'd look good in silk'.

"I'm on it. You know Annalise is here this evening?" she asks.

"Yes, I'm on my way now. Where is she?"

"In a private room with Alex and Mr. Collingham." I close my eyes to contain the anger that rises within me. If she carries on, she'll ruin everything. I cut the call and make my way downstairs, Annalise's collar tightly gripped in my hand.

I burst into the private room unannounced, and I catch the delight in Annalise's eyes when she spots me. She wanted this reaction. Clive Collingham is on his knees, his cock in his hands, watching Annalise play with herself while Alex touches her. They all stop to look at me, then Alex grins and moves away from her, holding his hands up to indicate he was just following her instructions.

"Up," I order her, and defiance dances in her eyes. Reaching across the bed, I grip her by the arm, hauling her to her feet. I hold the collar up in front of her. "Aren't you forgetting something?" I grit out, and she shrugs, another show of defiance. I place the black leather collar around her neck and hold it tight until she coughs. "You think you can come into a playroom without your collar, without permission?" I growl. She gives a nod, and I pull harder. "Oh, Annalise, you're pushing me too far," I warn, and she arches her brow.

I spin her away from me and bend her over the bed, slapping her bare arse hard and delighting in the red handprint I leave on her pale skin. "How many?" I growl.

"Ten," she hisses. I slap her again in the same spot, and she jolts forward.

"Have you forgotten yourself this evening, Annalise?" I ask.

"TEN, SIR!" she cries out.

I feel the beast inside me stepping forward and I look to Alex and Clive, who are watching everything. "Out!" I order, and they go without question. I hit the button to clear the glass in case they want to watch from the attached room.

I stand between Annalise's legs and use my foot to kick them farther apart. Running my finger along her opening, I feel that she's turned on already. I haven't even begun yet.

Chapter Five

Alivia

There's a knock on the door and I peep through the hole to see the office manager. I frown, wondering why she would be here at this time of night. I open the door and smile. "Clarisse, you're working late."

She holds out a package of pink tissue paper tied with a pink ribbon. "Courtesy of The Luxe," she says politely.

I take it, admiring the pretty wrapping. "Okay, thanks. What is it?"

"Silk," she says. "Vass asked me to bring it to you."

When she doesn't move, I give her an awkward smile. "Do you want to come in?" I ask, and she shrugs, then nods. I step to one side so she can enter the room. I lay the parcel on the bed, and we stand awkwardly for a second. "Drink?" I ask, and she nods again.

"Did Vass give you free reign on the bar and room service?" she asks. "He usually does for his guests."

"Yeah, but I don't want to take advantage of him. He's been so kind," I say, but Clarisse is already opening the minibar and grabbing bottles.

"Forget that. Do you know how much the guy is worth?"

"Not really," I mutter. "It makes no difference."

"He's my best friend, so he's used to me spending his money." She shrugs, laying the miniatures on the bed. She settles on vodka and opens two bottles, pouring them into tumblers and topping them with Coke. She hands me one, and I take a sip and wince. It's strong.

"That's the Polish in me, I like vodka super strong." She grins as I splutter. "Go on then, ask me. I know you're dying to," she says, sitting back on the bed and crossing her legs. When I stare at her blankly, she rolls her eyes. "Am I fucking him? Are we in a secret relationship? Do I love him?"

"It's none of my business," I say without admitting that I do want to ask all the above to settle my curiosity.

"No, I don't fuck him," she starts. "Not anymore," she adds with a wink. "Yes, I love him a huge amount because he's kind and funny and amazing, but only as a friend. I'm not *in* love with him, and our only relationship is purely platonic. We went out together when we were young and stupid, but we have the same taste in women now, which effectively means that we occasionally share a threesome, but he doesn't come near me cos that would be weird." She shudders at the thought.

"But seeing him naked and sharing women isn't weird?" I ask sceptically.

"No. We both love sex, and he hooks up with women who want a threesome. It's a win-win situation. No one bats an eyelid when he shares a woman with Alex or Curtis," she huffs.

"There's an awful lot of sharing going on between you all," I mutter.

"I suppose it would seem weird to someone like you."

"Like me?" I repeat, trying not to be offended.

She shrugs. "Well, yah know, plain."

"Wow, you have such a way with words."

She laughs. "Sorry, I didn't mean it like that. You're not the type of person Vass would normally hire."

"That's because his mother hired me on the promise of a career in her company if I helped out here first. What I don't understand is that Vass and The Luxe are doing extremely well. Why would she think he needs help with marketing?"

Clarisse falls quiet and chews on her fingernail. It makes me even more suspicious than I already am. I checked the memberships, and he has a lot of people on the books, so he doesn't need help pulling clients in. "I guess I'll find out eventually," I mutter, taking a drink.

"Vass is complicated. He has all kinds of pressures from family. It makes him do stupid things, like hook up with bitches like Annalise. I think you've been sent here to save him," says Clarisse. I wait for her to laugh, but when she doesn't, I begin to smile.

"You're kidding, right?"

"No. I believe in fate, Liv, and you're here to help him."

"So far, he's helped me. I haven't helped him at all."

"That isn't strictly true. Where was he all evening?" she asks with a cocky grin.

"He wanted to go to the gym," I say with a shrug.

"But he was supposed to be at dinner with Annalise. See, you're already working your magic."

I throw a small cushion at her, and she catches it. "You're crazy." Her comments have sent a small buzz of hope to my heart, though, and I can't deny that Vass is making a dent in the heartache I felt over Daniel cheating on me.

Clarisse leaves over an hour later. I like her. She's honest and to the point, and I could do with someone like that in my life. Opening the package she brought me, I hold up a light pink silk chemise with matching shorts. I've never worn anything as nice as this to bed. I hold it against me and smile, admiring how pretty it is. My thoughts turn to

Vass seeing me in this and I sigh. He isn't going to, of course, but a girl can dream.

I sit up, confused. I was having an amazing dream involving a Viking chasing me when something disturbed me. Looking around the room, I smile when I remember where I am. There's a loud banging on the door, and I jump out of bed, my heart hammering in my chest.

Looking through the peephole, I see Vass glaring at the door. I open it and poke my head out, quite aware that my hair is probably a mess and I'm wearing silk.

"Are you planning on working today?" he asks. I let go of the door and race to the bedside table, grabbing my phone. It's almost ten o'clock.

"Oh shit," I gasp. "I'm so sorry, Vass." When I turn, he's in the room, staring at me with a dark expression. I fidget and fold my arms, trying to hide my nipples that are desperate to get his attention. "The bed is so comfortable, I must have slept through my alarm . . . again."

"I guess the alcohol helped," he mutters, nodding to the empty glass bottles on the marble dresser.

"Well, that was Clarisse's fault. She turned up here and then we got talking and . . ." I trail off.

"I should've known she'd be involved." He sighs, rubbing his forehead. "Go shower and dress," he orders, heading to the French doors and opening them. He takes a seat on the balcony.

"You don't have to wait."

"Go," he repeats.

I shower in the luxurious walk-in wet room, regretting I didn't wake up as early as planned so I could take my time and enjoy it. I could get used to living like this. I feel like a queen.

I wrap myself in the fluffy white robe hanging on the back of the door and make my way back into the room. Laid out on the bed is a fitted black dress with a square-cut neck. To the side of that is a matching set of lace underwear. Vass steps from the balcony into the room. "I took the liberty of having clothes brought from a special boutique I know of," he says. "I thought you might want a fresh set of clothes."

"You think of everything," I say. "You really didn't have to, though."

"We have a meeting, so we need to leave." I gather the clothes and go back into the bathroom to change. I find a new hairbrush in the welcome basket and run it through my hair. Luckily, I have my tinted moisturiser in my handbag, and I quickly apply some.

Vass is speaking into his mobile phone when I go back into the room. He indicates for me to follow him and continues his call as we head down in the elevator. As we pass the reception desk, Clarisse hands me a set of keys and smiles.

"Have a great day," she says, and I look at the keys she's passed me. "Vass knows all about them," she adds as way of explanation.

Vass disconnects the call as we step out of The Luxe. "You can drive me for a change," he says, pointing to an Audi parked at the foot of the steps. "I believe my mother promised a company car."

I look back to the Audi in shock, the black paint gleaming in the sunshine. "That's my company car? It's brand new," I say, rushing down the steps towards it. I've never had a new car, second hand was all I could afford so this is a rare luxury.

"Well, usually, the company cars are Minis, but I think an Audi suits you better," he says with a wink.

"I love it, Vass, thank you." I'm genuinely lost for words. The car is pristine compared to the BMW I shared with Daniel, which he mainly used.

"Let's go. I'll give you directions," he says, getting in the passenger side.

We arrive at a warehouse where a man in a suit waits outside. He makes his way over with a huge smile on his face. When Vass steps out of the car, they embrace and pat each other on the back in greeting. I step out and straighten my dress. The man holds his hand out for me to shake, which I do. "This your new driver, Vass?" He laughs.

"This is Alivia, my marketing manager. Alivia, this is Mark. He's in sales."

Mark takes us through the warehouse. We go into a small office, and Mark closes the door. Before us, laid out on the desk, are boxes upon boxes of sex toys. I feel my face flush immediately, and I avoid looking at the desk as the men begin to pick up boxes and examine them in detail. Mark tells Vass about various toys and shows newer versions with in-depth explanations of what each one does for certain body parts. I stand rooted to the spot, wishing I could disappear. It's not that I'm a prude—I've used a vibrator—but I'm not used to discussing them and what they do. Vass holds up an angry-looking red vibrator, thick in width with veiny detail, and grins at me. "What do you think, Liv?"

"It's your area of expertise, Vass, not mine," I mutter.

"You have to get used to this sort of stuff if you're going to be around The Luxe. It's part of everyday life."

"My experience lies in the office side of things," I point out. Vass signs an order form for over five thousand pounds worth of toys.

"Why did you bring me here?" I hiss as we get back in my car.

"Because you need to know what sort of things The Luxe offers, toys and all." He smirks. "And because I love the way your face flushes red every time you're uncomfortable."

"You aren't funny, Vass. I was mortified," I groan.

"We have a brunch meeting now, no toys allowed," he promises.

Vass directs me to a grand hotel just five minutes up the road. It's the type of place that country club members would use, with a golf course leading from the back and a health suite boasting various spa treatments. Once inside, Vass gets the attention of a cute blond receptionist, so I take a walk around the lobby, looking at the beautiful artwork that hangs expertly on the walls.

"It's a beautiful piece, isn't it? I've tried to buy it so many times, but the manager here refuses to sell it to me, no matter how much I offer." I glance at the elderly lady who stands beside me, looking at the painting of a small child with her head resting on her dirty knees. She looks so sad.

"It's a sad painting, but very beautiful," I remark.

"The artist killed herself after painting this piece, so of course, it's worth a small fortune. Sad that art is worth more when the artist is dead," she says.

"Grandmother, I see you've met Alivia," comes Vass's voice, and we both turn. He leans down to kiss both cheeks of the elderly lady.

"She has a good eye for art," she says, smiling at me.

"Let's eat. I'm starving," says Vass, taking her arm and wrapping it through his own. I follow them into a large restaurant, wondering why the hell I'm meeting his grandmother and why he didn't warn me. A young girl shows us to our table and takes our coffee order.

"So, Alivia, how do you know my grandson?" she asks, stirring four sugar cubes into her coffee.

"She's my friend," says Vass before I can answer. When she looks to me for confirmation, I give her a weak smile. I hate lies.

"And what do you do for work?"

"I'm in marketing," I say.

"That's nice. A good job is important. Have you done anything I would've heard of?" she asks.

"Maybe. I worked for D.A. Property Services," I say.

"Yes, I know of them. An up-and-coming property guru, or so I've heard," she replies, and I inwardly groan. Of course, she would know of Daniel and his amazing company that I helped market. Clearly, I did a good job. I feel my bitterness rearing its ugly head.

"Actually, Grandmother, Alivia is helping me at The Luxe," says Vass.

She turns to him and gives him a pointed look. "Is there something I should know?"

"No. She came up with some great ideas, and I want to trial some of them, with the permission of the board, of course."

"Well, we'll hear them on Friday at our meeting and make a decision," she says.

We order brunch, and I listen as Vass tells his grandmother that he's thinking of putting a gym in at The Luxe. It would make sense for him to have a gym there, where he spends most of his time, since he likes to work out. She definitely isn't shy and spends some time asking me questions about my work and where I live. Vass tells her about creepy Keith.

"Well, give her a room at The Luxe," she says simply, and Vass nods.

"I'd like to, but Alivia insists she's okay there. She's too proud to accept help," he says, and I scowl at him for trying to get me into trouble with his grandmother.

"Alivia, life is too short. Take the help. This landlord doesn't sound very good. Are there other residents?"

"I think so. There're six rooms, but I haven't seen any other residents yet. I've only been there a few weeks."

"Well, consider staying at The Luxe. At least you'll be safe," she says firmly, and I nod, knowing there is no way I'll be accepting a room. As nice as it is, I can't rely on Vass to keep rescuing me. He must wonder what kind of mess he's got working for him.

By the time we get back to The Luxe, I manage a quick check of my emails before I head back to the bar area to meet the photographer. Khan is a friend from college, and I use him a lot for photographs. He's professional and discreet, which I like.

I tell him what sort of thing I'm looking for and how I want to portray The Luxe. We arrange for him to come back first thing tomorrow morning, so he can take photos when there are no clients about. "Actually, Liv, I could do with a huge favour," Khan says sheepishly. "I need a model."

"Me?" I almost choke.

"Yeah. I've told you a million times that I'd love to take your picture. I have a portfolio due for a job that I'm bidding for, and the model I was using dropped out this morning. The Luxe would make an amazing background for the shots I want. I'd consider dropping my fee to half," he offers with a grin.

"I'd have to ask my boss, but if he agrees, then I'll do it." He's asked to photograph me so many times that it'd be rude to say no after he agreed to come here on short notice to help me.

Khan hugs me excitedly. "Call me as soon as you've asked him so I can set everything up that I need. I'll bring the outfits."

When I get back to the office, Alex is sitting in Bianca's chair, spinning around. He steadies himself by grabbing the desk. "Don't go in there. He's got a 'do not disturb' sign on the door," he warns, pointing to Vass's office. I take a seat at my desk.

"Where is Bianca?" I ask, trying not to sound too interested. He points to the office again and grins wide.

"There's not many jobs where you can leave your duties to have sex," I mutter, and Alex laughs.

"I guess not." I note how he doesn't deny that they're having sex, and the thought pisses me off. It's natural for a girl to feel jealous even though she isn't with the guy in question and that said guy is the boss, I'm sure. "How's your first few days been?" asks Alex, resuming the spinning.

"Good. Everyone is really nice," I say. The office door swings open, and Clarisse saunters in. She glowers at Alex as he spins and shakes her head.

"Who's he with?" she asks, pointing to Vass's 'do not disturb' sign.

"His new trainee," says Alex.

"Stop spinning, it's annoying," she snaps, and he slows to a stop and rolls his eyes to me. "I think we should go out on Friday night," suggests Clarisse, sitting on the floor in the centre of the office and crossing her legs. "It's been ages since we all went out."

"I'm up for it if everyone else is," Alex agrees. They both turn to me with an expectant look on their faces. I thought they were talking amongst themselves.

"What?"

"You could come and celebrate your first full week of surviving Vass," Clarisse suggests.

"Oh, I don't think so. I'm sure Vass wouldn't want his new employee tagging along with his friends," I say, shaking my head.

"Firstly, Vass really won't mind, and secondly, Vass hardly ever comes out drinking because he doesn't drink, in case you hadn't noticed," says Alex. "Come out with us, Liv. We always have a good night."

I shrug. I'm pretty sure I'm right—Vass won't like me going out with his friends. I've intruded on his life enough this week, plus I don't have any money. "Vass is busy Friday night anyway. Doesn't he have the thing with his family?" asks Clarisse.

Alex shakes his head. "No, that's Saturday. I overheard Annalise telling someone."

I tap on my computer, ignoring the stab of jealousy in my stomach. I have to stop this. He's my boss, and I can't like a guy who owns a sex club. My mum would have a heart attack.

"If I can get the money together, then I'll come," I say, surprising myself. They both smile, and then Clarisse frowns.

"Money? Have you checked your bank lately?"

I shake my head. "No, I can't handle the negative balance on the screen. It makes me sick."

"Vass had me pay money into your account yesterday. He said to log it down as expenses," she says. I pull out my mobile and log into my online banking. Clarisse is right, my account is well in the positive with a thousand pounds showing in the balance.

I gasp. "Why has he paid me that?"

"Vass doesn't like to see anyone struggle," says Alex.

I suddenly feel uncomfortable. All the help he keeps sending my way is too much. He doesn't even know me, and now this. None of it makes sense. I stand and march over to the conjoining door. Alex stands too, his expression looking panicked as I reach for the handle and push it open. Stomping into Vass's office, I ignore the fact that he's sitting on his office chair watching Bianca touch herself in front of him on his desk. Bianca freezes, looking from me to Vass. Vass looks furious, but then so am I, so I glare at him to let him know I'm not leaving. His expression changes and his eyes go back to Bianca. "I didn't say you could stop," he snaps coldly, and she continues while looking highly embarrassed.

"What the hell is this?" I ask, holding up my phone.

He leans forward slightly and then sits back in his chair. "A cash deposit of one thousand pounds."

"I can see that, Vass. Why is it in my bank?" I demand.

He shrugs. "Because you needed money."

"It isn't pay day until the end of the month, and I only started on Monday!"

Vass rubs his forehead like he's trying to remain calm, when in actual fact, he wants to yell at me. He turns to Bianca. "Stop," he orders, and she does, looking thankful. "Go into the bathroom and get in the bath. I'll be there shortly." She nods and does exactly as instructed. I'm still reeling from the fact he has a bathroom with an actual bath in his office.

Vass stands, rising to his full height and squaring his shoulders. He walks around to my side of the desk and towers over me, his face a picture of rage. "How dare you march into my office like that when I'm otherwise engaged? If you weren't so fucking vanilla, I'd have you over my knee," he threatens. His words thrill me rather than insult me, but I glare at him, trying to make myself feel braver than I actually feel. "How dare you pay money into my account for no reason. Who even does that after three days?"

"Are you seriously pissed off that I'm helping you out?" he shouts.

"Yes," I shout back. "I didn't ask for your help, Vass. I'm not some charity case who needs you to swoop in and rescue me all the time. I eat and I have a perfectly good bed in my apartment."

He sighs in frustration, clearly annoyed by the whole conversation. "Fine, Alivia, message received loud and clear. Now, get the fuck out of my office, and next time you barge in like that, I'll fire you."

I take a step back. I want to cry and I have no idea why, but I feel it coming, so I storm out and head straight to the bathroom across from our office. I lock myself in the cubicle and lower onto the toilet seat, burying my face in my hands and bursting into tears.

I realise that I sounded crazy. Who yells at someone for trying to help? And who yells at their new boss when they've only known them three days? The thing is, I feel like I've known Vass for so much longer, and the feelings I get knowing he's with another woman burn me more than they should. I groan, grabbing a handful of tissue. I've officially lost my mind.

Vass

Who the hell yells at someone after they've given you a grand? Alivia is crazy, and now, I'm annoyed. Clarisse pops her head in and gives a little smile to test the waters. When I don't return it, she steps in farther. "Are you okay?"

"No, I'm pissed off," I snap.

"Some girls don't like money thrown at them," she says.

I sit back in the office chair. "I wanted to help her, Riss. She had a freezer full of microwave meals and she couldn't pay her rent."

"You can't help everyone, Vass. On the plus side, you know she isn't a money-grabbing whore like Annalise." I scowl at her comment. She doesn't make secret the fact she hates Annalise. "Liv yelled at you," she adds and then laughs. "I've never heard a woman yell at you."

"She's lucky I didn't put her over my knee." I smirk. "I really wanted to."

"I was waiting for the scary Dom voice to come out, but you kept yourself quite calm," she says, doing a small celebratory clap.

"I like having her around, Riss," I admit. "What does that mean?"

Clarisse shrugs but smiles. "I like her, Vass. I think she'll keep you on your toes."

"She makes me want a drink. No one's made me feel like a drink in a long time."

Clarisse's eyebrows shoot up in surprise. "But you haven't?" she asks, and I shake my head. "Well, that's good. You need a fuck. Take the afternoon and go down to the main room," she suggests.

"Maybe," I mutter. "I need to finish the session with Bianca. I told Tom she'd be ready by the weekend." Riss nods, leaving me to it.

I enter the bathroom, and Bianca is laying back in the bath. When I walk in, she scrabbles to her knees, causing the water to overflow. "I need an outlet," I mutter, and she glances at me, then remembers herself and looks back to her hands. "I'm going to let you touch me, Bianca. Are you okay with that?"

She nods eagerly. "Yes, Sir, I'd like that very much."

For two months, I've refrained from doing anything with her other than watch her. I'm training her to be a sub for a good client of The

Luxe after she came to me and asked for my help because she'd never subbed for anyone before. Since Alivia walked into this office on Monday, I've struggled to be with other women, apart from the receptionist. I can't lie, it's killing me, but all I can think about is Liv.

I unbutton my trousers and fist my semi-hard cock. I'm used to fucking every day, at least two to three times. Since Sunday, the most hard I've gotten is when I think up an image of Alivia in my mind and use my hand. I close my eyes and think of Liv in the silk pyjamas. I groan when Bianca runs her tongue along my shaft. She's hardly touched me, and I already know that I can't do this. I sigh heavy and step back. "Sorry, Bianca, I've changed my mind."

She almost looks disappointed, but it's worked out for the best because now I won't have to get rid of her.

Chapter Six

Alivia

By Friday morning, I'm feeling well and truly fed up. Vass doesn't need to drive me to and from work now that I have my car, and in all honesty, I miss that time with him despite the fact that at the moment, things are very professional between us. Gone is the flirty banter and the offers of lunch out. I know it's what I told him I wanted, but I'm starting to regret it. I miss him.

When I get into the office, Vass is waiting for me. His face changes whenever he looks at me lately. There's no more smiles or little winks here and there—now, it's a stony stare. "The board members are arriving. Have you got everything ready?" he asks coldly. I give a nod. I made sure I had everything ready before I left the office last night. He watches me as I gather the booklets I've prepared. Thanks to a last-minute rush, we now have a mock-up of a brochure. Khan took some amazing photos of things I wouldn't have even dreamed of. The close-up of the tassels from a flogger laying across silk bedding is personally one of my favourites. Considering I didn't even know what it was, I'm making progress.

Bianca arrives looking flustered. She gives us a weak smile, and Vass goes to her immediately, sensing she isn't herself. "Are you okay?" he asks gently. It's a bitchy thought, but I can't help feeling pissed that his whole demeaner has changed for Bianca, yet his attitude toward me is frosty.

Bianca sniffles and then bursts into tears. Vass wraps her in his big arms and jealousy pushes its way in again. He whispers into her ear, and she nods, then he turns to me. "You'll have to get started without me. I need to deal with this."

My eyes widen in panic. "What? On my own?" I almost screech.

He glares at me. "Yes, you're a big girl, I think you'll manage. I'll be there soon."

"Vass, I don't know any of these people. Can't Clarisse take care of Bianca?"

"Are you serious right now, Alivia?" he snaps, and I look away, not liking the anger in his eyes.

"Fine, whatever," I mutter, checking I have everything. Vass leads Bianca into his office, and I childishly stick my middle finger up at his closed door.

I make my way to the boardroom feeling completely sick with nerves and take a deep breath before making my entrance. Ten pairs of eyes turn as I enter, and I feel my face flush as I place my paperwork down at the head of the table. I finally look up and give my best confident smile.

"Good morning, I'm Alivia Caldwell. Unfortunately, Mr. Fraser has been called to something urgent, but he'll be here shortly. Until then, I'm afraid you're stuck with me."

I notice Vass's grandmother and give her a weak smile. She winks at me and gives me a thumbs up, which makes me feel like I haven't made a total twat of myself just yet. It's not that I don't like public speaking, I've done it many times, but this is a different kind of company than I'm used to and I have no notes prepared seeing as I wasn't expecting to do this. I start by handing out the mock-up brochure.

"I realised that The Luxe doesn't have any kind of brochure or anything to give to potential clients. Other places in this industry, although not near London, have a similar kind of brochure that hints at the things we cater to. As you can see, the brochure is classy, with nothing too in-depth but enough information to give someone an idea of what they can expect for their money. If you turn to the centrefold, you'll find the different memberships. We left the cost off the brochure because we don't want price to put clients off. Let the description lure them in and then hit them with the price."

I take a deep breath and let the board look over the brochure while they talk amongst themselves. So far, everyone looks impressed. "Mr. Fraser is in talks with the golf club, which is less than two miles away, about offering a discounted membership for their members. As you can see from the back of the brochure, there's a list of packages we would like to offer that do not involve the kind of things that the memberships do. For example, our bar area could be available for business meetings during the daytime. Our main room could be available for hire to businesses that need more room for conference meetings or training purposes."

Members nod in agreement, and Vass's grandmother looks pleased. The door opens and Vass enters looking dishevelled and rushed. He runs his fingers through his hair and takes off his suit jacket. "Sorry I'm late, office crisis," he mutters.

"Involving the removal of your trousers?" asks his grandmother, raising her eyebrows and looking directly at Vass's crotch area. Vass glances down and laughs when he realises his zipper is open. He fastens it and shrugs, causing the other members in the room to laugh. I, however, am pissed. How dare he leave me to start this meeting for a quick fuck? I continue charming the board with my ideas and then wrap it up because I have Khan arriving shortly to take photos of me on the grounds of The Luxe. I cleared it with Clarisse, seeing as Vass was being an arse to me, and she is the office manager.

The room begins to clear as I gather the scattered papers and brochures, and Vass's grandmother approaches us. "You have some amazing ideas. I'm very impressed, Alivia."

"Thank you," I say as she moves in to hug me.

When she makes her way out of the room, Vass takes a seat. "Wow, you melted the old crow's heart. I've never seen her hug anyone like that before," he says.

"I have a charm about me," I mutter.

"Are you mad at me?"

"I wouldn't say mad, Vass, a little annoyed maybe," I say, stopping to look at him. "You left me to run the meeting while you went and did whatever with Bianca." There, I said it. Yes, I'm jealous, but I think I've hidden it well.

"You're jealous," he says with a smirk.

"I am not," I almost screech. "I'm sick of doing all the work around here while you two have your training sessions," I say, using my fingers to make quote marks around the words 'training sessions'.

"My zipper was down because I went to the bathroom on the way up here," he says. "The board like to think I'm some sort of sex god, keeping the place going with my wicked ways, and I don't like to disappoint," he adds with a shrug. "And for your information, Bianca has handed in her notice, so I'll make sure to hire a harder worker."

"Why?" I ask, shocked. Bianca loves working here.

"Her mother called this morning. She needs her to go home to Leeds and help out with her father, who is terminally ill."

"Oh wow, poor Bianca," I mutter, feeling guilty. I glance at my watch. "Shit, I have to go, Khan will be here any minute," I say, gathering my stuff and heading back to the office.

Vass follows me. "I thought he got all the shots he needed?" he asks.

"Yeah, he did. I'm helping him out with some shots he needs for a new job he's going for. I okayed it with Clarisse, and he gave us money off our bill in return for my help," I say, dumping everything on my desk.

I get down to reception just as Khan is arriving. He looks trendy in his flat cap and tight jeans, and I can't help but smile at his quirky fashion sense.

"You are going to die when you see the outfits I have for you today," he says, grinning, then he leads me outside to a camper van. "This is your changing room," he says. "Katie is inside setting up outfits and makeup."

"Makeup?" I repeat.

"Yeah, this is going to be a proper shoot, Liv. Only the best for my new model."

"Khan, I'm not a model. I just thought you'd want a few pics of me smiling," I groan, wondering what I've let myself in for. Khan pushes me towards the door of the campervan, and I reluctantly go inside.

Katie is fantastic, my makeup is flawless, and I stare in the mirror in amazement. "I look so different," I gasp. "How did you do that?"

"Years of beauty school." She smiles. "Now, for the outfit," she adds with a grin. I watch in horror as she pulls out a red lace bodice.

"I can't wear that," I squeak.

"Don't worry, you won't see any of your private areas," says Katie, taking it off the hanger. "It has clever panels to hide everything."

I hold it before me. There's a low dip in the front that goes straight down the middle of my breasts, exposing my stomach to just below my navel. "I can't go out there in this. Isn't there something with more coverage?" I plead, and she shakes her head.

"Put it on. You'll feel better when it's on."

I step behind the partition that Katie kindly popped up and change into the barely-there bodice, noting that it's from Victoria's Secret. There's no mirror behind here, so I step out to where Katie is waiting, and she gasps in delight. "Oh my, you look stunning," she says, pushing the door open and shouting for Khan.

"No, don't bring him in here. I haven't even looked at myself," I screech.

Khan pops his head in and freezes. "Wow, Liv, that looks so much better than I could have imagined. You look gorgeous." He grins at me. I glance in the long mirror, and although the bodice is ridiculously revealing, Katie is right—everything important is covered. She passes me a pair of stilettos in black with the famous red bottoms, and it's love at first sight, despite them being much higher than I'd ever wear.

"Think of it as swimwear," Katie suggests.

"Let's go and take your picture, beautiful," says Khan, taking my hand.

I pull back, halting him mid-step. "No, I really can't go out there in this," I beg. We get into a tugging battle, which he eventually wins. "Is there anyone out there?" I ask before stepping fully out.

"No," reassures Khan.

I step out to find Alex and Clarisse waiting. "Khan!" I screech, and he laughs.

"Fuck, Liv, you're gonna cause me an injury," groans Alex, making a show of adjusting his trousers.

※

Khan leads me to the front of The Luxe and sits me on the wall, putting me in an uncomfortable pose with my head tilted at a certain angle. I thought it would be so much easier, but as it turns out, it gets harder and more exhausting as time goes on. I'm swapped into various outfits, some of which are less revealing than the first but still just as sexy. My makeup is changed over and over to accommodate the various daytime and evening looks.

I'm changed for the final shoot. It's a short black number that would probably look good for a night of clubbing. My makeup is dark and smoky, something I'd never be able to pull off if I did it myself, but it looks good and I vow to try it. Khan has my laying on the grass with my arms above my head and my knees bent slightly to the right of my body. He stands over me, a leg either side of my waist and points the camera down. "Look to the left," he instructs. I do, straight into the eyes of Vass. His stormy blues are fixed on me and he looks ready to pounce. I haven't seen that look since we had our disagreement.

"How about a photo of the owner and our aspiring model?" suggests Khan. I shake my head in protest, but Vass is already walking over. Khan scoops me up and stands me on unsteady feet. Vass doesn't need to spend hours in makeup—he's already perfect in his smart, expensive suit and neatly styled hair. Khan places Vass's large arm around me and turns us towards one another. He tilts my head so I'm looking up at Vass and places my hand over his heart. He positions Vass to look down at me, his face serious, and I almost swoon at his smouldering gaze. Khan snaps a few photos and then asks Vass to lift me under my arms so that I'm looking down at him. He does it with no problem, and I place my hands on his huge shoulders, trying not to squeeze his strong muscles that bunch beneath my touch. As he lowers me to the ground, he slides me down his body. I feel every hard, toned surface, and then I feel myself blushing.

"Am I pushing it if I ask you to kiss?" asks Khan, holding his camera up, ready for the shot.

"Yes," I snap, but Vass places his finger gently under my chin and lifts my head to look at him. He moves his lips so close that I hold my breath for the connection, but it doesn't come. He stays just a breath away, and Khan gets his shot of our pretend kiss. Disappointment sets in a knot in my stomach when he pulls away, seemingly unaffected, and heads back over to Alex and Clarisse without a backward glance.

Clarisse joins us in the campervan while Khan flicks back through the shots. I don't even recognise myself in most of them. I look confident, like I know exactly what I'm doing. He gets to the ones of me and Vass, and Clarisse grins at me. "Oh my god, look at the way you two are staring at each other. They are H.O.T.," she spells out.

"It was just for the pictures," I mutter, but she nudges me with her shoulder.

"Can she keep this dress for tonight?" she asks Khan, and he nods.

I forgot about the drinks with Alex and Clarisse, and I inwardly groan because It's the last thing I feel like doing.

I spend the rest of the day in the office. I feel like Vass is avoiding me and I hardly see him except for when he's dropping stuff onto Bianca's now empty desk. When five o'clock comes around, I pop my head into his office because the door is already propped open.

"Have a great weekend," I say with a smile. I figure he'll move on if I act normal.

He looks up from his computer and mutters, "And you."

Vass

Clarisse bounds into the office holding her iPad up and waving it in my face. "Oh my god, these are so hot," she says excitedly.

"What?" I ask, annoyance in my voice because I'm busy. She thrusts it under my nose, and I glance at the screen. It's the picture of me and Liv almost kissing. "How did you get this?" I ask. She's right, the photo is hot.

"I asked Khan to forward them to me."

"Why?" I sigh, flicking my finger over the screen to find more of the same.

"So that when you fuck it all up, I can torture you with them," she says with a laugh before snatching the iPad away and holding it to her chest. "Anyway, I have to go. I'm hitting the town tonight with Liv, Alex, and the gang," she says with a wide grin before flouncing out of my office.

I tap my fingers on the desk. I have plans this evening with Annalise, and there's no way I can cancel on her again after not turning up the other night. I have an overwhelming urge to be near Alivia, though, to make sure she's safe. I want to ensure that Alex doesn't do anything to threaten our friendship.

I take Annalise to the little Italian restaurant that Liv and I had lunch at. It's my favourite, and it's not too far from Annalise's place. She moans the entire time—service isn't fast enough, the spaghetti doesn't taste right, the wine isn't up to scratch.

"Next time, we should go into central London. There's a fantastic sushi bar that's to die for," she witters on. My phone beeps with a text, and I make my apologies to Annalise, who looks annoyed when I pull it out.

"It might be my mother about tomorrow evening," I explain, opening the text. It takes a second to load, but a picture opens of Clarisse and Liv holding up cocktails to the camera and smiling. She looks gorgeous, and I stare at it for a few seconds before Annelise touches my arm and gets a quick glimpse of what has my attention.

"Clarisse corrupting the new staff already?" she asks with distain.

"Seems so," I mutter, closing the picture and stuffing the phone in my pocket.

"How is the new girl working out?"

"Great. She has some fabulous ideas and she wowed the board with her plans today."

"When you get it all signed over to you, we can implement the plans and take all the profit," says Annalise with a wicked grin.

"I doubt she'll stick around for long. My mother offered her a position at her firm. If things go well tomorrow, there'll be no need for Alivia to stay.

It's not like the place needs marketing with the turnover we have. Not that I'm not grateful, I always like to make more money," I say.

"Well, let's hope tomorrow goes well. I've practised my best conversation, and I'm going to blow your grandmother away," she says confidently. "I'm picking my dress up early. Thank you for placing the order and taking care of that. What time is the stylist coming over?" she asks.

"Five o' clock, after the makeup artist. I'll have the car collect you at eight," I confirm, and she smiles. My grandmother had better be blown away, the dress alone cost me a good few grand.

When we step outside the restaurant, there's a photographer waiting. He snaps a few pictures of us, and Annalise plays up to the camera by holding onto my arm and looking up at me lovingly. As I drive Annalise back to her apartment, I ask, "Did you arrange that photographer?" She pouts.

"No, of course, I didn't. But it wouldn't hurt for people to see us together. Your grandmother is more inclined to accept it if we're splashed all over the papers. The press still thinks you're secretly in a relationship with Clarisse." I don't tell her that's how I like it, private. She leans over the centre console and places a kiss on my mouth. "Are you coming inside, Sir?" she whispers against my closed lips.

"I have somewhere to be. Maybe tomorrow," I say. She huffs like a spoilt child not getting her own way and then exits the car, slamming the door and stomping off inside. I roll my eyes and drive away. I hate drama.

I use the multi-story car park across from the nightclub, Las Deux. I know this is where everyone will be, it's where they always end up. I walk straight inside, nodding to the door staff as I pass the line of people waiting to get in. Heading to the VIP area, I sign my name in the guestbook. As predicted, Clarisse and the gang have all signed in.

I go inside and make my way to the bar, where I'm handed a bottle of water. "Have you seen any of them?" I ask the bartender. He points over the crowd to the booths at the back of the room. I nod my thanks and move away from the bar so I can watch from a distance.

Clarisse is dancing with some guy. The girl can't make her mind up, insisting she's drawn to people by their aura, not their looks or their sex. By the way he's pressed against her, I think the guy's aura is trying to get inside her. Alex is sitting in the booth, his eyes fixed on Alivia, who's chatting to Lexi. I make my way over, and Alex looks at me in surprise. "Wow, what brought you out of your cave?" Then he laughs and gives a nod towards Alivia. "Oh, I see." He grins as I take a seat opposite him.

"I thought you'd have made your move by now," I murmur, glancing back over my shoulder to check out the short dress that Liv is wearing from the photo shoot earlier. It barely covers her backside.

"It isn't the same if the competition isn't here to see me make the move," he says with another laugh.

"I'm not the competition, Alex. I've got bigger fish to fry. But you still aren't going near her," I say with a warning glare.

"Why?" he screeches like a child. "If you don't want her, why can't I?"

"Because she's too nice for the likes of us. Plus, she wouldn't satisfy your sick sexual needs," I say.

He smirks. "I dunno, I think our little Liv is secretly turned on by the thought of being tied and fucked."

I curl my fist and take a deep, calming breath. I don't like him talking about her like that. "Shut the fuck up, man," I mutter.

It's another twenty minutes before Liv drops down on the seat next to Alex. When she spots me, she looks shocked, and I like that she didn't expect me. "Are you having a good night?" I ask.

"Sorry, should I go?" she asks, grabbing my arm and giving me her sad eyes.

"No, why would you go?" I ask, confused.

"Because I'm here with your friends," she wails. "I don't want to intrude."

She's clearly drunk, which makes me smile. "No, Liv, it's fine. I just came for a catch-up with the guys."

"They're a great bunch of friends," she says. "You're so lucky." I look around at the group of people I've known for as long as I can remember. They are good friends, and they don't treat me any different just because I have money or The Luxe.

Alex places an arm around Liv's shoulders, and she rests her head against him. "He's lucky we put up with his miserable arse," he jokes, and Liv grins at me.

"His arse is cute, not miserable," she says, and then slaps her hand over her mouth and giggles. Alivia's phone lights up and she looks at it closely, trying to focus. "Oh crap," she mutters.

Alex peers at the screen. "Who's Dan?" he asks.

"I drunk texted him," she groans, holding the phone to her chest with a horrified expression. Alex laughs hard, but it pisses me off that she's thinking about him after everything he did to her. She stands on wobbly legs. "I'll just go somewhere and take this."

Alex looks to me for an explanation. "It's her ex," I mutter bitterly.

"Shit, never speak to your ex when you're drunk," he says as I watch her leave the VIP area.

I decide to give her a few minutes and then I head out to find her. I go out the front of the club and look around. It's busy with people still queuing up to get inside and others flagging down passing taxicabs. I spot her leaning against the wall, talking to Dan in the flesh. He's standing in front of her, holding both of her hands, his face close to hers. They look deep in conversation, so I stay back for a moment.

Chapter Seven

Alivia

I'd stupidly texted Dan to see how he was. It was an innocent text, but one I never would've sent if I was sober. He'd texted back saying he was out with friends, and then I'd replied telling him I was at this club, and lo and behold, here he is. He's holding both of my hands and is way too close to my face. We're both drunk, which is never a good combination.

"Becca was just there, and we were so busy that we lost track of who we were and what we were to each other," he goes on, "but after you left, I couldn't breathe properly, it hurt so bad." I want to believe the bullshit that comes from his mouth, but I'm pretty sure it's the alcohol talking. "When I saw you with that arsehole, it broke me, Livvy. I didn't expect you to move on so quickly from us. That's not like you, baby."

"Well, you moved on before you'd even moved off from me, so you can't really judge," I mutter.

"Livvy, you're wife material. Becca is the kind of girl who's fun in the bedroom, but to actually talk to, there's not much going on there. I miss lying in bed chatting with you," he says, squeezing my hands.

"You used to tell me to stop talking because I was getting on your nerves," I point out. "In fact, you once said if I fucked as much as I talked, I'd be able to do it as an Olympic sport."

"We had good banter, didn't we?" He smiles wistfully like that's a good memory.

"What are you doing here, Dan?" I ask.

"I miss you. I want you to come home. I figure we can work on the sex, and I'll show you what I like. We didn't communicate enough before," he explains, and then he leans in and kisses me. It's clumsy and wet, and I pull back in disgust.

"What the hell was that?" I snap, wiping my mouth.

"Livvy, I want you so bad. Look what you do to me." He grabs his crotch area.

Vass appears behind Dan, taking me by surprise. He looks smooth and calm, and before I can react, he leans close to Dan's ear. "I'm gonna let that slide and put it down to you being wasted. But you touch her again, and I'll make you regret it."

Dan spins around angrily. "Too bad for you, cocksucker, she belongs to me, so back the fuck off."

"Alivia," says Vass firmly, his tone clipped but commanding. I step away from Dan and move to Vass's side. Vass smirks at Dan.

"Livvy, baby, come home."

"Alivia is happy. Leave her alone," Vass warns.

"Your parents don't even know we've split up. I'm giving you a chance to make this right, Livvy. Come home and we don't even have to tell them. You know how much your mum worries, and this will send her over the edge."

I open my mouth to speak, but Vass punches Dan in the face, shocking me into silence. Blood splatters from his nose, and I scream as it splashes up my arm. Doormen from the club rush over, grabbing Dan and marching him away despite his protests. I stare at the splattering of blood and a funny feeling bubbles in my stomach. I lurch forward uncontrollably and vomit all over the pavement, horrified to see it splash onto Vass's polished black shoes. I slap a hand over my vomit-covered mouth and mutter what sounds similar to an apology, but even I can't understand what came out. A white handkerchief is held under my face, and I take it gratefully, wiping my hand and mouth. I slowly stand, awkwardness filling the silence.

"I'm taking you home," Vass demands in a clipped tone. He grabs my hand, despite my protests about having vomit on it, and leads me to his car, handing me a plastic bag in case I decide to cover the interior of his nice car with my bodily fluids.

I can't keep my eyes open as he drives us to my apartment. Feeling myself being lifted from the car, I snuggle into Vass's chest as he carries me up the steps. I'm aware of an exchange of words between Vass and Keith, and then I'm being laid on my bed. I feel him remove my shoes, and then I hear him rummage in my drawers. "Alivia, where are your pyjamas?" he whispers.

I shove myself up into a sitting position and pull at my dress, lifting it over my head and chucking it on the floor. "I sleep like this," I say, grinning. He leans closer to pull the blankets over me. I lurch forward and grab him, forcing my lips against his and kissing him. He's too stunned to respond, and as I pull away, smiling, I mutter, "Goodnight, Dan," before flopping back onto my pillows.

"It's Vass," I hear him reply, and then my bedroom door closes, and I fall into a deep sleep.

※

The following morning, my head hurts so bad that I'm scared to open my eyes. I know the light streaming through my broken blinds will hurt my head more. Reaching over to my bedside cabinet, I feel around until I find my alarm clock. Opening one eye, I check the time. It's almost twelve o' clock. I've slept in later than I ever have. After a five-minute pep talk in my head about getting in such a state, I manage to sit myself up. I glance down at my lace underwear and then have a horrible flashback of me taking my dress off in front of my boss, right before kissing him with my vomit-smelling mouth and then calling him Dan. I cover my face and groan. I'm such an idiot.

I reach for my mobile phone and find there's a text from my mother and four missed calls. I forgot to tell her I wasn't going over to see her this weekend, so I send her a text apologising and telling her I'm hungover and that I'll call her later.

Then, I take a long shower and get into some comfortable joggers before collapsing on the sofa to watch reruns of my favourite sitcom and wait for my hangover to pass. The only time I move is to eat.

I lose count of the amount of times I drift in and out of sleep, but it's early evening when I wake to a loud banging noise. I sit up and look around, grabbing the television remote and muting it. Another round of banging sounds like someone knocking on the door downstairs, but this time, it's followed by some yelling. My heart beats faster, thumping hard in my chest as I rise to my feet to peek out the window. But before I can, there's knocking on my own door. I jump in fright, letting out a small, surprised screech. When I open the door to find two police officers, I'm confused.

"Are you the only occupant in here?" one of them demands to know, and I nod. "We have an arrest warrant for Mr. Kenneth Elmwood."

"I don't know who that is," I say.

"We have him downstairs in custody. If you could just sit tight up here, someone will come and speak to you shortly." I close the door and take a seat. Pulling out my mobile, I send a text off to Clarisse telling her that I'm freaking out. She texts me back saying she's bored and free, so she'll come over and see what's going on.

It's half an hour by the time the police come back to speak to me. Clarisse has already arrived, and the policewoman takes a seat. "How well do you know your landlord?" she asks.

I shrug. "Not very well, he's a bit creepy to be honest. He told me he was called Keith."

"His real name is Kenneth, but he has a lot of aliases. Did you know you're the only person renting a room from him in this building?"

"No, I never asked about the other rooms. I just assumed they worked during the daytime, like me."

"Why have you arrested him?" asks Clarisse.

"We've been looking for him for a while," says the officer. "He attacked a former tenant. He's quite a nasty piece of work." She clears her throat before adding, "We found some things that are concerning. Have you noticed any of your belongings going missing?"

"No, I've been preoccupied, I guess. I started a new job and I recently split from my ex, so things have been a little hectic." I feel sick at the thought of creepy Keith having anything of mine.

"What kind of things?" asks Clarisse.

The officers look uncomfortable. "Personal items, such as underwear."

"How the hell would he have my underwear? How do you know it's mine?" I gasp, my mind racing, trying to picture my underwear drawer and whether anything might have been moved.

"I think perhaps you should come and take a look at what we found."

Clarisse holds up her mobile up. "I'm just going to make a call. I'll come down right after."

I follow the police officers to the ground floor where Keith or Kenneth lives. The apartment is a mess. There are dishes built up on almost every surface. There are discarded newspapers and unopened letters on the floor, and dirty clothes scattered about. It smells of damp and dirt. My hangover isn't completely gone, and I place a hand over my mouth to stop myself from vomiting. Clarisse appears "Jesus Christ, it stinks," she mutters, taking my hand.

We step over the piles of crap and go through to a room at the back. I freeze. Every wall is covered with photos of me. My eyes scan over the pictures—me leaving for work, me talking to Vass outside the building, me asleep in my bed. I pull the picture from the wall and hold it to the officer. "How did he get this?" I ask. "This was me last night. This is what I wore in bed last night."

"We think he may have been watching you from day one. He takes in vulnerable women who need a place quickly. He offers the rooms without a background check, without references, and they're available straight away. Of course, for people who have just been kicked out of a property or people experiencing a difficult time, it appeals to them," explains the officer. "He has spare keys to all the apartments. We found pictures of other women. Are those items yours?" he asks, pointing to a table.

Some of my pyjamas are screwed up with different sets of my underwear. There's a hairbrush and a pair of my heels. I nod, folding my arms and hugging myself. "He was watching me when I slept," I mutter, a shiver running down my spine. I feel violated.

"It appears so," confirms the officer. I scan over the various pictures of me sleeping. Bile rises, and I make a run from the apartment just in time, vomiting in the garden.

"Liv?" It's Vass, marching up the steps. I take in his evening suit, a bow tie unfastened but still hanging around his neck, and I wipe my mouth. *Christ, what's he doing here?*

"The second time you've watched me throw up," I say, smiling weakly.

"Riss called me. What's going on?" he asks, gently rubbing my arm.

Clarisse appears in the doorway. "I'll show you," she says, taking him inside. When he reappears moments later, he looks angry. He pulls me to him and wraps his arms around me. The safety of his hug releases something inside me, and I burst into tears, burying my face in his chest.

"Riss, go and pack her a bag. She can't stay here," he says.

"She can stay with me," she offers. I begin to protest, but the look in Vass's eyes tells me I won't get my own way on this. And he's right, I can't stay here now I know about this, even if Kenneth has been arrested.

Vass follows us in his car to Clarisse's place. It's an old Victorian-style house not far from The Luxe, and I fall in love with it immediately. She's kept a lot of the original features, giving the house a homely feel.

Clarisse shows me to her spare room. It's comfortable, with a huge king-sized bed. I get changed into some pyjamas and make my way back downstairs. I hear Vass and Clarisse whispering, which makes me pause and sit on the stairs.

"She hated her, Riss, like really hated her. She point-blank refused to engage further in the conversation," he mutters.

"I get where she's coming from, Vass. She's a bitch, and it's obvious to everyone but you."

"But if I married her, I could carry on as normal. My life would stay the same. It's hard to find a woman who shares my lifestyle and isn't after my money," he whispers.

"Maybe you don't need that lifestyle as much as you think. There're better things out there."

"I have to go back to The Luxe. She was raging that I had to leave her."

"Vass, this isn't you. You don't run when some bitch calls. You say this is all for the end game, but you act like she's already your wife. I miss the old Vass. Walk away, because she isn't the one."

"She is the one, Riss. I'm marrying Annalise and everyone, including you and my grandmother, will have to accept that."

I'm frozen to the spot. I can't deny that my heart hurts to hear those words. It's stupid really—I've only known the guy a week and we shared one drunken, vomit-tasting kiss that I don't even remember properly. So, why am I upset that he's with someone? He told me he didn't do relationships, so he's been lying all along.

I'm still sitting there when Vass comes back through to leave. He looks up and sees me. "Hey, are you okay?"

I nod and fake a smile. "Thanks for coming. You didn't have to. Apologise to Annalise for me."

"You heard me," he says with realisation.

"I wasn't listening in," I mutter and then laugh. "Well, I was, but it was an accident. I heard you whispering and was trying to give you a moment. Anyway, it's nothing to do with me. She's nice, and you look good together." I fiddle with the edge of my pyjama shorts. "Look, Vass, I'm really mortified about last night..."

He shrugs. "Don't be. You were drunk, I get it. We all make bad choices when we drink. Forget it ever happened. I have."

I nod, feeling disappointed. "Okay. See you on Monday, if I still have a job?"

"See you Monday, Alivia," he says, leaving, and I sigh. I miss him calling me Liv.

Vass

So, my plan failed, much to my mother's delight. Her heart is set on Liv, but she doesn't understand how sweet and innocent Alivia is. My life will swallow her whole and spit her out, and I can't hurt her like that. Besides, once I ask her, she'll not only be horrified, but it might change her opinion of me, and I can't handle that. It's been one week . . . one . . . and I've never felt so out of control around a woman as much as I do when I'm with her. My whole adult life has been about me getting control—over myself, over sex, over alcohol, and yeah, I guess over women too. I control how I feel all the time, but with her, I lose it, and I don't like feeling like that.

I get back to The Luxe and head straight for Annalise's room. She turns to me as I enter, anger still present on her face. "So, what was so important that you felt you had to leave me to make my own way back here?"

"I arranged a car to bring you back, Annalise. I wouldn't have left you if it wasn't important." I sigh, pulling off my bow tie and dropping it, along with my car keys, onto her dresser.

"What the hell do we do now? The old bag hates me," she huffs.

"I'll speak to her tomorrow. She'll accept it," I mutter.

Annalise reaches behind her back and unzips her dress. The grey silk pools to the floor and she steps out of it. "Heels on or off?" she asks, swooping down to pick up the dress, putting it neatly on the chair.

"On. Is your father still flying into London next week?" I ask, unfastening my shirt.

"Yes. I'll arrange brunch for the day after he arrives and email the details to you. Bed or shower?"

"Shower. I've got meetings most days, so make it lunch." I remove my shirt and unbuckle my belt, following her into the bathroom. She leans into the shower and turns on the water, then she faces me, placing her hands on my shoulders.

"She has to come around before you speak to my father," she says, pressing a kiss to my lips. "You need to shave this," she adds, rubbing at the shadow of stubble across my jaw. "Father likes men who are clean shaven. He thinks it makes for a good businessman."

I lift her, and she wraps her arms and legs around me. "I'll book in to having a shave especially for it," I say and then freeze. Annalise looks at me, her smile fading as I lower her to the floor.

"What's wrong?" she asks.

"This," I mutter, pointing between us. "Riss is right. What the fuck is going on?" I say, more to myself than her.

"I don't understand." She follows me as I go back to the bedroom and begin to collect my belongings.

"We just acted like a married couple," I say, alarm on my face. "We did what married people do. We were going to have regular sex, and we talked like married people. Fuck."

She sighs. "You're overreacting, Vass."

I open the door, and she tries to close it again. "I have to get out of here," I say, pulling harder and practically running out of there.

I manage an hour's sleep before I decide to give up trying and head out to the gym, needing to work off this build-up of testosterone before I explode. I run until my heart feels like it's going to burst from my chest, and then I spend an hour lifting weights, pushing myself harder than I ever have. By the time I leave the gym, my whole body is shaking.

I pick up a coffee and sit on a bench nearby, pulling out my phone and flicking to the celebrity gossip app to check out pictures from last night's charity event. I usually ignore the gossip, but

I want to see if they've written about me and Annalise. I glance over the headline above my picture and groan. What a clusterfuck. As I begin to read, my phone flashes with a call from Clarisse.

"Morning, gorgeous," I say.

"Don't you fucking gorgeous me. Have you seen it?" she demands.

"Yeah, just. Has Alivia seen it?"

"No, she's still asleep. She really doesn't need this shit right now, Vass."

"It isn't my fault, Riss. You know what the press are like," I mutter.

"It never is," she growls, disconnecting the call.

Chapter Eight

Alivia

I rub the sleep from my eyes. Clarisse is eating toast at her breakfast bar, reading the newspaper. "Good morning," I say.

She jumps in fright and then laughs. "Did you sleep okay?"

"Yeah, surprisingly. I thought I'd struggle with everything that happened, but my head hit the pillow and I was gone. Thanks for letting me stay over."

"You know you're welcome to stay as long as you like. My friend moved out two months ago, and I haven't gotten around to renting out her room. It'll save me a job," she suggests.

"What about Vass?" I ask. I don't want to piss him off by hanging around his friends.

"Forget Vass. I like you and I think we could be good friends. It'd be stupid to go and rent somewhere else when I have a free room right here."

"I'd still prefer to run it past him first before I commit. Is that okay?"

"Yeah, of course." She pauses and then turns the newspaper towards me. "You should take a look at this."

I stare at the newspaper spread and gasp as my eyes run over the words.

'Love triangle for sex addict Vass raises concerns for his future with wealthy model.'

The photo beside it is the one Khan took of me and Vass almost kissing, but it looks like we're locked in a deep lip-to-lip battle in print.

Underneath is a photo of Vass and Annalise walking hand-in-hand on a red carpet. It must have been last night because it's the suit and bow tie he had on. It's followed by a photograph of Daniel looking sorry for himself with a cut on his nose from where Vass punched him.

"Holy shit," I mutter. I proceed to read the story with horror, tears filling my eyes.

'It was only Thursday when we brought you the story that London's eligible bachelor was off the market. Thousands of hearts broke when pictures emerged of Vass Fraser with his new beau, Annalise Collinsworth. The model was recently reported to be in financial difficulty when bailiffs turned up at her Knightsbridge apartment to remove items. Questions were raised about her motives for announcing her relationship to Vass less than 24 hours after the bailiff incident. The couple appeared happy and in

love at last night's charity bash, Help the Children, held at the London Royal by Vass's grandmother, millionairess Lady Fraser. She refused to comment on her grandson's new relationship, but insiders report that she isn't taken with the penniless model.

'Further questions have been raised about Vass's inability to commit after he was spotted several times this week with new employee, Alivia Caldwell. Rumours have it that Ms. Caldwell is not Vass's usual type, giving hope to all of us single ladies in London.

'We spoke to Ms. Caldwell's ex-boyfriend, Daniel Hatchet. In a tearful interview, he told us that he was left heartbroken when Alivia finally announced her love for her new boss, after just one week of knowing him. She left Mr. Hatchet, telling him she could no longer live a lie. He says that the business they

built together, D.A. Property Services, has an uncertain future ahead while he tries to get over his shattered heart.

'Vass has previously been reported to be dating childhood sweetheart, Clarisse Underwood.

All we know for sure is that Vass Fraser has them queuing up. Is it his bad boy image from years of lavish parties and a string of broken hearts, or the reported net worth of one billion pounds that attracts the hordes of women just dying to get some of the action?'

Clarisse places her hand over mine. "It'll blow over. I wouldn't worry too much. By tomorrow, it'll be someone else in the gossip column."

"But today, it's me. My parents read this Sunday paper and they don't even know that I've split up with Daniel," I cry. "And now, it looks like it was my fault."

"Maybe it's time you told them?"

"And say what exactly? Sorry I didn't tell you a month ago, but I've left Daniel, been stalked by some psycho old guy, moved in with a girl I've known a week, and I have a new job. Oh, and please don't believe the papers, I'm not shagging my playboy boss."

Clarisse laughs and then presses her lips together when I glare at her. "Well, perhaps don't say it like that."

I bury my face in my hands and groan. "This is all Daniel's fault. Why would he speak to the newspapers? And where did they get these pictures?" My mobile vibrates to life. "Oh god, it's my mum," I groan.

"Answer it. Get it out of the way," insists Clarisse.

I take a deep breath and accept the call. "Hi, Mum," I say, making sure I sound bright and breezy.

"Alivia Jayne Caldwell, you'd better start explaining," she says sternly.

"You've seen the newspaper." I sigh. "It's all lies, Mum."

"So, you haven't left Daniel?"

"Well, that bit is true, and the bit about me getting a new job," I explain. I hear a sob on my mum's end. "Don't get upset, Mum, I'm fine. I promise."

"Poor Daniel. You left him for a man who's always in the paper with different women," she cries. "He's a manwhore."

"No," I screech, "I'm not in a relationship with Vass, Mum. He's my boss. Daniel lied to the papers to get his five minutes of fame."

She sniffs. "That poor boy must be heartbroken."

"I'm the one who's heartbroken. Daniel cheated on me," I snap.

"Oh my god, there is so much you haven't told us," she wails. "Are you okay?"

"I'm okay now. I didn't tell you because I didn't want to worry you and Dad. I've got a new job, and I'm sorting myself out. I'll come over and tell you everything soon. Just don't listen to the papers, it's all lies."

I disconnect the call after reassuring her over and over that I'm fine and I'll go over to see them next weekend. Clarisse gives me a sympathetic smile. "Being friends with Vass comes at a price," she says. "You get used to it."

"At least my parents know about Dan and me. I was dreading telling them, and I guess the story made it so much worse, meaning the truth felt better to them," I mutter.

The door swings open and Vass enters the kitchen. His face is dripping with sweat, and from the shorts and vest, I can only assume he's been running. "Morning," he huffs, placing a brown paper bag onto the worktop and helping himself to a bottle of water from Clarisse's fridge. I watch open-mouthed as he unscrews the bottle top and drinks it in one go, crushing the plastic and putting it in the bin. He turns to us both and gives a cheeky smile. "Breakfast," he says, nodding to the bag.

Clarisse opens the bag and smiles. "You're creeping," she says, glancing at him.

"Maybe," he grins. "Am I forgiven?"

Clarisse hands me a freshly baked chocolate croissant, and it smells amazing. "It isn't up to me. I haven't been plastered all over the Sunday papers," she says. They both turn to me.

"It's not Vass's fault," I mutter. "He didn't go to the press. It's Daniel I'm mad at," I say. He knew my parents didn't know, and he thought to tell them in the worst possible way.

"So, anyway, you were right, Riss. Annalise and I aren't going to work," announces Vass.

Clarisse looks at him in shock, her croissant paused halfway to her mouth. "What? You dumped her?"

"There was no relationship to dump, but yes, I walked out of there this morning realising that she's seeing too much into it."

"Thank goodness for that. You knew your grandmother was never going to accept her."

"It makes no difference now, does it? Time's running out, and I need to face the fact that I'm never going to be the full owner of The Luxe."

"Why?" I ask, suddenly intrigued.

"Nothing for you to worry about, Liv. You have enough shit going on right now. Who the hell thought creepy Keith would be that crazy?" he asks.

I shudder, wrapping my arms around myself. "I wasn't expecting that. Do you think he would've hurt me if he hadn't been caught?"

"Don't think about that, it isn't worth it," says Clarisse. "Let's just be thankful he was caught when he was."

"Why don't I take you girls out for lunch today? My way of apologising for the newspaper bullshit. I think we all need cheering up right now."

I nod in agreement. "That would be lovely." We agree on a time, and Vass leaves, saying something about getting rid of Annaliese from the club.

Lunchtime rolls around and Vass sends a car to collect us. It drops us at an expensive hotel in central London that usually takes weeks to book a table. We find Vass already sitting in the bar area with his usual glass of water, and he has a bottle of Champagne waiting for us on ice. He greets us each with a kiss on the cheek. He looks handsome in his shirt and jeans, the sleeves rolled up to reveal his tattoos.

"Who did you fuck to get a table here at such short notice?" asks Clarisse with a smirk.

"I don't have to fuck to get a table, Riss, just my name is enough," he says with a cocky wink.

"Of course, the amazing Vass Fraser gets anything he wants. Did you get rid of Annalise?" she asks.

Vass groans dramatically. "It was not a pretty scene. She's going to cause me all kinds of shit, I just know it."

"Did she sign a gag order to stop her talking?" asks Riss.

"Of course. I warned her before she left that I'll take her for everything if she goes to the press. I don't think she'll do that, but I know she's going to get at me in other ways."

"It isn't your fault. You were straight from the start, and she knew the deal. Stupid her for thinking you'd fall madly in love."

I want to ask about the deal, or what exactly Vass and Annalise were up to if it wasn't a real relationship, but I don't feel like they'd tell me. Instead, I listen to them talk while I drink the Champagne.

Thankfully, lunch soaks up some of the alcohol because I'm starting to feel a little tipsy, but once the plates are cleared, another bottle of Champagne arrives. Riss tops up our glasses and it feels rude to not drink it.

"Riss asked me to rent her spare room," I say. Vass looks between us and then shrugs. "I didn't want you to think I was stepping on your toes. She's your friend," I add.

"And now, she's yours," he says simply. Riss gives me the thumbs up.

"I just need some air," I say, standing on wobbly legs and heading outside. I want to move in with Riss, but I'm not sure how I feel about seeing Vass like this, outside of work. I get the impression that he pops in to see Riss all the time, and it's hard enough working for him and not being able to pounce on him. Which brings memories of our clumsy kiss, causing me to groan out loud. A man standing nearby looks over with alarm, and I smile weakly. "Sorry, bad day," I mutter.

He steps closer. "I saw you inside," he says, adding a smile. "I'm Guy." He offers his hand, and I shake it.

"Alivia," I reply.

"Just a bad day, Alivia? Or a bad week?"

I laugh dryly. "At the minute, it feels like a bad year."

"I don't want to seem like I'm hitting on you, even though I totally am," he says, grinning, and I can't help but return it. "Fancy a drink?"

"I need a distraction," I murmur, and he pulls the door open for us to go back inside.

We sit at the bar, and I look over to where Riss and Vass are seated. Riss grins, but Vass looks less than impressed. I guess it is a bit rude coming for lunch with them and having a drink with someone else but I'm single and I need a distraction from my disastrous life.

"I'm staying here for the week," says Guy.

"Nice. Bet that's costing you a fortune," I say. "I live Tower Hamlets way."

The bartender takes our drinks order and we go back to the conversation. "I'm here on business."

"What kind of business?" I ask.

"I'm a writer," he says. "And you?"

"Marketing," I say, taking a large gulp of my drink.

"And you and your gentleman friend are just . . ." He waits for me to fill in the blank.

"Oh, Vass?" I ask, "No, Vass and I are not together. I work for him. He's my boss."

"And you're out on a Sunday, drinking Champagne?" he questions with a laugh.

"We have mutual friends. Vass is totally not my type," I lie, adding a small laugh.

"Really? So, good looking, fit bachelors are not your type?" he asks, and I frown. His statement confuses me. How does he know Vass is a bachelor? I mean, I know he's well known, but it seemed such an odd thing to say. And then a realisation hits me.

"Oh my god, you're from the press," I hiss.

"Talk to me, Alivia. It's better to print an honest story rather than lies. Are you and Vass an item?"

"No, I just told you we aren't," I snap.

"But you like him. Who wouldn't? Poor wench from the dregs of London meets rich playboy and tames him—it's a great story," he says with a shrug.

"Poor wench?" I repeat. "How dare you?"

"Your parents live in a council-owned property. You weren't rich growing up. You wanted a rich guy, and when Daniel wouldn't add your name to his business, you moved on," he summarises.

I stand, outraged by his lies. "What are you talking about? I helped Daniel build his business, and he cheated on me," I snap. "I walked away with nothing."

"And you wanted revenge? Is that why you're following Vass like a puppy dog? Of course, if you walked away with nothing, then the billions Vass has will help."

Tears fill my eyes. "It doesn't matter what I say, does it? You want to paint me as the money-grabbing poor girl."

He shrugs. "If you don't talk, I can only go on the facts I have in front of me."

I feel Vass approach before I even see him. Something about his presence makes itself known. The reporter looks up at him and smiles. "Mr. Fraser, how's things?"

"He's from the press," I mutter with a sniff.

"Do you make a habit of going around harassing women and making them cry"? asks Vass calmly, wrapping an arm around my shoulder.

"I was simply asking for the truth."

"The truth is, I'm single. I have been for a long time. Ms. Caldwell is my employee and we're having a business lunch with my office manager. There's nothing between Ms. Caldwell and I apart from business, and there never will be." I shut down the sudden emotion that his friend-zoning statement evokes inside of me. "Now, if you'll excuse us, we have a meeting to get back to," adds Vass, leading me away.

"Sorry, Vass, I didn't know. I thought he was a nice guy," I tell him.

"Do you make a habit of letting strangers buy you drinks?" he hisses.

"No, but he seemed nice," I mutter, "and I needed a distraction."

Vass

I'm not sure why I feel so mad at Liv for having a drink with some guy she just met. It's not like she's in a relationship. She's entitled to drink with whoever she wants.

"You girls enjoy the rest of the afternoon. I have to go and see my grandmother and give her the news she's been wanting." Alivia looks upset still, but I cant be around her right now. I might do something reckless in front of the moron reporter, like kiss her until I bruise her lips and take her breath away. Cos fuck knows I want to.

My grandmother is at her usual Sunday hangout. She likes to tell everyone she's a member of the tennis club, but she doesn't actually play any tennis. I take a seat, and she looks up in surprise.

"Vass, what a nice surprise. Jean is winning this match," she says, nodding to the two ladies playing tennis on the court in front of us.

"Great. You didn't like her?" I ask, and she sighs heavily.

"It's not that I didn't like Annalise, Vass. I'm sure she is a lovely girl, but I know it's not real."

"It is real. What do you want to see exactly before you'll accept my choice?"

"She doesn't look at you with the love and devotion you deserve. You think you can fool me that you're settled and in love by bringing the daughter of a billionaire? She might not be after your money, Vass, but she isn't a good person," she says. "And then there're the rumours she's bankrupt, and I hear her father is refusing to bail her out."

I groan. "I don't know what you want from me."

"I want it to be real."

"Well, thanks to you and your appalling behaviour, Annalise and I have split up," I tell her.

She smiles. "Oh, that's good news."

"No, it isn't. I'm coming alone to dinner this evening."

"Bring Alivia. She's perfect for you," she says.

"Alivia is my employee," I snap.

"Not according to the newspapers," she says with another smile.

"You really have to stop this meddling. Between you and my mother, you're driving me mad."

"Your mother agrees with me. She doesn't want you to end up alone. Finally, something we agree on."

"But you're forcing it. How can it be real when you're forcing it?" I ask. "Maybe I'm happy as I am."

"You're looking in the wrong place, just like your father and your grandfather."

I groan in frustration. "I'm coming alone this evening," I repeat and stand. I know this will piss my mother off because it's a couples dinner and she likes things done properly.

That evening, I arrive late to dinner. My mother's driveway is cluttered with cars, and I hand my keys to the parking attendant. I go straight to the large, white tent that was erected especially for this event. The theme is white, so inside, I'm not surprised to see most of the females in white. Wanting to avoid the whole John Travolta look, I opted for a white shirt and black trousers.

The seating attendant looks at her chart and then walks me through the throng of tables to my seat. The charity speeches have begun, so I fix my eyes to the stage as I lower into my seat, avoiding any glares at my late arrival from my mother.

It takes me a second to realise the seat next to me isn't vacant, though It should be because I didn't bring a guest. I manage a quick glance to my left and my eyes widen in shock. Alivia stares awkwardly at me, and I glare at my grandmother, who's sitting opposite me at the large round table. She gives me a little wave and a smug smile.

"I am so sorry. I thought you knew I was coming," whispers Alivia into my ear.

"My friends move you in, my family invite you to their charity functions . . . you really are moulding yourself into my life," I hiss.

She doesn't reply, instead pushing her chair back. It makes a screeching sound, which causes those nearby to look over. Alivia's cheeks colour, and then she turns and walks out. I sigh, groaning. It isn't her fault that everyone else is using her as a pawn in this ridiculous game. "That's all your fault," I growl across the table at my grandmother before rushing after her.

I catch a glimpse of Alivia storming across the garden and towards the house as I step out of the marquee. "Alivia, wait," I shout, but she continues. My leg muscles scream in protest as I turn my walk into a jog to catch up with her. My earlier workout has left me aching and sore. I reach out to grab her arm, but she pulls loose and continues towards the house. I stop, frustration coursing through me. Then, I feel the Dom inside me step up. "Alivia, stop now," I order, and to my surprise, she does. I give a satisfied nod as I step in front of her. "That was out of order and I apologise."

"Well, thank you for the apology," she snaps and then goes to walk around me. I block her, placing my hands on her shoulders to hold her still.

"Wait," I say. "I don't feel like that at all. I honestly don't mind that you're moving into Clarisse's, you'll love living there. I'm pissed at my grandmother, not you, cos she keeps meddling in my life."

"Why?" she asks, placing her hands on her hips. I like the sassy attitude she's giving off.

"Because she's asking for the impossible and pushing me to find it."

"What's so impossible?"

"She wants me to settle down." I huff, and Alivia laughs. "It isn't funny."

"I thought it was something terrible." She grins. "You said impossible."

"Impossible for me. I don't want to settle down. I like my lifestyle, and I don't understand why she can't just let me be happy in my own way."

Alivia takes a seat on the grass, hitching her long dress to her knees and folding her legs. She points to the space next to her. "On the grass?" I ask doubtfully. When she nods, I sigh and lower myself next to her.

"What's so impossible about settling down? I mean, how old are you now, like thirty-five?" she asks with a cheeky wink.

"Thirty." I scowl at her. "And every man in my life, my father, my grandfather, all thought they wanted that settled down life, and all it brought was misery and grief. This lifestyle doesn't allow for vanilla relationships with a boring sex life and," I huff, "children. It's not for me."

"So, just tell her you don't want to settle down," she says with a shrug. A passing waitress is carrying a bucket of Champagne, and I stop her and take it.

"I'll also have some water, please," I say to her, and she rolls her eyes and stomps back towards the house. I pop the cork on the Champagne and hand it to Alivia.

"Why don't you drink?" she queries. I knew this would come up, but I'm not ready to answer that.

"I do, water and coffee," I joke, and she rolls her eyes.

"You know what I mean."

"Alcohol and I just don't have a good relationship," I say with a shrug. She senses my reluctance to talk, which I appreciate.

"So, going back to your grandmother, why is she so desperate to see you settled?"

"She owns half of The Luxe," I explain, noticing the surprise in Alivia's face. "She wants to sign it all over to me so I'll own a hundred percent instead of fifty, but there are conditions."

"Those being that you settle down?" she asks, and I nod. She takes a drink from the bottle and the bubbles spill over the rim and run down her hand.

"I can get you a glass," I offer, but she shakes her head, giggling. I like the sound, it warms my soul.

"No, I like to slum it sometimes. It reminds me of when I was a teenager drinking in the park with the local hoodrats," she says with a grin.

"Hoodrats?" I query.

"Yeah, you know, the local bad boys," she says. "Although, we weren't drinking Champagne back then, more like cheap cider."

"I never did that," I admit. "I feel like I missed out."

"You really did. Cheap cider shared from the bottle between ten kids and a quick, sloppy snog with some boy who thinks he's a gangster, my life rocked back then." She nudges her shoulder into mine, and we smile.

"My grandmother doesn't want me to be like my father or grandfather. She thinks The Luxe ruined them and their relationships. She doesn't see that by forcing me to marry, just to get the other fifty percent, is going to cause the same problems. What woman is going to marry someone who spends half his time participating in orgies or nipping off to see his submissive every night?"

Alivia thinks for a moment. "Maybe she thinks that if you find the one, then you won't turn to those things anymore?"

"But I like those things. I want that life."

"Well, she doesn't want it for you," says Alivia. "It sounds like she just loves you and wants the best for you. You might not agree it's best right now, but twenty years down the line, when you're balding and overweight, you'll thank her for the backup plan," she says with a smirk.

"I will not be fat or balding!" I laugh. "Would you want your husband to be like me?"

She shakes her head. "I'm not sure I could handle a man who goes to have sex with other women. I don't know a woman who does," she says honestly, and I'm surprised how her comment bothers me.

"That's why Annalise was perfect. She'd have put up with that because she liked it too," I say.

"For now," she replies, and I give her a quizzical look. "Well, maybe it works now, but eventually, when you're both old and grey, what then? This life isn't forever, right? What about when it all stops and it's just the two of you? Sometimes you need more than just a connection in the bedroom."

"Maybe so, but the future wasn't on my mind. The here and now is. Anyway, my grandmother didn't fall for it, so it's not an issue. Apparently, she can spot real love, like a modern-day bloody cupid." I roll my eyes and shake my head.

Alivia takes another sip of Champagne, spilling a little down her chin. She smiles bashfully, wiping it away, and my heart beats a little faster. She's so damn beautiful.

"My mother was mortified when she thought I'd hooked up with you," she admits.

It's not unusual for parents to hate me when they first find out I'm in their daughter's life. I don't blame them—I wouldn't want my daughter to be with someone like me. I usually win the mothers around with my charm, but fathers never fall for my bullshit. Men have that knack of knowing an ulterior motive when they spot one.

"Now, I have to spend the weekend with them to convince them I haven't lost my mind or given my heart to a playboy," she adds, laying back and looking up at the sky. "So, thanks for that."

"Did you do this with the hoodrats in the park when you were being young and reckless?" I ask, laying on my side so I can see her face illuminated by the white of the moon. *Fuck, I want to kiss her.*

"Of course. I wanted to be popular, and to do that, I had to make sacrifices. Letting Tommy Oakham grope my breasts, over my top, of course, was one of those sacrifices," she says with a laugh.

Hearing her laughter brings me some kind of joy, and I find myself laughing too. "Tommy Oakham was the man. I'd high five him if I ever met him."

"He was a twat in the end, told everyone I stunk of fish down there. I was mortified and spent the rest of that term being called 'fishy'." I press my lips together to keep my laugh inside, but she catches it and lightly hits me on the arm. "I did not smell. He wanted to go further, and I said no."

"Typical boy, making up rumours when he got his ego bruised," I say, shaking my head in mock disgust.

"I can't imagine that's ever happened to you," she adds, arching her brow.

"I've had hard times. Maybe I didn't feel up a girl in the park while drunk on cheap cider, but I got caught having sex by my headteacher once. It was embarrassing . . . mainly because it was his wife I was fucking. The fact that she was my English teacher really didn't help."

Alivia gasps, pushing up on her elbows. "No way, that did not happen," she screeches, giggling.

I nod. "It really did. Just one of the moments in my life when my mother compared me to my father. She seems to think it's in the Fraser DNA."

"Wow. That shocks me. It shouldn't, knowing you like I do after just one week, but my god, I hope she was fit and not some eighty-year-old teacher."

"Of course, she was fit, what do you take me for? She was newly qualified, and it ended her career before she'd even completed her first year."

"Ouch, I feel bad for her."

"I was just a kid." I shrug. "She should've known better."

"Um, somehow, I don't feel like you were the innocent party in any of it. She was swayed by your boyish charm and enticing eyes." She gives me a playful wink.

"Ouch, Liv, victim shaming is a terrible thing." I lean forward, my face inches from hers. "Why don't my eyes work on you?" I feel the tension hit up a notch, and she inhales a shaky breath.

"Because I know they're dangerous," she whispers.

I fight everything in me that's telling me to kiss her, and instead, I pull back. She exhales like she's almost relieved. "You're right, so dangerous," I say with a shrug, "Maybe we should get back to the party."

I push to stand and hold out my hand to her. I think I detect a look of disappointment in her eyes, but she shuts it down quickly, smiling wide and placing her delicate hand in my own. I pull her to stand, causing her to crash against my chest. Her free hand rests there for a second, and I stare down at her. It's like the fucking Lord of love is there himself, trying to get me to kiss her.

"Right... inside..." I mutter, shaking my head to clear the voices screaming at me to do it. I lead her back to the party as quickly as I can. As we take our seats, I catch my grandmother smiling smugly at us.

Before the main meal arrives, I'm pulled off to meet various associates of my mother. She likes to drop that her son is Vass Fraser to all those who don't yet know. I glance back to the table and find my seat has been filled by Evan Johnstone, a lawyer who often chats to my dates—not that she's my date, but still—in the hope it will piss me off. I fucked his wife, it was years ago, but the guy just can't forgive and forget. He's still with her, and I'd bet my life savings she's also here tonight chatting with another rich bachelor, talking him into her bed.

I continue my conversation. If I rush over, he'll know it's bothering me. When I look back, the seats are empty, and I immediately scan the room, trying to find them. My eyes finally catch a glimpse of Alivia in Evan's arms on the dancefloor. He's holding her close, too fucking close, and I clench my fists, trying to tame the anger I feel building.

"They look cute together, don't they? Is she the type to hook up?" whispers Savanna, Evan's wife.

"He's still pissed about us, Savanna. Can't the guy move on?" I sigh. "It's getting boring, his constant need to chase my dates." Savanna runs her hand down my back and rests it against my arse.

"I still think about us. It replays over and over." She sighs, dreamily. "You're like an addiction."

"It was a mistake, Sav. We both know it, and I deeply regret it."

"I can only imagine how good you are now after all that practise," she adds, placing a well-manicured hand to her chest. "If the newspapers are to be believed."

"Excuse me, I have a date to rescue," I mutter, making a beeline for Alivia. "May I cut in?" I ask politely. They stop their gentle swaying, and Evan takes a step back, smiling smugly as I take his place.

I sweep her away from him, keeping her close as we move through the other couples dancing. She smiles up at me, a question that she doesn't voluntary air playing on her mind.

"What?" I ask gruffly.

"Are you jealous?" she asks, smirking.

"No, don't be silly. I just hate him."

"He predicted you'd get jealous and cut in," she says, wiggling her eyebrows playfully.

Something about the haunting music the band is playing and the playful gleam in her eyes has me pulling her closer. I knock a small breath from her and heat returns to her eyes. She wants me to kiss her too. I lean in so that our mouths are almost touching again. "I don't like other men dancing with my dates," I whisper.

"I wasn't technically your—" she begins, but I can't take the tension a second longer. I slam my mouth against hers. She's hesitant at first, but when I don't pull away, she melts against me, letting me take what I need. And fuck, I need her. My body tingles with want as my tongue sweeps into her mouth, tasting the remnants of tonight's Champagne. I'm vaguely aware the music has stopped and I pull back. Alivia continues to stare up at me in shock, or maybe it's a lustful haze. Either way, I need a second to process what the fuck just happened. I've kissed a lot of women, and not once have I felt the loss of control that just took over me. She's dangerous.

Chapter Nine

Alivia

"I have a few people I need to speak with before I call it a night," says Vass, taking a few steps back. "I'll make sure there's a car out front to take you home whenever you're ready. Just give your name to the doorman."

I'm confused as he marches away, his strides long and purposeful, like he can't wait to get the hell away from me. I gently touch my fingers to my swollen lips, still tingling from our kiss, and those butterflies are swirling around my stomach so hard, I feel nauseous.

The dancefloor begins to clear as the band announces they're taking a break. I spot Vass chatting to a group of women who are all enthralled by whatever he's saying. Regret hits me hard as I realise I've got to face him tomorrow in the office. *What the hell was I thinking?*

I make my way back to the table, deciding to get out of here. Vass catches my eye as I pass but doesn't say a word.

Our table is empty apart from Vass's grandmother. She smiles kindly, patting the seat beside her. I glance over to check Vass is still talking before I sit. "Alivia, thank you so much for coming this evening. I hope you've had a nice time."

"It was an amazing night. Thank you so much for inviting me. I have to go now, though. I have work tomorrow."

"Is Vass escorting you home?" she asks, looking around for her grandson.

"No, he's arranged a car," I say with a tight smile.

"A car? He's been raised better than to kiss a woman with that amount of passion and then send her home unescorted in a car," she mutters dryly. "I must apologise on his behalf." I feel my face burn bright with embarrassment as she pats my hand. "Don't feel embarrassed. He's charming, isn't he? His father and grandfather were the same. But he likes you, Alivia. I can sense it. He just hasn't worked out how to deal with that. Be patient with him. I have a good feeling about the two of you."

I shake my head. "Vass doesn't like me like that. You have to let him live his life the way he wants. He's happy."

She rolls her eyes. "He isn't happy. He thinks he is, but once he falls in love, that's when he'll know what true happiness is."

"Most men find it, eventually, and Vass will too. He's only thirty. That's considered young these days."

Her expression turns solemn. "I don't have long left . . . less than six months. I'd love to see him settled before then."

I stare wide-eyed. Vass never mentioned it was his grandmother's dying wish. I feel terrible for her. "I'm so sorry," I mutter. "I didn't realise."

"Don't be, I've accepted it. But you can't deny a dying woman her one wish," she says, adding a playful wink.

"Me?" I ask, laughing. and she nods. "I don't understand."

"You're the one. You can make him see there's more to life than that club and his party lifestyle."

I laugh again, shaking my head as I stand. "No, I can't. Did you see how fast he ran after he kissed me? He sees me as an employee, and maybe a friend, but nothing more. I mean, he's Vass Fraser, and I'm just... I'm just me. I have to go," I mutter, stumbling away from the table. "Thanks again for tonight," I throw over my shoulder as I rush out of there.

As I climb into the back of Vass's car, I feel a sadness pass over me. His grandmother is dying and her last wish is to see Vass settled. I'm sad it'll never happen, not in six months at least.

I don't sleep well,. spending most of the night tossing and turning, Vass's kiss weighs heavy on my mind, along with the revelations of the evening. By the time six a.m. comes around, I'm irritated and tired. I shower and decide to go into work early. I have lots to do today, so the early start won't do any harm, and maybe it'll distract me from the dread I feel at seeing Vass at work today.

By the time Vass rolls into the office, I've made a good dent in my to-do list and given myself at least a hundred pep talks on how to appear cool and calm. "Good morning," I say, putting on my bright and breezy tone.

"Morning," he mutters as he shuffles some papers on Bianca's old desk. "I just wanted to speak to you about last night," he adds, looking uncomfortable.

No, no, no. "Okay," I say, closing my laptop and folding my arms. "I'm listening." Panic envelopes me. *What if he sacks me?*

"It shouldn't have happened. I'm your boss, and if things like that were to happen, I'd have to fire you. I don't want to do that."

I go over his words in my head before frowning and asking, "What do you mean?"

"Well, just that if we did . . . yah know," he nods instead of adding the words 'have sex', "I'd have to let you go. We couldn't continue to work together."

I tip my head to one side. "Why?"

He looks more uncomfortable. "Because it wouldn't work, would it? Things would be awkward."

"It worked for you and Bianca."

"That was different. We didn't have sex."

I slowly nod, understanding dawning on me. "Right. But you and Amy, you slept together and then you fired her?" He nods, wincing with what I hope is shame. "I'm sure there are laws you're breaking right there, but whatever. So, you sleep with employees, fire them, rehire, and the cycle continues?"

"When you put it like that, it sounds bad."

"Because it is bad." No wonder his grandmother worries about him. "And that's why you never fall in love. You don't let them stick around long enough for you to feel anything."

He scoffs. "Not true. I don't *want* to fall in love."

"Your mother chose me, didn't she?"

He frowns. "You know she did. She employed you on my behalf."

"I mean, to fulfil your dying grandmother's last wish."

He eyes me angrily. "Who told you she was dying?"

"We spoke last night and she told me. She tried to convince me I could change you." I laugh. "And now, I've put two and two together. I'm right, aren't I? Your mother hired me for you marry, to appease a dying old lady."

He looks pissed, which tells me I'm right. "So, what if she did? I didn't ask you, did I? I haven't made a move, and when I did, I regretted it," he snaps.

I feel a small triumph that I'm right. "What do I get out of marrying you?" I ask, twirling a pen in my fingers. Vass pauses his paper shuffling but doesn't look up. "If I was to make an agreement with you, what would I get?" My heart hammers in my chest. This wasn't in my plan, but I'm curious.

"What are you saying?"

I shrug because, honestly, I don't know. "That I feel bad she's dying. I like her, and I think she should get her wish, or at least think she has." Vass pulls Bianca's office chair towards my desk and sits down opposite me. "I know it wouldn't be a real marriage because that's not what you want. And it would have to be secret from the limelight. My parents can't ever know."

"Why would you do that?" he asks.

"I couldn't stop thinking about your grandmother last night, it kept me awake. She wants this so badly for you, and she seems to think I'm the one who can make it happen. I don't want her to pass away worrying about you. Maybe we can give her some peace. And we're friends," I pause, shrugging, "I think. You've helped me so much recently, been so kind, so maybe I can return the favour."

He sighs, rubbing his face. "It's a massive thing to ask of someone."

"You haven't asked me, I'm asking you."

"What about your parents?" he asks. "I don't know how secret I can keep a relationship from the press."

"Maybe I can tell them we're seeing one another, but marriage? That's too much to lie to them about, even if I'm doing it with good intentions. They take all that very seriously, and once your grandmother passes, it'll break them to know we've separated."

My parents were married young. My father has always said he loved my mum from the day he met her and didn't want to risk losing her, so he proposed a month after they met. Six months later, they were married. They're inseparable and still so in love. "We'll need to come up with rules.

Why don't you come over to Clarisse's tonight and we can go over some?" I suggest.

Vass stands and rounds the desk, then he leans down and kisses me on the top of the head. "You have no idea what this means to me, no one's ever done something so massive for me without ulterior motives. It means so much."

I smile proudly. I feel good about this, and I know his grandmother will be so happy.

⊰⊱

I tell Clarisse about my offer over lunch. "Oh my god, that's huge," she screeches, running around to my side of the desk and hugging me.

"We might need your input on the rules later. I have no clue what to implement so we both know the boundaries."

"Don't worry, I'm great at that sort of thing," she reassures me.

The afternoon drags slowly. I don't see Vass at all as he's in and out of meetings, so it gives me a chance to make a rough list of rules. Number one being no sex. It may be a marriage but only a pretend one, and if we engage in intimate relations, then I know without a doubt that I'll end up falling for Vass, and that'll only end in heartache for me. I sigh, realising I must be crazy agreeing to this. I'll be a divorcee before I'm thirty.

By the time I get home, I'm talking myself out of this crazy idea. Clarisse freezes when I walk into the kitchen, dumping my bag on the worktop. "What's wrong, Liv?" she asks, concerned.

"Am I crazy?" I blurt out, and she looks taken aback.

"I hope not, since I've said you can live here now," she says with a small laugh.

"I mean about the Vass thing. I've known him for such a short time and I'm offering to marry him to appease his dying grandmother. That's crazy talk, isn't it?"

Clarisse takes my hands in hers and pulls me to sit down. "No, Liv, it's not crazy. You have a kind heart and you saw a dying woman wanting the best for her grandson."

"But it's a lie. We're lying to a dying woman," I groan. "She's going to look down from heaven when I sign that divorce and put a curse on me."

Clarisse laughs. "It's a massive thing, I get it, and I know you don't know me well either, but I can vouch for Vass. He's a sex-crazed manwhore, but he's such an amazing guy. He cares so much about others. Look how he took you out to eat because he knew you didn't have the money. He's a good man, and his grandmother wants the best for him. So, what if the marriage is a lie? Your fondness of each other isn't. Let her die happy knowing that Vass is happy. And he will be, just in a different way to what she wants. You've made a friend for life in him, and he won't ever forget that you helped him out like this."

I feel a sense of calm wash over me. She's right. "Thanks, Riss," I say, giving her a hug.

Vass arrives an hour later with takeout Chinese and a bottle of wine. Once we're all settled at the table, I pull out my list of rules. Vass raises his eyebrow and laughs. "You're taking this really serious, Liv."

"Aren't you?" I ask.

"Well, yeah, of course, but I'm not great with rules. Just ask my mother."

"If this is going to work, Vass, you need to respect Alivia's terms," snaps Clarisse, and I smile, knowing she's on my side.

"Fine." Vass sighs. "Hit me with it."

"Sex," I say, and his eyes widen. "There'll be none between us." He rolls his eyes.

"Way to get my hopes up, Liv," he mutters.

"We have to keep the wedding a secret. I don't want my parents to know." He nods in agreement.

"Once your grandmother has . . ." I trail off. "Well, yah know, you file for the divorce and pay the costs."

Vass nods again. "And what do you want to walk away with?" he asks.

"Me?" I ask, confused. "Nothing."

Vass frowns. "So, you're going to marry me, stay married until my grandmother passes away, let me divorce you, and you want nothing? Not a house, not a car . . . just nothing?"

I nod and shrug. "Yeah. I'm doing this for your grandmother, and you've helped me out so much already. I owe you this."

"Liv, you can't do this for nothing. I have billions. I can give you cash, get you a house, anything you want."

"No," I say with a shudder. "It makes it feel seedy when you offer things like you're my sugar daddy."

Vass laughs. "We'll talk about this further. You have to walk away with something, so have a think."

"Lastly, other women," I say, knowing this could be the deal breaker for Vass. "I don't mind what you do, but don't do it around me, mainly because if anyone else sees you behaving like that, it looks disrespectful to me. I don't want to be seen as some little wifey who gets cheated on and turns a blind eye," I state, and Vass nods. "And don't get caught out, not by the press, not by employees, which means you taking part in sex at The Luxe could be an issue."

"I haven't joined in for a while now. But you're right, I can do that stuff privately."

Vass

Alivia stares at me for a moment and then shrugs her shoulders. "Any rules from your end?" she asks.

I'm still in shock that this beautiful woman has chosen to do this for me. She'll never understand how grateful I am. "What about your dating life? It'll have to be put on hold for a while." I can't deny this pleases me, because thinking about another man touching Alivia in the way I crave makes me want to rip shit apart.

"What dating life?" She scoffs. "I can wait until we divorce." That one word, divorce, doesn't sit well with me. Of course, that's the natural end to a fake marriage.

"What about the important stuff?" asks Clarisse.

"Like?" I ask.

"Well, like what's acceptable and what's not. Who's making the announcement? How are you going to convince your grandmother that Alivia is the one? Will you move in together? Will you share a bed?"

"Christ, no," Alivia says in a high-pitched tone. "We're not sharing a bed. Go back to my first rule—no sex. And his grandmother won't be a problem. She saw us kiss and she told me she thinks I'm the one to change him."

"Kiss?" Clarisse repeats, looking back and forth between us.

"Never mind that," I mutter. "But you're right, we'll have to move in together." My grandmother will expect it before she hands over The Luxe. "I'll tell my grandmother in a couple of weeks. Until then, maybe we need to be seen together, so it looks like a natural progression. Once we've announced the engagement, then you can move into The Luxe. I'll come with you to see your parents on the weekend, so they can get used to seeing us together and it won't be a shock if the papers then get pictures of us."

"No. No way are you coming to my parents'. Let me talk to them, ease them into the idea of us being a couple," says Alivia. I nod, not wanting to push her too hard but knowing full well I intend to see her parents. I finish my glass of water and stand. "Where are you going?" asks Alivia.

"Jesus, woman, are you getting into role already?" I ask with a smirk, and she blushes. If I didn't know better, I'd think she was sad to see me leave. "I have a private room with my name on it." I wink, and Clarisse rolls her eyes and scowls at me while Alivia nods. I wish I could explain why I need what I need. I promised I wouldn't get caught having sex, and I won't, because honestly, since meeting her, I haven't wanted anyone else. But this . . . this I can't give up.

Once I arrive back at The Luxe, I go straight to the bar, where I spot Ava. She feels the moment

I'm approaching because she turns to face me, a smile on her plump red lips. When I scowl at her bright smile, she lowers her head, realising we've already begun and I'm in full Dom mode. She rises to her feet, keeping her head lowered. I pull the silk collar from my pocket and place it around her neck, then I put out my hand expectantly. I see the hesitation, but she reaches under her skirt and shimmies out of her underwear. It's not uncommon in here, so no one bats an eye. I take the scrap of black lace from her and place it in my pocket.

"Take it off," I growl in her ear, not missing the shudder that races through her. She enjoys this. She wipes at her lips and the red stains her hands. She wore red on purpose to defy my instructions. She wants to be punished.

I take her by the hand and lead her through the bar and towards the main room. I make her stand to my side while I take a seat near the back of the room. I like to keep in the shadows. "Watch," I order her, and she looks up to the stage. Two women are taking centre stage. One sits on a high stool with her legs open and wrapped around the head of the other. She screams in pleasure as the girl on her knees eats her pussy. I run my hand up Ava's inner thigh, stroking her leg and tracing small circles along her soft skin.

A man comes onto the stage, and the girl on her knees turns her attention to him while he kisses the girl on the stool. Ava fidgets. She wants my hand to move higher, but I ignore her and continue my slow, torturous circles. I let Ava watch for another five minutes while the man takes turns fucking each girl.

I stand and take Ava's hand again, leading her to the doors where we can watch private shows. I pop my head into the closest room. It's perfect because there's a threesome behind the glass. I pull Ava inside and stand her near the glass, her hands pressed against it. I kick her legs apart and leave her to stand like that for a few minutes. When I finally run my hand back up her inner thigh, she's soaking wet. "Do you like the show, Ava?" I ask.

"Yes, Sir," she whimpers.

"You wore red lipstick," I say, and she nods. My hand slaps hard against her backside, causing her to lurch forwards.

"Sorry, Sir," she gasps.

I slide my finger into her, and she shudders. I bring it to her mouth, wiping her juices along her lips. "Lick," I tell her, and she does. Then I cram my finger in her mouth. "Why did you wear the lipstick, Ava?" I ask.

"Because I wanted you to punish me, Sir," she admits.

"How?"

"I wanted you to spank me, Sir," she whispers.

Too bad. I won't give her what she wants, it's not how this works, so I push a finger back into her, and she cries out. I try another, stretching her, and she rocks against me, trying to get herself off.

I use my other hand to free her breasts, pulling her dress down at the front. I gently massage them, occasionally squeezing her erect nipple. I feel her inner walls squeeze my fingers and I know she needs to climax. I pull my hand away, and she cries out in protest, then I slap her peachy backside again and push my fingers into her mouth. She licks them clean before I push them back into her, repeating this over and over until she's a quivering mess, desperate for a release. I turn her to face me, and she places her hands on my shoulders for support while I bring her to climax, rubbing her vigorously until she's crying out in pleasure. My cock aches to be inside her, but my mind is too full of Liv and the sacrifice she's making for me. I pop my fingers into my mouth, tasting Ava's release, then I allow her to pull me into a deep kiss, tasting herself on my tongue. Reaching around her neck,

I unclip the collar. She pulls back to look at me. "Are we done?" she asks, and I nod.

"I have stuff to do, sorry," I say. "Go and play in the main room. Enjoy the rest of the night." I kiss her on the head and leave the room. I need to have a cold shower.

Once I'm dried off, I slip on a pair of jeans and a T-shirt. I head to the second floor and knock on the door. "Come in," says Ella. I open the door, and she smiles. "Vass, I didn't expect you. It's been a while."

"I'm desperate," I mutter, and she nods, indicating for me to come in farther.

"I'm free."

Chapter Ten

Alivia

"Mum, where are you?" I shout as I enter my childhood home.

"In the kitchen," she answers. I head through and find her with her hands in a bowl of dough. "Bread," she says as a way of explanation.

I go behind her, wrapping my arms around her waist and pressing my cheek against her back. "I missed you."

"I missed you too, sweetheart." She smiles. "Your dad's gone to the shop to get us a bottle of wine for tonight. I'm doing salmon for tea, your favourite." I love coming home to homecooked food, and nothing beats my mum's cooking.

I sit at the breakfast bar and watch her knead the bread. "So, tell me what the hell's been going on."

I fill her in about Daniel and what he did to me, how he then begged me back and Vass hit him on the nose. Mum presses her lips together to keep her smile in. I tell her all about my new job, omitting that The Luxe is a private sex club and opting for an elite hotel. She has no clue how to use the internet, so I'm not worried. I tell her how Vass has helped me so much and how great he is.

"He has a terrible reputation for being a womaniser," she reminds me.

"I know. But I haven't seen that side of him, Mum, and I'm not willing to judge a person on what the newspapers print."

"They've been printing rubbish all week," she says, nodding to a pile of papers on the worktop. I reach for one and open it to the celebrity gossip section. I scan the text. I've been avoiding looking at them all week as Vass said they were only printing bullshit and to ignore them. This one talks of a love triangle involving me, him, and Annalise Thankfully, there are no more pictures. I drop it back onto the pile, "Just ignore them all, Mum, none of it's true."

"I know. One said you were a money-grabber trying to take Vass for everything he has. I told your father that I have a good mind to go and speak to them. How dare they paint that picture of you?"

I smile at her in protective mum mode. "I haven't read them because they annoy me, and I suggest you do the same."

"Are you dating him?"

The big question, and now, I feel bad because I have to lie to my mum. I shrug my shoulders. "I wouldn't say dating. We see each other a lot, and I'm open to getting to know him more, but I don't want to rush anything."

"I rang Daniel's mum," she suddenly blurts out.

I gasp. "Oh, Mum, why?"

"Because of what he did. She knew all about your split, but he blamed you. She was so upset when I told her what he'd done. Anyway, she told me something," Mum says, and my ears prick up. "Daniel cheated on her too, on that Becca girl."

"That doesn't surprise me."

"With her sister," hisses Mum, like she's sharing top secret government news.

"Wow. That's low even for him."

"That's not all. She got pregnant, so he's having a baby with his girlfriend's sister," she almost shouts.

"Jesus Christ, what a dick."

"Alivia," gasps Mum, "do not take the Lord's name in vain and then say dick in the same sentence."

"Sorry," I apologise, even though Mum isn't religious.

We have dinner and it feels good to catch up with my parents. My mum monopolises the conversation with gossip about the neighbours, and every so often, my dad chips in with a snippet of information. I love seeing them together like this and witnessing how happy they are. It's the future I eventually want with a man that loves me.

After dinner, I go and change. I've arranged to meet Jenna, my childhood friend. Things were awkward for a while when I first got with Daniel because she didn't like him and predicted he'd break my heart. We kept in contact by text, but I haven't seen her in over a year. I'm excited about catching up. I kiss my parents goodnight with the promise of coming in quietly and not waking them.

I take a walk to the city centre. Our house is literally a five-minute walk, which was handy when I first started partying.

Jenna is already waiting in the swanky bar, Capers. I get my drink and join her at a small table by the window. "It's so good to see you. You look amazing." She smiles, hugging me tight.

"So do you. Thanks for meeting me at such short notice," I say, taking a seat opposite her.

We spend time catching up on gossip, just like old times, and it feels like we've never been apart. The alcohol sneaks into our system because we're so busy chatting, and by the time we stand to move on, we're both swaying.

We go to a nightclub so we can dance off the vodka. My phone flashes with a text from Vass. I open it, smiling. I like hearing from him.

Vass: Be good tonight.

I frown. How does he even know I'm out? I only arranged to meet her yesterday.

Me: *I'm always good. No orgies your end either, please.*

We soon get chatting to a couple of guys who insist on buying us drinks. They seem nice, and I have my eye on the taller of the two. He's good-looking, not on the scale of Vass, but still someone I'd usually go for. We dance, chat, and laugh the night away. My cheeks hurt from smiling, and I realise how much I've missed being home.

At the end of the night, they walk us to the taxi rank. Even though I only live close by, I never walk alone at night, and Jenna has to pass my house to get home, so we always share a cab.

As I'm about to get in, the guy I was talking to spins me to face him and places a hard, deep kiss against my mouth, I'm shocked, but it's not a bad kiss, so I don't pull away immediately. When we finally part lips, I smile up at him before diving into the cab, giggling with Jenna like schoolgirls.

I get home and crawl into my old bed, comforted by my great night out with my childhood friend.

Something whacks gently against my head, and I groan as it blows my hair across my face. It happens again, and I swat whatever it is with my hand.

"Morning, Ms. Caldwell. Care to explain this?" I dive up to the sound of Vass's amused voice. He stares down at me, looking fresh and smelling of his usual woody aftershave. I'm aware I still have on last night's dress, which is currently wrapped around my waist, as well as the makeup that I couldn't be bothered to wipe off. I straighten my hair in a failed attempt to look half human. "The hair is the least of your problems," says Vass with a smirk. I wipe under my eyes, trying to clear any black that may have smudged down my face.

Vass thrusts his phone closer for me to inspect, and I move back slightly so my eyes can adjust. It's a picture of me and the guy last night. "Oh my god," I wail. "How did you get that?"

Vass pulls his phone back and smiles while reading from it. *"Vass Fraser's latest love breaks his heart on a drunken night out,"* he says dramatically. *"Alivia Caldwell was spotted out in Brighton last night, miles apart from her new beau, Vass Fraser. It raised questions that the pair are already having difficulties after reports that Caldwell ran off to her family home in the well-known beach town earlier today. Mr. Fraser declined to comment on his current relationship status, although he did confirm that Ms. Caldwell had gone home to visit her parents, adding that she would be back to work as normal on Monday. Ms. Caldwell finished off her night out with a lip-locking kiss from an unknown stranger, fuelling rumours that the pair have in fact split after only a few days together. Ms. Collinsworth, the recent ex-partner of Fraser, was too upset to comment but confirms that she and Fraser are no longer in a relationship."*

Vass pulls my hands away from my face. "Oh god, why were they following me? And why are you here?" I groan.

"I told you I was coming to meet your parents. How's the head?" he asks, handing me a bottle of water and a couple painkillers.

"I told you I didn't want you to come yet."

"You'll soon realise that I never listen. I always do what I want, and I'm one bossy motherfucker. Anyway, your mum has breakfast on, so get up."

"Jesus Christ, you've already spoken to them," I moan.

"Yes. How do you think I got in?"

"I wouldn't put it past you to let yourself in, Vass. Have they seen that?" I ask, pointing to the phone.

"I can't even discuss it with you right now, Liv. I'm crazy mad that you broke one of your own rules already, and I can't punish you for it." I watch in astonishment as he leaves the room. What is he so mad about? I didn't know the press would follow me here to my home. I sigh and throw the covers back, taking in the state of my rolled-up dress and smeared fake tan.

After a long shower, I head downstairs to find my parents in deep conversation with Vass. I watch from the kitchen doorway, confused that they've welcomed him with no hesitation, and so much better than I thought they would.

"Here she is." My dad smiles. I give a small wave as my mum and Vass turn to me. Vass rises to his feet and strides over, placing a kiss on my head. I frown as it feels weird acting out a lie.

"You've met Vass," I say sarcastically, moving around him and taking a seat.

"We sure have. He brought me flowers," says my mum wistfully, pointing to a ridiculously large bouquet by the sink.

"Wow. You haven't even brought me flowers yet," I point out, raising my brows.

"I was just telling your parents how seeing you with that man last night woke me up. You were right to give me the ultimatum. It wasn't desperate or needy, like I said, and I didn't mean any of that." He turns to face me and grabs my hand. I scowl at him, daring him to carry on with this charade. "I want to try . . . for you. I know you're in love with me, and I," he pauses dramatically, and I glance at my mum, who is literally swooning, "think I can learn to love you one day. I accept your jealous ways, and if you need to constantly check up on me to quench that green-eyed beast inside you, then I'm willing to let you."

I pull my hand away and groan, "What the hell are you talking about?"

He smiles wide and gives a wink. "Sorry, I should say all of this in private."

"You should stop talking before I stuff my fist in your face," I warn.

"Alivia, don't be so aggressive," snaps Mum, and Vass smiles at her gratefully.

"Don't believe him, he's winding you up. There's no way I'm desperate enough to beg him to give us a try, and I'm definitely not jealous of the floozies who follow him around, begging for attention."

Vass gives me a condescending smile and pats my hand. "It's okay, Alivia, no one's judging you." My parents exchange an amused look.

I let out a frustrated growl and stomp from the room. I can't believe how quickly my parents have let him in, seeming to accept him right away. They took ages to warm to Daniel.

I sit outside on the front steps, the fresh air helping my hangover. The door opens and Vass lowers beside me, smiling. "You're not funny. I asked you not to come here because my parents needed time to get to know about us before you bombard them," I huff.

"They love me. I brought your dad a signed England Football shirt and your mum a bunch of flowers and an expensive bottle of wine."

"You can't just buy my parents, Vass. We aren't like you. We don't need material things."

"Ouch, bitch mode on," he mutters. "It was payback for you breaking the rules. Don't set them if you can't stick to them, it breaks me out in hives."

"I didn't know the press would follow me around. I didn't even realise they thought we were together. They were speculating, like always, the last I read."

"They're desperate for a story," he says. "Speaking of which, we're being watched." I panic, and he sees it, taking me by the chin and forcing me to stare at him instead of our surroundings. "Relax, calm down," he instructs firmly. "I'm going to kiss you now. Look happy about it," he whispers, and before I can respond, he leans in and plants the gentlest kiss against my mouth. "Smile," he urges against my lips, then he wraps me in his arms and holds me. It's a nice embrace, one that screams security and safety. One that tells the press we've made up. "We're taking your parents to lunch today, and I'm going to tip the press. We need to smile and act loved-up. The show begins now," he whispers, reminding me this isn't real. His embrace is for show. *What have I let myself in for?*

Vass

I knock gently on Alivia's bedroom door and wait for her to tell me to come in. Pushing the door open, I find myself transported back into the late nineties. This is Alivia's childhood bedroom, posters of boy bands are stuck to the wall, and there are photographs on a pin board of a younger Alivia posing with friends. "Don't judge me. I was a typical teenager, and boy bands and friends were my life," says Alivia, smiling. She looks amazing, her golden tan standing out against the white of the dress she's wearing.

"You look beautiful," I say. She does a spin and takes a bow.

"I was going for virginal, innocent, and nice. Will I be judged?" she asks.

"Only by the haters, and it doesn't matter what you wear for them, they'll still come for you. You look amazing. Let's give them a show that leaves no doubt that we're together," I remind her.

I drive us to the restaurant I found searching online. It has top ratings, so I'm hoping it's impressive, although I don't get the impression that Alivia's parents are the kind of people to bother about that. I could've quite easily taken them to a local bar and they'd have been grateful. It's refreshing. As soon as I step from the car, I'm bombarded with questions from the small group of reporters I'd tipped off. I smile without answering and round the car to open the door for Alivia and then her parents. I grab Alivia's hand, and we head inside, continuing to ignore the questions and flashing lights.

"How exciting," says Alivia's mum with excitement dancing in her eyes.

"Really, Mum?" asks Alivia. "You don't find them intimidating?"

"No. I can't wait to see what they say in the papers," she says. "I hope it was a good picture," she adds, straightening her hair. Alivia shakes her head and rolls her eyes.

We're quickly shown to a table by the window, also requested by me specifically so the press can get some good shots of us looking happy. "Caroline, Mark, after you," I say, letting Alivia's parents take their seats. We're handed menus, and I take Alivia's from her hand and place my arm around her shoulder, sharing my menu with her. I kiss her head just in time for a photo. "This is embarrassing," she mutters.

"It's necessary," I reply quietly.

We order our food and drinks and fall into a comfortable chat about the Caldwell family. I discover Mark has his own small business of cab drivers, and Caroline is a shop assistant for a clothes retailer. We talk about Alivia, much to her annoyance, but I love hearing stories of her childhood and find myself laughing at their tales.

Alivia sighs. "Vass doesn't want to hear about me and my unfortunate teenage years."

"Oh, I really do," I reassure her. "I find it fascinating that you weren't always this nerdy."

"If that's an insult, it didn't work. I'm a proud nerd," she says indignantly. I watch her swallow some of her wine, paying close attention to the way her throat moves and the way her lips press together before she runs her tongue over them. "What?" she asks, eyeing me suspiciously.

I place a finger under her chin gently and kiss on her lips. "I like watching you," I whisper, realising it's the truth. I find her fascinating.

"Oh, Mark, isn't he just the cutest?" Caroline sighs, placing her hand over her chest and tilting her head to the side. It's something I've never been called before, but I'll take it. "You're perfect together."

We finish our food and relax as the coffees are brought out. I find myself constantly touching

Liv, even hooking our little fingers together. Before long, it's a natural move. Then, after a short battle with Mark, which I win, I pay the bill and we head back out to the car. A photographer stands in front of us. "Can we have a picture, Mr. Fraser?" he asks politely, so I give a nod, and he smiles in delight.

I straighten my jacket and pull Alivia into my side. Placing her hand against my chest, I stare at the camera. He takes a couple of shots. "What about one with your future in-laws?" asks the photographer. Instead of protesting that they're simply Alivia's parents, I smile at them and invite them to join us. "How do you feel about your daughter dating Mr. Fraser?" the photographer asks as he snaps away.

"I'm delighted," shrills Caroline. "He's a real gentleman, and I've not seen Alivia this happy in a while." I feel smug knowing my plan is working.

"Any future plans?" he asks me.

I smile down at Alivia, and he captures the shot. "We're taking things one day at a time, but I'm very happy at the moment," I confirm.

"And you, Ms. Caldwell?"

"I'm waiting to wake up from this dream," she says wistfully before smirking up at me. "It just seems too good to be true."

We get into the car and head back to the Caldwells' home. Once there, they get out but I remain seated. "I need to find a hotel."

"Okay, I'll call you later," says Alivia, trying to close the door, but Caroline sticks her head back into the car, preventing her.

"You're not staying in a hotel. You're our guest and you'll stay with us," she insists. Alivia shakes her head at me, prompting me to refuse, but instead, I smile wide and Alivia groans dramatically.

"That is so kind of you, Caroline. I'd love to stay with you."

"That's settled then. Alivia, show Vass to the spare room," says Caroline, before heading off into the house.

"Haven't you got to work tomorrow?" asks Alivia. "I booked a day's holiday to relax with my parents, and now, you're crashing my day off."

"I need a day off anyway. We can read the papers together over breakfast. It'll be fabulous," I say, stepping out of the car and taking my bag.

The spare room is directly across from Alivia's room. It's comfortable and homely. Once I'm showered, I go back across the landing and tap on Alivia's door. "Yes?" she shouts, and I enter. She's sitting cross-legged on her bed, and when she sees me wet and wrapped in just a towel, her eyes bug out of her head. "What are you doing? My parents might see you dressed like that and they'll think we've been up to no good," she hisses.

I grin. "You wish," I say. "What're you doing?"

"I'm checking my social media. Why aren't you on here?" she asks.

"Have you been trying to stalk me?" I grin, and she rolls her eyes. "I don't have time to keep on top of social media. The Luxe page is run by Clarisse. If I go on there, I'd be inundated with messages. It gets ridiculous. Have you changed your relationship status?" I take a seat next to her on the double bed.

"No, don't be weird."

"You have to. The press will check that kind of stuff," I say. I take her mobile and change her status to 'in a relationship'. I then take the opportunity to go through her friends list. "You have a lot of guys on here," I mutter, laying back until I'm resting against the head of the bed.

"Vass, give it back, that's my privacy you're going through." She makes a snatch for the phone, but I move it and she falls against my chest. I wrap my arm around her and pin her there so she's lying against me. After a few struggles, she accepts her fate and watches as I flick through her friends list.

"How do you know this guy?" I ask. His profile picture is of him and her together, and it stirs that jealous beast inside me once again.

"He's a friend from school." She shrugs. "We met up a few times after Daniel."

"Do you talk to him?" I ask, and she nods. "About?" I probe.

"You remember this isn't a real boyfriend and girlfriend situation here, Vass. It's none of your business."

I open up her messages, and she tries to take the phone again but misses a second time. I roll her so that she's under me, and then I sit up over her so she can't escape. She hits out at me playfully, but I catch her hands in mine and hold them above her head. Looking around, I spot the cord to her dressing gown. I reach for it and then bind it expertly around her hands, pulling them above her head and securing her to the bedframe. "This isn't fare," she says, laughing and trying to pull free.

I ignore her, remaining seated over her just in case she manages to slip a hand free. I find a message from a man and open it, arching a brow as I scan through.

"It was great to see you. You looked so amazing, and I regret not going in for the kiss," I read aloud, and Alivia blushes. "Maybe next time, we can have dinner at my place," I continue. "Wow, he's keen," I add, cocking an eyebrow.

"You're being a total prick right now, and I'm going to write a new rule about respecting boundaries and privacy," she mutters, tugging on her restraints.

"Rules have already been written, so you can't add, change, or amend. And, Liv, I should warn you that if you keep moving like that, I'm not going to be responsible for my actions." She stills, eyeing my towel warily. "Who's Carl?"

"Oh my god, Vass, stop now. I can't help having a past or chatting to other guys. We aren't really together, so this isn't cool."

I stare down at her flushed face. If I didn't know better, I'd think she was enjoying being at my mercy. I lean down so my mouth is to her ear and I hear her breathing hitch. "The things I could do to you right now while you're tied up like this." She inhales sharply, and I smile. "I think you like that idea, Liv. Do you want me to do things to you?"

"Vass, I said no sex," she whispers, but she doesn't sound at all like she means it.

"But you didn't say no sexual contact. Your rules really need to be clearer," I say, running my finger down the middle of her chest, towards her stomach. She holds her breath in anticipation.

I smirk, moving my hand away from her body and adjusting my towel to keep the erection I'm now sporting covered. She licks her lips subconsciously, and it takes everything I have to untie her arms. "I'm going to sort," I look down at my obvious erection, "this. And you should get dressed. I'm taking you out this evening for a few drinks." She sits up and rubs her wrists, and the slight red marks turn me on even more. I feel her disappointment as I turn away to leave, freezing when she gasps. I close my eyes momentarily, knowing what's coming next. *Why the fuck didn't I put a top on?*

"What have you done to your back?" she whispers.

"It's nothing. Get dressed," I say firmly, leaving the room.

Chapter Eleven

Alivia

Those marks on Vass's back were not nothing. The angry, red welts looked painful, and there were so many. It's all I can think about, and even now, sitting across from the gorgeousness that is Vass, I can't stop the questions that fill my mind.

"You're very quiet tonight. Are you okay?" he asks. I nod and give him a weak smile. "You may as well talk about whatever's bothering you, Alivia. I can't do moods or sulking," he adds.

"I'm not in a mood or sulking. I can't stop thinking . . ." I trail off. He doesn't want to talk about it, which was obvious from his very first response. "What the papers will print tomorrow," I lie.

"Don't worry about it. They print what they want, and nothing we do or say will change that. It gets easier to ignore after time."

"We really can't let it leak out about us getting married, Vass. When we go our separate ways, they'll have a field day, and I can't handle that without you."

"Why would you have to? I'll be here to support you through it," he says, frowning.

"Once we split, you won't," I say. "And I'm sure they'll paint me out to be the money-grabbing bitch."

"Of course, I'll be there for you. Won't we still have a friendship?" he asks, and my heart squeezes with hope. Maybe Vass is becoming a real friend. I like that idea. "So, tell me, do you like being tied up?"

I almost choke on my own saliva. "I'm not discussing my sex life with you, Vass," I mutter with a slight smirk.

"It's a genuine question. Someone might ask me this information to verify that I really do know you."

I roll my eyes. "Let's talk about your sex life," I suggest, drinking down my vodka.

"Let's play a game. I answer a question and then you answer one," he says. I consider it and nod. "Me first," he continues. "Do you like being tied up?"

I laugh. "I've never been tied up before today, but I guess I'd be open to try it. It wasn't terrible, and I liked the idea of not being able to control what was going on."

He raises his brow and then smirks. "The things I could show you," he utters with a gleam in his eye. I shudder at the suggestiveness in his voice, and I find myself wanting him to show me everything.

"Are you a Dominant?" I ask, though I'm pretty sure I know the answer to this. Bianca told me a lot about the stuff they did together before she left.

"Yes," he says, and we stare at each other.

I'm not sure where to go from this, so I nod. "Continue."

"You asked a question, and I answered."

"I want to know more," I argue.

He ignores me and thinks for a second. "How many sexual partners have you had?"

"Three," I say confidently. Most girls my age have at least doubled that figure, but I'm glad I haven't. Now, Vass looks at me expectantly, waiting for me to continue. When I don't, he sighs.

"Fine, yes, I like to dominate. I realised when I was a teenager that it turned me on to be in charge. Now, I get paid a lot of money to train girls who want to be submissive for members of The Luxe. I'm very experienced, and it's something I'm good at." I have no doubt about it, as I sometimes get a slight glimpse of that side of him.

"Three guys. Dan, who was my childhood sweetheart and the person I gave up my virginity for. We got reacquainted at a school reunion. I gave him four years of my life, and he repaid that by cheating with my friend. Then Mark, he was after teenage Dan. It was a short relationship, and I used him mainly to piss Dan off and make him jealous. Finally, Jacob. He was someone I dated for a while before I met back up with Dan. I ended it. What about you?"

Vass laughs. "A lot more than three."

"Do you know how many?" I ask, and he looks embarrassed before shaking his head. "Wow, so there's been a hell of a lot?"

"I own a sex club, Alivia, it comes with the territory. Why do you think I haven't settled down or had a steady girlfriend? Are you good at sex?"

"What kind of question is that?" I ask, laughing hard. "I don't know. I haven't had any complaints, but I've not had anyone tell me I'm amazing in the sack either."

"Has a man ever made you orgasm?"

"Hold on, it's my turn, and that question is way too personal. Why do you like to dominate women? What do you get out of it?"

He thinks for a minute. "I get pleasure from their pleasure. Bringing a woman to orgasm is satisfying, and controlling how and when it happens is even more so. But it's also about the trust a woman puts in me to know what she needs."

"A man has never made me orgasm," I answer truthfully. "I've faked it every time."

Vass laughs at my brutal honesty. "Liv, you don't know how much I want to take that on as a challenge." He groans, and I laugh at his pained expression.

"Why don't you drink alcohol?" I ask, and Vass's smile fades. He sits straighter and fidgets uncomfortably.

"That's not about sex," he mutters, and I can see him closing off.

"You didn't say it had to be. I guess I could look online. Would I find a story there, Vass? Because if there's a chance someone could make a comment about it, and I don't know the truth, it could make people question how a marriage will function with secrets and lies."

"It comes back to control, Alivia. Being drunk makes me out of control and I don't like that feeling." He sighs. "There's no big story there."

"But one drink wouldn't hurt. You never drink a drop."

"Oh, I do," he says, avoiding eye contact, "just pray you never see me like that." He takes a breath before asking, "Do you fancy me?"

"If you want an ego trip, go visit your club," I say, and Vass laughs, the awkwardness of my last question lifting.

"I fancy you," he says honestly, and I blush. "It's hard wanting something you know you can't have." I'm flattered. Vass is gorgeous and here he is telling me that he fancies me.

Vass stands. "I'll get us a drink. Same again?" he asks, and I nod. I pull out my phone and flick through my social media while I wait for Vass to come back. A shadow falls across the table, and I look up into the eyes of the guy I met last night.

"Alivia, right?" He smiles, and I nod. I can't for the life of me remember his name, so I just sit there with a blank expression.

"Curtis," he reminds me.

"Of course, sorry. How are you?" I ask politely.

"I'm good. I didn't get your number last night, and I was wondering if I could get it now?"

"Erm, I don't think that's a good idea, Curtis. I'm here with a friend, and he can be..." I trail off. Vass is approaching with my drink in his hand, his eyes fixed on Curtis's back.

"This has to be fate, though, right? Seeing you like this is my second chance to get that number, and you said last night you were available," he continues.

Vass places the drink down in front of me and takes his seat. "Did you?" Vass asks me.

My mouth is suddenly dry. "Erm, I don't think they were my exact words. Maybe, I—"

"Aren't you that rich guy?" asks Curtis, smiling at Vass.

"I am. The same rich guy who is out on a date with his fiancée," says Vass coldly. Curtis looks back and forth between us, and his eyes widen as he gets the message.

"I'm so sorry, man. She totally led me on last night," he splutters.

My mouth falls open in shock. "I really didn't," I hiss.

"She tends to get a bit out of control when she's off her meds," says Vass dryly. "I apologise. I'll keep her under lock and key from now on."

Curtis gives me an unsure look before making his excuses to leave. Vass glares at me. "Available, are you?"

"Come on, Vass, I was drunk. And besides, I am single. I didn't know we were starting the lie so early, and it's happened faster than I expected."

"From now on, you are not single. You need to believe that, or you'll slip up."

I nod and mutter, "Okay, sorry."

I wake the next morning with another headache. Hangovers seem to get worse the older I get. I groan and turn to my alarm clock. It's only seven in the morning but I decide to get up and dress.

Downstairs, I find my parents and Vass huddled around my dad's laptop at the kitchen table. "What's going on?" I mutter, reaching for a glass and filling it with water.

"We're looking at the newspapers," says Mum excitedly.

I take a seat away from them and rest my head on the table. "How thrilling," I mutter.

"Vass Fraser stepped out with his new girlfriend, Alivia Caldwell, in a show of unity after pictures emerged of Caldwell with an unknown male while visiting her hometown. The pair smiled and posed for photographs and appeared very much in love. Caldwell's mother, Caroline Caldwell, told us it was the happiest she'd seen her daughter in some time. Vass Fraser confirmed he was taking things one day at a time with Ms. Caldwell, adding to rumours that they are under strain. A close friend

of Fraser's told us the pair are still getting to know one another. It's no secret that Ms. Caldwell is new to Fraser's lavish lifestyle and only time will tell if she can handle the storm that is Vass Fraser," Mum reads aloud.

"Oh, Jesus," I grumble against my arm.

"You know, you really should drink less if it makes you feel so ill," Mum comments, and I look up in time to see Vass nod in agreement.

"Being with a man so popular drives me to drink, Mum. It's the pressure," I say, scowling his way.

"Don't be ridiculous, Alivia," she mutters. "Get some breakfast, that'll sort you out."

"Don't you have to go back to London?" I ask Vass, and he shakes his head, still peering over my mum's shoulder at the laptop.

"I've invited him to come with us to see Gran today," says Dad, and I glare at him.

"Dad, Vass is a busy man. He doesn't have time to visit Gran. She doesn't even know who we are, so having Vass there will just confuse her," I argue. Both my parents give me the look that tells me to be quiet and stop arguing with their decisions.

An hour later, we all traipse into the care home that's currently taking care of my Gran. Dad goes to speak to the nurse while the rest of us go through to Gran's room. She's propped up in bed, looking at the newspaper. She glances up and gives us a vacant look.

"She has dementia," I whisper to Vass. "She doesn't always remember us."

"Hi, Doris, how are you today? You look well." Mum smiles, kissing Gran on the cheek. "We brought Alivia to see you," she adds.

I give her a small wave. "Hi, Gran." The blank look she gives tells me she doesn't remember me. We make small talk while we wait for Dad to return. When he does, he looks annoyed.

"Mum caused problems last night, and the nurse in charge isn't very happy. They're thinking of transferring her again."

"Oh, not again." Mum sighs. It's been a constant battle to keep Gran in a care home. She can be violent and tries to escape a lot. No one seems to be able to cope with her, but it's not her fault, she just gets confused and frustrated.

Gran suddenly smiles brightly at Vass. "Mark, you came to see me."

"Go with it," Mum whispers to Vass.

"Have you been misbehaving?" Vass asks Gran sternly, and she gives a guilty look. "You don't want to get kicked out of here. They're doing their best for you."

Gran nods. "I know. I just want to go home."

"This is home," says Vass gently, sitting on her bed and taking her hand. Mum pats my hand and gives me swoon eyes. I guess it's cute to watch. He doesn't even know her yet he's being so kind.

"I want to live with you and Caroline," says Gran.

"You'd hate it with us. Alivia comes to stay, and you know how loud and annoying she can be," says Vass.

Gran playfully taps his arm and smiles. "Fine. I'll try to behave."

An hour later, As we leave the care home, my mobile pings with a news alert. I'd set it to notify me if Vass came up, so I discreetly open it and gasp. In bold letters, the headline reads, **'*Is Vass Fraser about to tie the Knot with girlfriend Alivia Caldwell?*'** I quickly shove my phone in my pocket and take a few deep breaths. How the hell do they know everything?

Vass

I left Alivia with her parents an hour ago. She wasn't happy with the latest press story, but there's not much I can do to stop stories getting out, and I told her as much. Besides, her parents loved me. The visit was a hit, and I don't think they'll be too upset when we marry.

Once back home, I shower and change and then head straight back out. I'm meeting my mother for dinner and she hates tardiness. I arrive on time, and she's already seated, waiting, which is no surprise.

"Good weekend?" she asks as I take my seat and shrug out of my jacket.

"Yes, thanks. You?" I ask politely.

"Yes, though not as good as yours by the sound of it. Any announcements you'd like to make?"

"Mother, don't be so smug. You were right, okay, Alivia is perfect."

She smiles triumphantly. "It's not often you admit that I know best."

"It's not often that you do know best," I say dryly.

"Have you agreed on a price?" she asks.

"No. She says she doesn't want anything." Mother looks confused. "I told her she could have anything, but she said she was happy to just help me out."

"No one does anything for free, darling. Set a price."

Before Alivia, I'd have agreed with her. No one ever does anything for nothing, but with Liv, I'm certain she really is doing it to help me. She has a heart of gold, and in my social circles, that's rare to see. "The press seems to have grabbed onto it. Alivia doesn't want them to know about the wedding."

"Darling, there will be no hiding it. Vass Fraser is no longer a bachelor, and that's big news in the gossip columns."

"I know, but I respect her wishes, Mother, so we need to do our best to stop that happening. She doesn't want her parents finding out," I explain.

Our food arrives and I tuck into my steak. My mother stares at me and says, "Her parents have to attend the wedding, Vass."

"Why? It doesn't have to be a big affair," I say through a mouthful of food.

"Of course, it does. Do you think your grandmother is stupid? She'll insist on a grand affair, and she'll want to meet Alivia's parents."

"Alivia won't agree to it. She feels strongly about this. She doesn't want to upset her parents when the divorce comes through."

"It won't work. You'll never keep it quiet," she warns.

I think her words over. Deep down, I know she's right. This will hit the papers the second Alivia steps into a wedding shop. And if I want my grandmother to believe this marriage is real, Alivia's parents need to be at this wedding. I need a plan, because Alivia backing out on this agreement can't happen. Not when I'm this close.

After dinner, I head back to The Luxe to work on a plan. As I walk through the reception area, I hear heels clicking behind me. I glance back in time to see Annalise. "Vass," she says, falling in step beside me, "my father's been trying to contact you."

"I'm aware, Annalise, but I've been busy. What does he want?"

"To speak with you about us," she says, following me up the stairs.

"But there is no us." I sigh, and she grips my arm to halt me.

"He's not very happy you ditched me like that. He's threatening to pull some of the members from The Luxe."

"And how does he plan to do that?" I ask. "There's no other club like this around here."

"Well, you know Daddy. His influence stretches quite far," she says innocently. I shake my head in annoyance and then continue my walk to the office. She follows. "Vass, don't be angry with me, it isn't my fault. When he saw the news this morning about you and that geeky girl in the office, he hit the roof. You should be thanking me because I calmed him down." We reach the office door and I unlock it, then grip Annalise by the upper arm and pull her inside. A fire lights in her eyes, but I shove her away from me.

"I don't like threats, Annalise," I growl.

She lowers her eyes sadly. "Like I said, it isn't my fault."

"I told you that if my grandmother didn't agree, then it wouldn't go ahead. Why you told your father in the first place is beyond me."

"Because I thought your grandmother would like me. Everyone likes me," she says, sounding exasperated.

"Well, she didn't, so get over it. Go back to your father and explain that you're happier without me. I won't allow him to try and ruin my business because I wouldn't marry his daughter when it was never a real wedding to begin with."

"I tried that already, but he wouldn't listen. Have you thought about this properly, Vass?" she asks, taking a seat.

"I'm not discussing this with you. Go home." I pour myself a water and drink it in one go. The sound of Annalise clicking her false nails on the wooden arm of a chair grates on me and I close my eyes briefly in irritation before taking a deep breath and turning back to face her.

"She doesn't get you like I do. She isn't our sort of person. Will she let you carry on with the club, training the subs?" she asks. "She's so vanilla, can you imagine her on her knees for you, Vass, letting you boss her around?"

I close my eyes again. Imagining Alivia on her knees gives me all kinds of happy thoughts. "I think you should be leaving now."

"You'll come crawling back, Vass. We all know how much you need this lifestyle, and she's not going to sit back and let you have sex with other women, fake or not. She'll fall for you, and you'll panic. When that happens, Vass, I'll be there, on my knees, ready." I watch her saunter towards the door, then she looks back over her shoulder. "Oh, and Vass, I'm with Alex in the private rooms, number ten, if you want to watch . . . or join . . . whatever." She leaves, closing the door quietly.

I pace the office. What I really need right now is a drink, and that feeling doesn't come too often these days. Without giving too much thought to it, I let my feet take me to the room I'm becoming so familiar with. When Ella opens the door, she frowns. "Again?" She sounds concerned. I nod, pushing my way inside.

"Make it hard," I mutter.

Chapter Twelve

Alivia

I stumble against the door as Clarisse falls about laughing. "Those shoes need to go in the bin. You seriously can't walk in them."

"They'd be great for Bambi On Ice, though," I say, pulling myself up and holding onto the door while I pull the ridiculously high heels from my sore feet.

We go inside, and Clarisse runs for the stairs. "You pour the drinks, and I'll just get out of these jeans," she says. I head into the kitchen and drop my heels and bag to the floor. Turning the light on, I jump back in surprise to find Vass sitting at the breakfast bar with his head resting on his arms, face down on the worktop. He looks up slowly, blinking like he's just woken up.

"Shit," I curse. "You scared the crap out of me, Vass."

"Where's Clarisse?" he asks gruffly.

"She's getting changed. Are you okay?" He lays his head back down on the worktop, not bothering to answer my question. I pull a bottle of wine out of the fridge and two glasses from the cabinet. Vass peers up again, but this time, he looks alarmed.

"Put it away, Liv," says Clarisse from the kitchen doorway. I screw the lid back onto the bottle, looking from her to Vass. "What do you need, Vass?" she asks seriously.

"Sleep," he mutters. I watch her go to him and gently take his arm. He stands and winces with the movement.

"Bad, huh?" she asks, leading him from the kitchen.

I take a seat on the nearest stool. Somehow, I feel like whatever just went down has happened many times before. Clarisse knew exactly why he was here. I wait around, but Clarisse doesn't reappear. He needs her right now, and so I decide to go to bed with my mind full of questions.

The following day, my alarm screams at me at six a.m. sharp. I groan and whack it to shut it off. After my shower, I get dressed for work and head downstairs. I'm surprised to find Clarisse and Vass sitting in silence, eating breakfast, both staring at their mobile phones.

"Good morning," I say brightly, pouring myself a coffee.

"Morning. Sorry I didn't make it back for the wine," Clarisse says, glancing at Vass, who still hasn't looked up.

"That's okay. I needed an early night anyway. Everything okay now?" I ask. She nods, but Vass doesn't respond. "Well, I'm heading into the office early. Does anyone want a ride?" I ask.

"No, we'll see you there," says Clarisse. I shrug my shoulders and then leave them to it. I can't help but feel shut out, which is ridiculous. They're great friends and they clearly lean on each other for support. But my mind is so full of questions right now and I hate not knowing what's going on.

At the office, I throw myself into work. The new brochures have arrived, so I put together a welcome letter and prepare them for delivery to local businesses. It's almost eleven when I check my watch. I haven't seen or heard from Vass yet, which is odd because he pops into my office every day when he arrives so I know he's around.

Vass will need to check them before I send them out, so I grab a copy of the letter template and the brochure. I swing open his office door and come to a sudden stop. Vass is standing with his back to me, his shirt off, and Clarisse is standing behind him. It's hard to ignore the angry cuts that mark Vass's skin. His back is covered in deep welts, worse than the ones I saw the other night, and Clarisse is gently rubbing cream into them. They both look over their shoulders when they hear my gasp. Vass quickly grabs his shirt from a nearby chair and pulls it on. "What the fuck have I told you about just walking in here?" he yells angrily.

I'm taken aback by his tone. "I didn't think you were in," I mumble, slowly backing out.

"Get out!" he shouts. "Get the fuck out!" I rush back to the safety of my own office, slamming the door. I throw the brochure on my desk and go straight to the bathroom, locking the door and taking a shuddery breath. There's nothing I can do to stop the tears that spring to my eyes and slowly roll down my cheeks. I hate that he yelled at me like that, and I hate that he's hurt, and I especially hate that I don't know what the hell is going on. And so I remain in the bathroom to wallow in sadness.

Ten minutes pass before there's a loud knock on the door. I jump in fright and grab a handful of tissue paper, wiping my wet cheeks and swiping under my eyes to remove smudged mascara. "I'll be a minute," I say, trying to sound happy.

"Alivia, you have a meeting. Reception just called up to say your appointment has arrived," Vass says through the door.

"Okay, I'm on my way," I say. I count to ten before taking a deep breath and unlocking the door. Vass is leaning against the opposite wall, his arms folded across his chest. He pushes off and comes towards me slowly. "Do you need me in the meeting?" he asks.

I force a smile and shake my head. "No, I've got this."

"I'm sorry I shouted back there," he begins, but I wave him off and walk towards the office so I can gather what I need for my meeting.

"Don't worry, it's fine." He follows me, watching as I gather my things together.

"Liv, please . . . hear me out," he mutters. He steps in front of me, blocking my exit. "I shouldn't have yelled."

"I said it's fine, Vass. Now, leave it."

He sighs heavily but takes a step to the side, allowing me to pass.

My meeting starts off well. I wow the hotel manager with my plans for lunch meetings and special events to be held in our large, staged room. I flirt my arse off and make him feel like we're offering him an amazing package, one he'll only get with us. Vass stands over by the bar, watching my every move, and I'm beginning to feel self-conscience when he makes his way over.

Luke stands, grasps Vass's hand in a firm grip, and they shake, "Luke Moore. I'm from Moore's Hotel in central London. It's great to finally meet you, Mr. Fraser."

"Is Ms. Caldwell looking after you?" asks Vass, glancing at me.

"She certainly is. She's charming her way into my wallet," jokes Luke, taking his seat again.

Vass lowers into the opposite chair. "Please, carry on. Don't let me stop you."

I take a deep breath. There's nothing worse than being watched when you're trying to impress, especially if that person watching is your boss. "As I was saying, the top price is high, but when you consider what you'll be getting within that, it's a great deal. We have a fantastic team coming together that'll take all the stress out of the arrangements," I say confidently.

"It sounds great, Alivia. I'm impressed, and if your boss wasn't sitting right here, I'd be trying to get your number," says Luke with a wink. I feel myself blush and laugh to hide it.

"Fiancé," says Vass firmly, and Luke looks his way. "You said boss, but actually, I'm her fiancé." Luke looks flustered and stammers out an apology, clearly embarrassed that he's practically hit on me.

"Please, don't worry at all," I reassure him. "I'll show you out."

"No need. I'll be in touch," he mutters, gathering his things and rushing for the exit.

I glance at the brochure he's left behind and groan. "What the hell was that?" I snap. "I had him. He was looking at the top package."

"He wanted you, Liv, not the package. His body language was off. I didn't like him."

"You don't have to like him as long as he's paying us money," I say angrily.

"I like almost everyone who walks in that door. I get a gut feeling and I go on that. I've never been wrong."

"I can't have you assess every client I pull in based on your gut feelings."

"I'm the boss, and I decide who enters The Luxe. Luke isn't welcome."

I gather my things and mutter, "You're being ridiculous. I can't work like this."

"What's that supposed to mean?" he snaps.

I shake my head and make my way back to my office. I don't know what it means, but I feel emotionally drained. Since agreeing to this crazy marriage idea, nothing seems to be going right.

Vass follows me, watching from my office doorway as I lay my files on my desk and take a seat. "I've agreed to help you, so maybe I can stop working here and go back to your mother's business," I suggest. Vass's frown is back, and I remember how he yelled at me earlier. I take a calming breath. "You never needed me here. It was a ploy to get you to ask me to help. Your mother promised me a job at her firm."

Vass shakes his head. "No. I like the way you work, and I want to see you implement the ideas you've come up with."

"You just ruined my first potential booking, Vass. It isn't working out."

"You're staying at The Luxe, Liv. No arguments." He goes into his office, slamming the door.

I avoid Vass for the rest of the day. He's clearly got a lot going on and he's taking his mood out on me. I'm about to leave when the joining door between our offices opens and a woman sticks her head around the door. "Alivia?" she asks with a friendly smile. I nod, hoping this isn't one of Vass's 'girls'. "Fantastic. We're ready for you." She realises from my confused expression that I haven't a clue what's going on. "Mr. Fraser booked you in for makeup and hair," she explains.

"Why? I'm not going anywhere." The woman turns back into Vass's office to ask him.

"Get in here, Alivia," he shouts, and I roll my eyes. The woman laughs at my small show of defiance and opens the door wider for me to go inside.

"I have a charity event at seven. You can use my shower, it's through there," he says coldly, pointing towards another door in his office.

"I'm going home. I have a date with the couch and my pyjamas, but you have a great time," I say, heading to the exit.

"Alivia, don't make me come and get you," he mutters, his voice low and menacing. A thrill shoots through me, and I bite my lip to stop smirking. I'm testing him, which will probably just annoy him further, but I feel like he should work for it. I'm doing him the favour yet he treats it like the other way around.

I continue my walk through the door and hear him growl. I pick up my pace, rushing down the stairs. I'm halfway across the reception area when I'm hauled back against a hard body. "You had to push me," he growls in my ear, then he spins me around and I let out a surprised yelp as he hauls me over his shoulder, slapping my arse. Clients turn to see what the commotion is, and I bury my face in my hands, trying to hide my embarrassment as he carries me back up the stairs. We go through his office to his private room. He reaches past me and turns the shower on. "If you aren't out in ten minutes, I'll be back to get you," he warns and leaves me standing there, shocked and slightly aroused.

I know he'll keep to his word, so I shower in record time. I don't want him carrying me out there naked. Just to get under his skin, I wrap myself in a white fluffy towel and head back into his office. He glances up and does a double take, a smirk forming on his lips. The woman from earlier is standing by a chair, waiting patiently for me with a hair dryer in her hand. I turn the chair to face Vass and take a seat, ready to be primped.

"I have nothing to wear, but I'm guessing you've sorted that?" I ask.

Vass sighs and drops his pen onto the documents he's working on. He steeples his fingers and looks at me. "Alivia, you were going home to sit alone in Clarisse's house to watch television. I'm taking you to a charity function, and it'll be a nice evening. Why are you behaving like a brat?"

The comment burns me. "I actually like staying home and watching television. You should try it sometime. Maybe you'd be a little less uptight."

"Umm, I think I'll give it a miss. I like my kind of relaxation techniques much better," he says.

"Are they the same techniques that cause you back injuries?" I snap, and then press my lips together. I didn't mean to say that, and by the enraged look on his face, he isn't happy that I blurted it out. He picks up the pen, completely ignoring my remark, and goes back to his paperwork.

I spend the next hour and a half having my hair curled and styled followed by my makeup. By the time the woman has finished, I don't even recognise myself. I show her to the door, thanking her over and over for the amazing transformation. Once she's gone, I turn and walk straight into Vass, who's standing directly behind me. I inhale sharply, surprised by his sudden closeness, and try to step back, but he follows, trapping me against the door.

"Your smart mouth will end up getting you in trouble," he growls.

"I'm sorry, I wasn't thinking," I mutter.

"No, you weren't. You'll pay for it later, though, I promise." He steps back, and I exhale in relief. Sometimes, he's so intense that I'm not sure whether to jump on him or run the other way.

Vass reaches for a clothes bag hanging on a hook and unzips it. He pulls out a pink silk dress. It's long and flowy, and I fall in love immediately. "Underwear is in the bathroom," he says, handing the hanger to me.

Vass

When Alivia reappears from the bathroom, I'm already in my tux and waiting for her patiently. As she steps out, I have to grip the edge of my desk to stop from grabbing her. She looks amazing.

"Who chose my dress and shoes?" she enquires, spinning around to show me the back of the dress. It's low-cut, the dip stopping just above her arse.

"Me."

"And the underwear?" she asks.

"Also me. Do you like it?" Knowing she's wearing white silk under the dress is clouding my mind, and I push up off my desk and offer her my arm. She hooks her hand through it, and we head out.

"I love it all. You have very good taste."

The limo comes to a stop outside the large hotel. This charity event has been organised by a popstar to help raise money for poverty-stricken areas in London. There'll be a lot of media attention and it's the perfect opportunity to show that we're together officially. I turn to face Alivia, holding out a small, black velvet box. "I also chose this," I say, handing it to her.

Alivia opens the box and gasps. "Oh, Vass, it's gorgeous," she whispers.

"I thought tonight might be a good time to put it on, make us more official. My grandmother is going to be here tonight. If we cross paths, we can tell her our good news."

Alivia looks troubled as she closes the box, leaving the diamond ring inside. "If you want to make her believe us, Vass, we should wait. It wasn't that long ago you were shoving Annalise under your grandmother's nose. Will she really believe you're now in love with me and engaged?" she asks.

Alivia's right, there's no way things would happen that fast, but seeing her with my ring on in a room full of famous men would relax me. I give Alivia a nod. She's right to slow it down, it'll look too obvious, but I can't hide the disappointment I feel.

We step out of the car and we're met with the flashes of cameras and shouts from the awaiting press. Alivia takes my arm, and we step onto the photo backdrop advertising the charity to pose for a few photos.

"Is it right that you're pregnant, Alivia?" shouts a photographer. I roll my eyes at the absurd questions being fired our way.

"Don't respond, just smile for the photos," I say into her ear.

"Where do they get this crap?" she asks, turning back to the camera and smiling.

"Alivia, can we have one of you both kissing?" someone shouts.

Alivia laughs, and when she looks up to me, I place my finger under her chin and lower my mouth to hers. I feel her intake of breath as I sweep my tongue against hers, testing her willingness to engage in this. When she responds by gripping my jacket and standing on her tiptoes, we share a slow, gentle kiss, much to the delight of the press. As I pull away, I place a single kiss on the end of her nose and smile. There's a strange look on her face, but before I can analyse it, she turns back to the cameras.

Once we're safely inside, I take a glass of Champagne from a passing waitress and hand it to Alivia. She accepts it gratefully and drinks down the entire contents, dumping the glass on the same waitress's tray and taking another. When she sees me watching her warily, she shrugs her shoulders. "Is there a rule on how many I can have?" she asks.

"No, help yourself," I say. There's a nearby table with bottles of water, and I take one before leading Alivia to the seating arrangements to find our table. I groan when I see we're sharing with six other guests, all of whom are members of The

Luxe. On the table directly behind me is Annalise. "Great," I mutter, leading Alivia to the hall where the tables are situated.

I'm relieved to see that Annalise isn't yet seated, and I'm praying she doesn't turn up. She hates these kinds of events. The tables are close together, and she'll be able to talk to me from her seat. Our table is full. Grayson has his sub with him, one I trained a couple of months ago, and her eyes light up as I pull out Alivia's seat for her. I shake hands with all the other gentlemen and kiss the hands of their plus-ones.

When I get to Keely, she stands and kisses me on the cheek. "It's so lovely to see you, Sir," she whispers.

"Not here, Keely. It's Vass," I mutter, and she nods once.

"Of course, sorry." She lowers into her seat, and Grayson whispers in her ear, probably making promises of all the things he'll do to her later as a punishment for getting out of her seat to talk to me.

Chapter Thirteen

Alivia

I don't remember a time when I've felt this uncomfortable. I drink down another glass of Champagne, they're only small glasses and I can swallow the contents in two large gulps. Glancing around the crowded room, most of the tables are full and some of the faces are familiar, not that I know any of them personally.

Vass is in deep conversation with the man sitting next to him. He's hardly paid any attention to me at all, only occasionally asking if I'm okay. I desperately wish I was on the couch watching a film and eating my way through a pizza.

I stand, needing movement before I drop dead from boredom. Vass looks to me, but I ignore him. He hasn't bothered with me so I let him wonder where I'm going as I head in the direction of the bathroom, which seems to be quite a walk.

"Alivia, I thought that was you." I spot Luke Moore, the guy from the hotel when Vass ruined my meeting today. He stands and kisses me on each cheek.

"Luke, lovely to see you again," I say with a genuine smile. I felt bad for how rude Vass was earlier. I glance back and see Vass has turned in his chair and is in a deep conversation with Annalise. My heart beats a little faster. *When did she arrive?*

"Fancy sitting with me at the bar? I'm so bored here, my table is made up of bankers and politicians," says Luke.

"Yes," I say, feeling relieved. "I also need rescuing before I fall to sleep," I joke. "I'll pop to the bathroom and see you back at the bar." I don't want to sit beside Vass while he chats about old times with his ex. Besides, maybe I can salvage my deal with Luke.

When I get back to the bar, he's already ordered us each a drink and grabbed a table by the window. "I hate these events," he says as I sit down. "I know it's all for a great cause, but I wish they'd just send an email asking for a pledge. The amount of money they spent renting this place could have helped quite a few children."

"Do you hold events like this at your hotel?" I ask.

"Yes. I quoted for this one, actually, but I lost out."

"At least you can leave here when you feel like it, though. If you were hosting, it would've been a late one."

My handbag starts to ring, and I dig around inside for my mobile. Vass's name flashes on the screen. I've only been gone five minutes, so I press cancel and turn it off. I know it's petty, but I'm pissed that he's ignored me tonight after he suggested this was another chance for us to show unity.

"Fiancé?" guesses Luke.

"Yes, he loves this sort of thing. I was getting bored being his silent partner while he did the social butterfly thing. Sometimes I feel slightly out of my depth at big events like this," I admit. My head feels lighter, and I think maybe the Champagne's catching up with me.

"It's good for business, networking with all these rich people. You should've brought your brochures. Speaking of which, I left mine behind. Maybe I can pop by and get it sometime?" I'm relieved he realised.

We spend the next half-hour talking business. He's very interested in The Luxe and what we can offer. When the conversation begins to run dry, I stand. "Let's sit at the bar and drink shots," I suggest. Shots make the dullest conversation brighter, and I want him to trust me. Half my strategy in marketing is building good relationships with clients.

Luke laughs and shrugs his shoulders. "I'm game if you are, but be warned, I can hold my drink well."

By our sixth shot, I'm really beginning to feel the effects. Even Luke gags at the seventh. We take it in turns to choose the shot, and the other has to drink it, no excuses. I'm still giggling at his overreaction to a lemon meringue flavoured one when I hear a cough from behind me. I glance over my shoulder, and Vass is there, his arms folded across his chest and anger written all over his face.

"I've been trying to call you, but you turned your phone off," he says coldly.

I press my lips together to hold in my nervous giggle. "My battery must have died," I whisper, wincing. Luke laughs aloud, and I nudge him in the ribs with my elbow like we're teenagers in trouble. Vass catches the movement and arches his eyebrow.

"Shall we go and take our seats? The auction is about to start," Vass growls.

"Actually, I'm having a great time here. Come get me after," I slur as I turn back towards the bartender. "Absinthe, please," I order, holding out my cash.

"Alivia," Vass snaps, clearly irritated, "remember what happened last time you ignored my request?" I roll my eyes, hand the money over, and slide a shot to Luke. We clink our glasses and knock the absinthe back, coughing as it burns.

"Come on, Liv, let's call it a draw. We'll have to have a rematch another time, of course." Luke grins, standing.

"No, don't go. We're having fun," I whine, and he laughs, walking away and leaving me with a pissed-off Vass. "Do you want to play?" I ask, waving my empty shot glass at him. I cover my mouth and widen my eyes. "Oops, I forgot, big bad Vass doesn't drink, does he?"

"I think you've had enough for one night," he mutters, taking me by the upper arm and guiding me off the stool. I grab my bag, laughing at his overdramatic reaction.

"I saw you talking to her," I say sulkily, the alcohol controlling my mouth.

"Did you?" He manoeuvres me through the room towards the exit. Vass stops us by the main reception desk, where a young blonde girl smiles sweetly at him, and I roll my eyes, earning me another scowl from Vass.

"I know it's really short notice, but do you have any rooms available for this evening? My fiancée is feeling a little . . . sick and she needs a lie down."

The girl taps away on her computer. "We only have our honeymoon suite free, I'm afraid."

Vass nods, handing her his platinum plus bank card. She smiles and takes Vass's details and then hands him the key. Vass grabs my arm again and marches me towards the elevator. "Vass, I'm not staying here. I have nothing with me," I hiss.

"I can't take you out there, can I? Not in this state. The press will have a field day," he hisses angrily.

I hadn't really thought about that. They already think I'm out to get Vass's money, so the last thing I need is them telling the world I'm a drunken mess. "Sorry, I didn't think about that."

"No, you really didn't," he mutters, shoving me into the elevator and then standing in front of me, keeping his back to me. "You've embarrassed me tonight, Alivia. That won't happen again."

"I said sorry. I'm not used to all this. I don't know the etiquette at these sorts of things," I say.

"It's quite simple—act like a fucking educated lady and not some cheap, drunken hooker," he snaps, and I rear back like he's slapped me. A stab of pain hits my heart and I blink to keep the tears from coming to my eyes. "Why were you even talking to him anyway? I told you, I don't like him and I don't want to do business with him."

I take a moment to reply, trying hard to get my feelings in check. "We got talking, and he was bored like me," I mutter.

"It's a charity function to raise money for underprivileged children and you two sat huddled at the bar, getting wasted on cheap shots. It's disrespectful not to mention in poor taste."

The elevator finally opens, and I breathe a sigh of relief. I just want to be away from him. I follow him into the hallway. Our room is the only one on this floor, so he goes straight to the door to unlock it.

Inside is beautiful. The large four poster bed is huge, and there's a piano in the corner of the room. Across from that is a hot tub with unlit candles floating on the water. If I was a newlywed, I'd be very happy with this room. I go straight to the bathroom and get undressed, leaving on the underwear, and wrap myself in the complimentary robe. Luckily, toothbrushes are provided.

When I go back into the room, Vass is sitting up in bed. His clothes lay folded on the chair, and he has the television remote in his hand, flicking through the various channels. I take in his broad, muscled chest and bite my lip. I can't share a bed with this man, mainly because my body has been craving his touch since that steamy kiss for the press earlier, but also because he hurt me with his words yet again and I'm mad at him for that. I take myself off to the couch.

He sighs. "What are you doing, Alivia?"

"Getting some sleep. The minute I wake up, I'm out of here," I mutter, laying down and wrapping the robe tighter around me.

"Don't be ridiculous. You can sleep in the bed with me, there's more than enough room."

"I'm not sharing a bed with you," I snap.

"I won't touch you, don't worry about that," he says firmly, and it sends another stab to my heart. I snuggle down. The couch is comfy, though not as comfy as the bed looks, but I refuse to share with Vass after the way he spoke to me. "I didn't like seeing you talking with that guy tonight," admits Vass.

"You'd ignored me all evening, Vass. Next time, take someone else to these things. I don't fit in here."

"Of course, you do, Liv. I have to attend a lot of things like this. You'll get used to them. Next time, I'll make sure I don't ignore you. I was pissed because of earlier today."

I prop myself up on my elbows so I can see Vass. He's staring at the television, still channel hopping. "Vass, what are those marks on your back?" I ask, my voice quiet.

His eyes remain fixed to the television, and just as I'm about to give up on any sort of answer from him, he says, "A cane."

I sit up farther. "A cane? I don't understand."

"And you never will. It's just something I have to do once in a while, but you wouldn't understand why or how it helps."

"If we're going to get married, don't you think you'll need to start letting me in, Vass? How will I ever understand your world when you won't show it to me?"

Vass sniggers and shakes his head like he's thinking of a private joke. "It's safer you stay in your perfect world, Alivia. Goodnight."

I lay back down, feeling deflated. I want to get to know the real him, yet he shuts me out. And every time I think I'm making progress, he closes down again. I don't know why he intrigues me so much, making me want to know every little secret he holds, but it's becoming an addiction.

I wake to shouting. I slowly open my eyes and look around. Vass's voice hurts my head, and I wince every time he speaks. He's pacing around the room with his mobile pressed to his ear. "I don't care. I want to know who the hell sent them those pictures. It's like I'm being followed." He pauses for a second while the person on the other end of the phone speaks. "But I was told that no press was invited inside the venue, so it makes no sense. Just call them and threaten legal action. I'm pissed off with this circus." He disconnects the call and chucks his mobile phone onto the bed, then he notices I'm awake and scowls deeper.

"Do you want breakfast? There's a tray over by the window," he mutters, pointing in that direction.

"Is everything okay?" I ask, sitting up.

"No. The gossip column is bursting with bullshit today." I pick up my mobile phone and check for the news alert' I'd signed up for. Sure enough, there are several. "Don't even look, it's not worth it," he warns me.

I place my phone back on the table, deciding I'll look when I'm next alone. I don't want to annoy him further. "Get showered. We'll head off to get a change of clothes and then spend today together," he says.

"I might have plans," I mutter. I don't, but he can't just assume he can take up my time.

He pulls on his jacket. "Then cancel them, because you're spending the day with me."

Vass takes me home to change. I find it odd that he has a change of clothes at Clarisse's place, but I remind myself that it's none of my business.

We spend the entire day shopping. It's not that I don't like shopping, but I feel a bit like Vivian from *Pretty Woman*, and it makes me feel cheap. I have my own money now that I'm being paid, but Vass insists on buying my clothes. He insists on cocktail dresses and other dressy kinds of garments. It's all things I wouldn't normally buy for myself, but they're beautiful.

As the day flies by, I can't stop the doubt creeping in. All these posh clothes just aren't me. Somebody like Annalise would dress like this, but I like my jeans and vests. Obviously, my workwear is smart, with dresses and typical office wear, and I have a great evening wardrobe of the usual things someone my age would wear, things I can pick up on the high street that are fashionable and affordable.

We pass a jewellers, and Vass grabs my hand to stop me from walking past. "Would you like to choose your own ring? I never really thought about it, but the one I picked up might not be to your taste," he says.

"Suddenly you care about my taste?" I ask. "No, the ring you picked is fine. I'm not a jewellery kind of girl."

"I noticed," he says, raising his eyebrows. I feel like it's another dig at my lower-class ways and, quite frankly, I'm sick of it. My hangover is bad and I'm out of patience.

"Is that a problem?" I ask.

"No, why would it be? I was just saying I've noticed you don't really wear any kind of jewellery," he explains. "Maybe we should grab a coffee and take a quick break," he suggests, taking my hand again and pulling me across the road to a coffee shop.

I leave Vass to place the order as I get us a seat by the window. There's a queue and it's a good opportunity to check the online gossips, so I pull out my phone and click on the news alert. There's a photo of Vass and Annalise kissing, and I feel like I've been punched in the gut. The headline reads, ***'Vass Fraser embraces his split from Annalise well.'*** I go on to read how the pair were spotted at last night's charity event locking lips, while his current beau was spotted propping up the bar. This is followed by a photo of me looking drunk and upset at the bar. It must have been a lucky picture while I was mid-blink because I look terrible, and it's been taken at an angle as if I was sitting alone and not with Luke.

Fury fills me, and I glance up in time to see Vass walking towards me with our coffees. He stares at the mobile in my hand and must sense that I'm pissed because he slowly lowers into the seat opposite me and cautiously passes me a coffee. "You saw the gossip column, didn't you?" he asks.

"You should have warned me, Vass," I hiss angrily. "I look like an idiot."

"It wasn't how it looked, Liv."

"Now you call me, Liv?" I snap, and he looks at me confused. "You've called me Alivia for the last twenty-four hours, but now you want to placate me, you call me Liv."

"I'm not going to argue about this with you. It isn't what it looked like, so take my word for it and ignore it." I get to my feet and grab my bag. He sighs. "Where're you going?"

"You might be able to just ignore it, Vass, but it's me the world is laughing at right now, so excuse me if I'm a little upset about that." I stomp from the coffee shop, almost knocking into another customer as I leave. Vass is hot on my heels, his hands full of shopping bags.

"Alivia, wait," he orders, but I'm too angry to listen to him right now. People look up as he runs to catch me, shouting my name. He gets in front of me, trying to slow me down. "Let's not do this now. I get that you're mad, but don't make a scene in the street. We can go back to my place and talk."

"I don't want to talk to you right now. If you don't want to make a scene, then stop following me."

"People are staring, Alivia. Please, let's go and talk about this somewhere quiet."

"There's nothing to talk about. Go and see Annalise. In fact, give her your charity clothes, she'd love them," I snap.

"What are you talking about?"

"All of those," I say, pointing to the shopping bags he's holding, "They're her, Vass, all of them. Not me. You clearly want her, so just leave me the hell alone."

He continues to walk backwards in front of me. "This is ridiculous. You're being dramatic." I stop, and Vass breathes a sigh of relief. "Thank you. Now, let's go somewhere quiet."

"If you don't stop following me, I'm going to really make a show," I warn.

"Look, if it's just about the clothes, then we can choose something else. I know you prefer high street brands, I just wanted to treat you to something nice," he says.

"Wow, the insults literally fall out of your mouth with no effort," I snap, and he groans aloud, clearly irritated by my lack of compliance. "Keep the clothes, keep the goddamn ring, and stay the hell away from me. It's off. The whole thing is off." I move around him and march in and out of the busy shoppers, making my way home.

Clarisse is in the kitchen when I get back. She smiles. "Hey, you, how did last night go?"

"Don't even ask," I snap. I take a seat, and she joins me. "Have you seen the gossip today?" She nods. "So, you know how pissed off I am with him right now. He's made me look like an idiot, and I realise I'm out of my depth. I can't do it, Riss.

I can't go ahead with it." I fill her in on the key points of the last twelve hours.

"Vass is a prick sometimes. He wouldn't have realised he was being insensitive. I'll talk to him." I shake my head. Vass is her friend, and I don't want to involve her in this. Right now, I just want to sleep off this hangover and spend my evening how I'd planned to last night, before Vass took control.

Vass

"Are you trying to blow this?" Clarisse yells down the phone line.

"She totally overreacted. That picture was staged. Annalise lunged at me, and someone clearly took a picture. I wouldn't be surprised if she did that on purpose. And I've never had a woman who hates going shopping and being spoilt. I thought she'd appreciate that."

"I suggest you get to know Alivia, Vass, because you're so used to women who want your money that you don't know how to appreciate a real woman, one who just wants to get to know you. This girl is willing to marry you just so you can keep The Luxe, and she doesn't want anything in return. She feels like the press are laughing at her, the poor girl from a council estate being cheated on by the great Vass Fraser. Whatever she does always backfires on her. Stay the hell away from Annalise, she's out for trouble."

"Don't I know it. I've already had six members cancel their membership because of her father's influence."

"Well, it's a good job you have an amazing marketing employee, isn't it?" she snaps before disconnecting the call.

I need to let off some steam. I keep seeing Alivia laughing with that arse last night, and it's evoking feelings that I've never had before. Feelings I've avoided for most of my adult life. Usually, I'd shut this shit down now and move on, but I can't do that with Alivia. Not only do I need her for the next few months, but I also like having her around, and I hate that I've let her down.

I wander from room to room throughout The Luxe. Nothing is appealing to me—not the couples fucking in the viewing rooms, not the two girls on stage, and not the Dom/sub shit going on in the playroom. I lean against the wall of the bar, resting my head back and wondering what the fuck is wrong with me tonight. "Hello, stranger. I was starting to think my best mate had gone and gotten himself loved up or something." I look up as Alex saunters towards me.

"Hey, I've had a lot on. What're you doing here tonight?" I ask. Usually, Alex hits the town on a Saturday night.

"I've brought a friend for a play around," he says, looking back in the direction of the bar, where a brunette sits, sipping a cocktail and looking around nervously.

"She doesn't look like the type, Alex. Where'd you find her?" I ask.

"A dating site," he says.

"You joined a dating site?" I laugh. I'm surprised because Alex is never short of females who want to entertain him. He also has the same problem as me—he can never find a woman who understands this lifestyle.

"I thought it was about time I tried to find a genuine person, think about settling down. I'm thirty years old," he says with a shrug of his shoulders.

I give him a sceptical look. "And you thought a dating site was the best place to do that?"

"Clarisse suggested it," he says, his eyes avoiding mine. Alex has been in love with Clarisse since his teenage years. We were all friends together, and I knew from very early on that he was besotted with her. It just never happened for them, and I thought Alex was over it, but the look on his face tells me he really isn't.

"Man, you still like Clarisse, after all these years?" I ask, surprised.

"No. Why'd you say that?" he questions innocently.

"Hey, I'm not judging, you know I love Clarisse. Have you told her?"

"God, no, can you imagine? She isn't into me like that, and I respect her for it," he says. "I'd appreciate it if you didn't say anything. We're working as friends, and I don't want to ruin it." I give him a nod. He's my best friend, and I wouldn't do that to him, but I think he and Clarisse could make it work. They both love this place, and they love this lifestyle. Clarisse has spent many nights with Alex and another girl, not that they've had sex, though, because it's always about the other girl. "How's things with Alivia? The press isn't being too kind to her right now."

"It didn't go down well when she saw today's shitshow. She's not used to it, and I get that, but if she's serious about this, she's going to have to suck it up."

"Maybe you need to step into her world and see it through her eyes, so you understand where she's coming from. If you want everyone to believe you've settled down, then you have to start doing the things you wouldn't normally do."

He's got a point, which gives me a good idea. I pat him on the back. "Thanks, Alex. Good luck with the date," I say and head out.

Chapter Fourteen

Alivia

It's the simple things I love in life—a cup of coffee, a good magazine to read, a romance on my Kindle, the odd drop of gin, and Saturday nights in my pyjamas watching my favourite romance movie of all time, *Dirty Dancing*. Clarisse went out to The Luxe, so I have the place to myself. It's been ages since I've had a night to myself.

I'm all set with a bowl of popcorn, but as I settle down onto the couch, there's a knock at the door. I decide it'll more than likely be for Clarisse, so I ignore it and press play on my movie. A second later, the knock comes again. I groan, pausing the movie and placing my bowl of popcorn on the table. Peeping through the spy hole, I'm surprised to see Vass and my heart rate picks up. I'm a complete slob in animal print pyjamas and my hair piled on top of my head.

"Come on, Liv, let me in. I know you're in there." I roll my eyes. The guy has a sixth sense or something.

"I thought you had a key?" I ask as I open the door.

"I was being polite. I know Clarisse isn't here," he says, pushing past me and heading inside.

I frown. "I was planning a night in alone. What are you doing here?" I follow him through to the living room, where he's made himself comfortable on the couch with my bowl of popcorn on his lap.

"I came to see you," he says, grinning.

I scowl. "We're not on speaking terms."

He shrugs. "I can do silence if you'd prefer."

"I thought you liked kinky nights at The Luxe," I mutter, taking a seat farthest away from him.

"Kinky nights?" he repeats, smirking. "Cute. I've never had a night in watching films, so I thought I would give it a go."

I can't deny I like the thought of him staying around for a while. "I'm watching *Dirty Dancing*. I don't think it's your kind of film."

"It sounds exactly my kind of film," he says, getting comfortable. "Now, come and sit here so you can see the television better," he insists, patting the space beside him. I reluctantly move and start the movie.

We watch the entire film without speaking. Vass is entranced by it and watching him makes me smile. I grew it anup loving this film, and I can't imagine not ever watching these old classics. Every so often, his knee brushes mine and I feel like a love-struck teenager again. When the credits roll, he looks to me. "I get why girls want the fairy tale. You watch this make-believe bullshit," he says.

"Vass Fraser, don't pretend that you didn't like it. I saw you blink away tears when Johnny had to leave her."

"Please," he scoffs, "I was relieved for him. Trying to impress her father was a pain in the arse."

"But so worth it when they got to be together. Love is worth fighting for," I say dreamily.

"See, these films make you want things that are impossible," he says.

"Love isn't impossible, Vass. Just because you haven't felt it, doesn't mean it's impossible. I'm sure if you found the right girl, you'd do anything for her."

"Right, that's enough talk of make-believe happy ever afters, let's order some food. I'm thinking Cantonese or sushi," he says, patting my leg.

"I say pizza." Vass screws up his face. "Look, if you're wanting to experience a real night in, then it has to be pizza. No one orders sushi." Vass groans dramatically, "You've had a pizza before, haven't you?" I ask, but I'm not surprised when he shakes his head. "Oh my god, you really haven't lived."

An hour later, I watch as Vass takes a slice of the cheesy delight that is pizza. He sniffs it and screws up his face again. He takes a bite, and I watch in anticipation as he chews it slowly. "Well?" I ask.

"It isn't bad," he says, still sounding unsure. "I prefer sushi, but I could eat this." I smile triumphantly. The sight of Vass enjoying junk food while sitting here with me warms my heart.

"You know, next time we hang out like this, you really need to lose the posh clothes," I say. Vass looks down at his pale pink shirt and dark blue trousers and then my pyjamas.

"You wanna hang out again?" he asks, adding a small smile.

"I haven't decided."

"And I have lounge clothes," he says, placing his pizza back in the box and heading upstairs. He reappears minutes later in a soft T-shirt and shorts and does a spin. "Have I passed the lounge wear test?"

I nod, smiling. He sits back next to me and takes his pizza. "Do you stay in Clarisse's room?"

"Are you jealous?" he asks, a small smile playing on his lips.

"No, of course not," I say a little too quickly.

"I have the spare room here. Sometimes I need to get away from everything and hide out. Clarisse and I are great friends. I love her, but not in a romantic way."

"But you've had sex?" I ask, and he almost chokes on his food.

"No, I mean, yes, but when we were a lot younger. I already told you, it didn't work out, but we remained good friends. I've had other women and she's joined in as the third person, but I haven't done anything with her in over twelve years at least. Clarisse is bisexual and we both like threesomes. It works." He shrugs. I don't like that thought, so I change the subject.

Seeing as he's in a talking mood, I approach another taboo subject. "Are you an alcoholic?" I blurt out.

"Yes," he confirms without hesitation. "I haven't had a drink for five years." I'm shocked by his willingness to admit what I'd already kind of guessed. "Growing up, I always had women throw themselves at me, and with that lifestyle came parties, sex, and alcohol. Before I knew it, I was spiralling and every night became a party."

"How did you stop?" I ask.

"I was out of control. Luckily, I had good friends to save me. Another film?" he asks, passing me the remote for the television. I'm happy that he's opened up a little, even if he did shut it down pretty quickly. I find our next film, *Love Actually*, and press play.

"Why did you kiss Annalise?" I ask quietly.

"I didn't. She lunged at me, and a second after her lips touched mine, I shoved her away from me. It was a set-up. She's pissed that she isn't you right now."

"I hate that the press make me out to be a loser. It isn't fair."

"You know, they do that to put pressure on. If I settle down and live happily ever after, who will give them their daily gossip? A married man, rich or not, is a crap story. They'll get bored eventually. We just have to ride the storm." He takes my hand and squeezes it reassuringly. "And I'd like us to ride the storm together, Liv, like we agreed."

He keeps a hold on my hand while we settle together to watch the film. I like that he turned up here tonight and has shown me a little more of himself. Maybe being married to him wouldn't be so bad, even if it's all a lie.

I wake the following morning to Vass sitting on my bed, nudging me. I'd left him asleep on the couch last night. He didn't even manage to watch the whole second movie. "Wake up, we need to go shopping."

I groan dramatically and cover my eyes with my arm. "No, no more shopping."

"Why do you hate shopping so much?" he asks, tugging my sheets away.

"I don't hate shopping . . . I just hate it with you."

He laughs. "I promise not to make you go in any store that you hate. Take me to the places you go to, show me what things you like."

"In the budget shops? Vass Fraser on the high street," I say, with a grin. "What will the gossips think?"

"Maybe it'll inspire more people to do it, and it'll give the high street a boost. Now, get up," he demands, tugging my arm.

Vass

Alivia takes me in so many shops that I'm starting to regret asking her. She doesn't let me spend a penny on her and insists on buying everything herself. She then takes me into a men's high street store, and when I pick up a shirt I like the look of, she takes it from me and purchases it. That's never happened to me before, and the most surprising thing is, I liked it. After an amazing night with her, and an interesting insight into her world, I'm finding that I really do like her.

We laugh and pose for photos on Alivia's phone, trying on silly hats and oversized sunglasses. I realise that it's the first time I've felt so relaxed and comfortable, and not once have I thought about needing a drink. I'm glad I told her the truth about that. Opening up to her seemed to help her to relax too.

Alivia makes no fuss when I ask her to come to my grandmother's for dinner. It's her birthday, and she always holds a family dinner. We head back to Clarisse's to change, and I pull on a pair of jeans and the T-shirt that Alivia purchased for me today. I don't often go anywhere dressed in casual clothes because I always end up back at The Luxe, where jeans or casual dress is not allowed.

"You look amazing," I say as I enter Alivia's bedroom. She spins around in fright, and I realise I should've knocked. Her short, chequered skirt flares out and reminds me of a school uniform. It's hot.

"Is this okay for dinner or am I too underdressed?" she asks, turning back to the mirror to scrutinise herself. I want to wrap her in my arms and make her see how stunning she looks right now.

Instead, I shove my hands in my pockets and smile. "It's perfect." Her own choice in clothes suits her so much better. She was right about the clothes I purchased—they weren't her style at all.

We approach my grandmother's large country manor, and as I ring the doorbell, I take Alivia's hand. The butler opens the door and ushers us into the living room. My mother sits awkwardly with a glass of wine, chatting to my aunt, my father's sister, whom she hates. My grandmother didn't make it easy for my mother once she split from my father, but over the years, they've learnt to get along, mainly for my sake. They came together to get me into rehab just over five years ago.

I kiss them both on the cheek, and when my grandmother breezes in with my cousins, Jenny and Alison, I greet them in the same manor. I introduce my aunt and cousins to Alivia, and then we head into the dining room for dinner.

The conversation flows well, so much better than when I brought Annelise over for dinner. My grandmother asks about the marketing for The Luxe, and I listen as Alivia speaks passionately about what she's done so far. After dinner, my grandmother pulls me aside. We head into her office, where she hands me a water and pours herself a whisky neat.

"I like her, Vass," she says, taking a seat.

"Me too. She's like a breath of fresh air. She made me watch movies last night. You know, I'd never watched a movie with a woman before. Today, she took me high street shopping, and I think I actually preferred it over places like Harrods. She's done some amazing things for The Luxe and . . ." I pause when she smiles wide and laughs.

"I've never seen you so besotted before, Vass. She's good for you," she says. It hits me suddenly, taking my breath. My grandmother's right—I am besotted. I didn't have to force those things from my mouth, they flew out without me thinking about them. I didn't create lies to appease my grandmother because it all came from the heart. "She's a keeper, Vass. Don't blow it."

※

The journey home is silent. My head is reeling from the realisation that I really do like Alivia, and I'm not sure how I feel about that. I've never felt like I wanted to settle down or stick with one person. I thought it would feel suffocating and boring, but all I feel is free and happy. If this is how it feels all the time, then would it be so terrible to give it a go?

"I've been thinking, Vass," she says, interrupting my thoughts, "I want to step into your world a little."

"What are you talking about?" I ask, taking my eyes off the road briefly to look at her serious face.

"Well, you tried my stuff, and I want to try yours."

"Alivia, watching films and shopping is not the same as you trying my world. It's not something you just suddenly turn up to. Usually, people know they want those kinds of things."

"I've never been exposed to kink before. I wouldn't know if it's something I want unless I try it for myself."

"I showed you around The Luxe when we first met. If you could have blushed any more, you'd have been redder than a stop sign. You hate being told what to do, so you couldn't sub for anyone. Have you even watched porn?" I ask with a laugh.

"I did once, but I found it funny rather than a turn-on."

For the first time in my life, the thought of seeing Alivia in the playroom with all those other men pisses me off instead of turning me on. I don't want to share her. "It's not something I want you to try."

I stop the car outside her home, and she turns to me. "Aren't you coming in?" she asks. "Clarisse is home tonight." I shake my head. If I go inside, I might act on these feelings and I'm not sure that's a great idea. Once I do, there'll be no turning back.

I'm pleased when she looks disappointed. "Okay, well, I guess I'll see you tomorrow then. I've had a great weekend, Vass, thank you." I watch as she slowly moves closer and presses her lips just to the side of my mouth. Acting on impulse, I turn my head so that our lips touch fully, and she gasps. We pause, lips almost touching and our breathes mingling together. I press another kiss to her lips, and this time, she opens up, letting me take it deeper. I swear this is the first time I've ever gotten an erection from a damn kiss. When she pulls away, she looks shocked, and without saying a word, she gets out of the car and goes inside.

I grip the steering wheel, staring straight ahead. Fuck, I want her so badly, I feel like I'm in hell. *What's happening between us?*

When I get back to The Luxe, I call Clarisse. "Hey, gorgeous, how was dinner?"

"It was good. Great, in fact. Did Liv not tell you?" I ask.

"No, she didn't say much. She went straight bed, so I thought it'd gone bad."

"Quite the opposite. My grandmother loves her." I inhale before adding, "I kissed Alivia tonight."

The line falls silent for a moment before she asks, "A kiss for show, or a private moment between you both that felt more than pretend?"

"The second one. Definitely the second one," I confirm.

She gasps. "What does that mean, Vass?"

"That I'm fucked, Riss. This doesn't happen to me. Right about now, I'd be fucking her, and tomorrow I'd be firing her so I'd never have to see her again."

"Is that what you want to do?"

I sigh, pinching the bridge of my nose. "No, I hate the thought of not seeing her again."

"Is it so bad if you like her, Vass?"

"Yes, it's bad."

"She's a great person. You could make one another really happy."

"I'm already happy."

"If you regret the kiss, then be honest with her. She's a big girl, she can take it."

The problem is, I don't regret it at all, but I don't tell Clarisse that. I don't need extra pressure to decide what to do about this clusterfuck. On one hand, I could try and see this through, but on the other, I know it wouldn't work. I'd screw her a few times, and then someone else would probably catch my eye. Then I'd hurt her, feel bad, and more than likely turn to drink to make myself forget.

I spend the next few days away from the office as much as possible. I visit Ella again, even though my back isn't completely healed from the last time. She insists on taking it easy, even though I ask for hard. But she's got to feel comfortable too, so I don't push it.

By Friday afternoon, I'm struggling. Clarisse spots me in the doorway of the bar and places a hand on my shoulder. "Let's take off," she suggests.

"To?" I ask.

"Anywhere. Let's get Alex and go somewhere, just for the weekend. Take your mind off whatever is going on in here," she says, tapping my head.

We used to take off at short notice all the time. It's been a while since that's happened. so I agree. The space will do me good. I need to get a handle on my feelings and find my self-control again.

We agree to go and pack a weekend bag, then I'll collect everyone. But when I get to Clarisse's, she's standing outside with Alivia, each holding a bag. Riss opens the car door and sticks her head in. "About time," she says, smiling.

"Riss, what's she doing here?" I whisper-hiss.

"Alivia?" she asks, and I nod. "I invited her."

"Jesus, why would you do that? You said us two and Alex."

"Do you want me to tell her she can't come?" I shake my head. How can I be that harsh when she's doing so much for me? I drive the entire way to Southend in silence. Clarisse and Alex make up for it with nonstop chatter of childhood tales, telling Alivia all about our teenage years. All I can think about is how I'm going to get Alivia off my mind now she's here with us.

Chapter Fifteen

Alivia

I've never been on a holiday with friends. Daniel and I went away to Scotland with his parents once and then we travelled to Greece with my parents, but we never went alone or with a group of friends. Clarisse said that she, Alex, and Vass often go for weekends away. I love the friendship they have, and if the tales that she and Alex are telling me on our drive to the sea are anything to go by, they have a special bond that'll never be broken.

We arrive at a cottage overlooking the sea, and Vass practically jumps from the car and heads inside. Clarisse gives my arm a gentle squeeze as if to reassure me things will be okay, but the fact he didn't speak a word for the entire journey makes me think I've made the wrong decision. I tried to tell her that Vass wouldn't want me here, but she was insistent I tag along, telling me Vass was going into a dark place and he needed us all right now. I guess I felt some guilt for that because I ended up agreeing.

Once we're unpacked, the others decide to go for a walk. I hold back, telling Clarisse I need to make some calls. In truth, I think Vass needs his friends more than me right now. I make myself a coffee and sit out on the deck, listening to the crashing of the waves. It's a beautiful place and I feel relaxed listening to the sounds of nature around me. It makes me wonder why I never did this before.

It isn't long before my thoughts turn to that kiss. It felt perfect, exactly how a first kiss should be, and it was real, not forced or for the press. I sigh heavily. I'm getting in way over my head, but something about the man makes me want to stick around to see what happens.

When the trio returns, the mood seems a little lighter. Clarisse insists we head out for dinner, and Vass chips in with the suggestion of a bar just down the road. So, we head off to change before taking a slow walk there.

He's right, the village around us is perfect, and the second we step into the bar, I'm transported back to when I was small and I'd go with my grandpa for his regular Sunday pint in his local.

We order our drinks and take a seat. "How was your date the other night, Alex?" asks Vass.

Clarisse looks up with interest. "You went on a date?" she asks.

He nods. "I used the dating site you told me to sign up to."

She looks disappointed for a second but recovers well, forcing a smile. "Fantastic. Did it go well?"

"Very well. She's into soft kink, we get along, and she laughs at my crap jokes," says Alex.

"Will there be a second date?" asks Vass, eyeing Clarisse with interest.

"We're on the fourth date, actually. I saw her almost every night this week," Alex says with a grin. Clarisse and Vass exchange surprised looks. "What?" asks Alex defensively. "I told you both, it was time I looked to settle down."

"We didn't think you were serious," says Vass. "Is this the only woman you've taken past date one?"

"Yes. I like her, she's nice. Anyway, have you guys set a date for the fake wedding?"

I glance at Vass, who nods, which takes me by surprise. "We have?" I ask, my stomach tying itself in knots.

"Two months. We'd better get ourselves out there and looking like we're in love."

"How are you both finding it?" asks Clarisse. "It must be weird acting like that."

"The press are making it slightly complicated by trying to put me back with Annalise, but once we get them on side, it'll be easier. In the meantime, we need to kiss and hold hands in public, all the things I'd never normally do so that they point out this is different." His words feel stern, like he's telling me exactly what he wants me to do, and I feel slightly annoyed he's disregarded everything I said before. He must sense it because he adds, "We'll talk about it further in private."

We order food, and I listen to more stories about their friendship. I feel moody since Vass's little announcement, so I remain silent. Once we've eaten, Alex announces that he's going to walk off his meal, and Clarisse decides to join him, leaving me and Vass alone.

After a few minutes of silence, I can't take it anymore. "Vass, should we talk about the other night?"

"What's to talk about?" he asks.

"Well, it feels awkward between us since we kissed. You've avoided me," I say accusingly.

Vass laughs, frowning like the whole thing's in my head. "I've been busy, Alivia. It was a meaningless kiss, caught in the moment. Are we going to analyse every kiss or touch? Because there'll be lots of that if we want people to believe our lie."

"Don't do that," I mutter. "It's what Daniel used to do. I haven't imagined it, and you making out I that have is out of order."

He sighs, rubbing his brow. "I've just been busy, Liv. That's all. You're reading more into it than necessary." I remain silent, so he continues. "When we get back to London, we'll need to step up the game. I've cleared it with Clarisse for me to stay at hers. Obviously, I'll be in the spare room, but no one will know that. And if the press stops you to ask questions, give them what they want to hear." I nod, suddenly feeling overwhelmed by the whole thing. I didn't consider the press's interest in Vass or the fact we'd be splashed over the gossip pages. "It means you won't be able to slip off for any more dates."

I arch my brow. "And no more sex at The Luxe with other women for you."

"Actually, I'm safe there. Phones aren't allowed inside any of the rooms, and the press can't get in so . . ." He shrugs.

"I'm pretty sure that wasn't in the agreement, Vass."

"The press already hates you. Do you want to risk them catching you with another man?"

"I quite like the thought of being the one who cheated on the great Vass Fraser," I say with a smirk. "Maybe I can date at The Luxe?"

He shakes his head. "That wouldn't work. First of all, every member of The Luxe knows I don't share, so seeing you there with someone else might set off rumours that'll leak to the press. And secondly, I'm expected to perform at The Luxe. It won't be anything new to see me with women. But if you show up draped over another man, well, it'll look bad."

"Fine, then you'll take me on dates." I arch a brow, knowing he'll hate that idea.

He scoffs. "I don't think so. I'm not grafting for a relationship that's fake."

I laugh. "You don't get to call all the shots here, Vass. I'm doing you the favour, so the least you can do is entertain me for a couple nights a week. Two dates, and charity functions or nights you require me to appear as your wife are extra."

"What?" he almost shouts. "Two nights as well as events? Why do I feel like you're taking advantage?"

"I'm in the position to make demands. You can't expect me to stay home all week until you need me."

"Do you usually go on dates two nights a week?"

I grin. "Sometimes."

He rolls his eyes. "Fine. Whatever. Two dates. Do I at least get a say in where we go?"

"Maybe," I say with a smile. "We'll discuss."

The rest of the weekend seems to pass in a blur. I'm sad we have to go back to city life because once we'd had our chat, things were good between me and Vass. We enjoyed hanging out with Alex and Clarisse, and I didn't want it to end.

The moment we get back to London on Sunday evening, we're met by three photographers waiting for us outside of Clarisse's. "How did they know?" I groan, unclipping my seat belt.

"I tipped them off," says Vass. "Minibreak is a big thing for a commitment-phobe, the press will eat it up. Now, lean over and kiss me," he orders.

I swallow down the fluttering in my stomach as I lean closer and place a quick kiss on his lips. He smiles against my mouth. "You can do better."

"Don't make me vomit," mutters Clarisse, getting out of the car and heading for her front door.

Flashes light up the car, and I kiss him a second time. It's soft and gentle and I almost forget the photographers are waiting outside for us. Vass pulls away. "Showtime," he says. "I'll come and open your door." He gets out and rounds the car to let me out. I take his hand, and we stand side by side, smiling for the cameras.

"Did you have a good break, Vass?" asks one.

"We certainly did, although we didn't get to see much outside the cottage." He winks for added affect, and the reporter laughs at his boyish joke.

"Alivia, what's it feel like to be the first female to get Vass Fraser on a minibreak?" asks another.

"I feel very lucky," I say with a smile. "Vass is a great man, and I love spending time with him." Vass kisses me on the top of my head.

"Is it love, Vass?" he asks. Vass smirks, and when I look up to him, he covers my mouth with his and gives me another heart-stopping kiss. The flashes bring me back down to Earth and then Vass leads me inside without answering.

Clarisse is already upstairs when we get inside. Vass drops my hand the second the door closes, and I try to hide the disappointment. "Shall we watch a film?" he asks, flopping down on the couch.

"Actually, I'm just going to go to bed. I'm exhausted," I say with a yawn.

"I'll lie with you. I can watch something on your television," he suggests, jumping up and heading upstairs. I follow after him, knowing I should refuse his offer because I'm giving my heart false hope. But the words don't come, and when I find him sitting on my bed, flicking through the channels, looking like he belongs, I decide I can deal with the heartache at a later date.

I shower while Vass finds a film to watch. When I'm done, I decide to be a little daring and slip into my silk shorts and vest set. I like the way it shows off my curves, and I feel sexy in it. I notice Vass glance up as I enter the room, running his eyes over me like a lion ready to pounce on his prey. I sit on the end of the bed and begin to dry my hair, ignoring his hungry stare. Why should I be the only one to suffer in his company? It's time I made it hard for him too.

Once my hair's dry, I crawl into bed beside him and turn my back, throwing my leg over the quilt so he's got a good view of my arse. I must fall asleep pretty soon after because I don't remember the movie he chose or the fact that he also fell asleep. When I wake feeling too hot, I realise he's wrapped around me, with his arm around my waist and his leg tangled around mine.

I try to disentangle from him without disturbing him, but he pulls me tighter against him, pressing his erection into my thigh and groaning. Vass's hand moves along the silk of my vest until it brushes against my nipple. I inhale sharply. It seems like forever since I was last touched. He takes my erect nipple between his fingers and gently squeezes it, sending shockwaves straight to between my legs. "If you knew how badly I want you, you wouldn't have dressed like this tonight," he whispers, his voice low and full of sleep.

"Sorry," I mutter, not feeling sorry at all as he gently tugs my nipple again.

"I think you did it on purpose," he whispers, running his hand down my thigh. "To torture me."

"Never," I whisper, closing my eyes as his hand moves towards the waistband of my shorts.

"It's a dangerous game you're playing, Liv," he murmurs, nipping the delicate skin on my neck.

"I don't know what you mean."

His hand slips into my shorts and he runs a finger over my opening, causing me to buck against him. He withdraws it and slips it in his mouth, sucking away my wetness. I've never had a man behave like he does, but it's driving me wild with need. "I'm gonna be the first man to make you come," he says, a hint of promise in his voice.

It's a pointless task, I can't orgasm with a man, but I don't protest as he slides down my body and settles between my legs. He slides my shorts down my legs, dropping them to the floor, then he hooks his arms around my thighs. "I told myself to resist you," he mutters. I try to close my legs, but he holds them open. "But you're like a damn drug calling to an addict." He swipes his tongue along my opening, using my thighs to pin me to the bed. "And now, you're gonna let me taste you until you come on my tongue."

He presses a thumb against my clitoris, and I cry out. It's throbbing with need as he replaces his thumb with his tongue, licking and sucking until I feel a build-up somewhere between pleasure and agony. He doesn't let up, and I writhe around until I finally fall over the edge into a screaming ball of ecstasy. My entire body feels like it's floating, and Vass pushes two fingers into me, hooking them slightly and rubbing vigorously against my already swollen clit. I arch my back off the bed as another wave of pleasure takes over, and this time, I feel wetness coating my thighs. I flop back, exhausted.

Vass reaches for a towel, wiping my thighs. "So fucking responsive," he mutters. "I knew you would be." Then he crawls up the bed and settles down beside me. He closes his eyes, and within a few minutes, he snores softly. I stare, confused. The tent in his shorts clearly needs attention, but he doesn't seem too bothered as sleep takes him. I close my eyes too, hardly believing what just happened.

When my alarm clock rings out the next morning, Vass is gone. I lie there for a few minutes, reliving the night. I find myself smiling as I get up and shower, and I can't wait to get into the office and see him. Maybe we've turned a corner.

I pop my head into his office when I arrive, but he isn't there, so I make a start on my work. It's almost lunch before Vass appears looking dishevelled and tired. He avoids eye contact with me while he sorts through the mail in my office. "Good morning," I say brightly.

He looks up like he's surprised I'm at my desk, and I wonder if he even saw me until I spoke. "Morning," he mutters.

"Everything okay?" I ask, and he nods, pulling out a couple of the letters before going into his office. I stare at the closed door, confused by his mood swing. I know last night really happened, but I find myself questioning if Vass was actually awake when he did those amazing things to me.

Clarisse comes in, disturbing my thoughts. "How's Vass seem today?" she asks.

"Tired, pissed off with the world, same as usual," I mutter.

"He was really hard on his sub downstairs just now. It's not like him."

As the words hit my brain, my heart squeezes. It's not like I expected him to confess his undying love today, but I expected him to acknowledge me at least. Then to find out he's been in the rooms after I told him I didn't want him to just makes me feel used and dirty.

"Really, in what way?" I ask, tapping away on my computer like I'm not paying any attention.

"She's new. Usually, he's softer the first few times, but he was stern, tough, and in full Dom mode. I haven't seen him like that. Has he spoken to you about anything?" she asks.

I shake my head. "No, he wouldn't talk to me about that sort of stuff. Go and ask him, he'll tell you."

"No, I tried to downstairs, but he shut me down. I don't like him in Dom mode, it's fucked up."

"Really? I asked him to show me that side of his world and he refused," I say. Clarisse looks surprised.

"He refused? Weird," she says, a thoughtful look on her face.

"Yeah. I was thinking of asking you or Alex to show me around one night so I can get a feel for it."

"We'd have to run it by Vass, Liv. If he's turned you down, he must have a good reason."

Vass comes into the office, and when he sees Clarisse, he frowns. "Haven't you both got work to do?" he snaps.

Clarisse raises her eyebrows. "Yes, I was just checking in on Liv."

"Well, now you've done that, you can get back to work."

She stands, glaring at him. "What's gotten into you?"

"Not now, Riss. Just go and get some work done. You," he says, looking in my direction, "can fetch me a coffee."

Riss and I exchange surprised looks. Vass has never asked me to get him a coffee. In fact, he's never told us to get back to work. I stand and curtsy with a sarcastic smile. "Of course, Sir. Any preference, Sir?"

He scowls at me, a fire lighting in his eyes. "Say it again," he growls. Clarisse shakes her head at me and mouths the word 'don't' before making a dash for the door and leaving. "Say. It," he grits out, punctuating each word clearly. I move towards him. How dare he talk to me like I'm his damn submissive?

"Any preferences, Sir?" I spit out angrily.

"My preferences involve you being on your damn knees," he growls, and I inhale sharply. Suddenly, this battle of wills has taken a different turn and all the feelings from last night rush back, causing butterflies to flutter happily in my stomach.

"Of course, Sir," I say quietly, then I lower to my knees.

"Fuck, Alivia, don't," he growls, his eyes pleading.

"Do you have any more preferences, Sir?" I ask again, and he groans, falling to his knees in front of me and wrapping my hair into his fist. His lips crash against mine in a hungry, desperate kiss, one that I return with just as much desperation.

"I can't get you out of my head," he pants, pressing his forehead against mine.

"Maybe you just need a release," I suggest, making a bold move and rubbing my hand over his erection.

"Subs aren't supposed to talk," he whispers.

"I'm not a normal sub," I say with a smile.

Vass stands and heads to the door, flicking the lock. As he walks back to me, he unfastens his belt. "We'll see about that. Do you trust me, Liv?" I nod, because I do, without a doubt, trust him. He moves behind me, pulling my arms behind my back and wrapping his belt around them. "You wanted to step into my world?"

When he comes back to stand in front of me, he has his erection in his hand, slowly rubbing his shaft. He grips my chin between his thumb and forefinger and forces me to look up into his eyes. "I like eye contact at all times," he says clearly, and I nod. "Open." My mouth falls open, and he presses the head of his shaft against my lower lip before moving away. My tongue darts out to taste the drop of precum on my lip. "Open," he orders again, and I do. This time, he fills my mouth with his hardness, pushing it in inch by inch. He gets halfway, and I begin to cough, my gag reflex protesting. "Just relax," he whispers, stroking my hair.

He continues to whisper words of encouragement, pushing all the time until I feel him pressing against the back of my throat. Vass closes his eyes and stills. He begins to move out again, and I suck in a breath, ready for him to push back in. With my hands behind my back, I feel vulnerable but fully turned on by his show of dominance. "If it gets too much or you want to stop at any time, you say the word 'Luxe' and I'll stop straight away, okay?"

"Okay," I say, wondering why I'd need a safe word. I find out minutes later, when he's thrusting so hard into my mouth that I'm coughing and salivating. My eyes water, but I'm determined not to use the safe word. I wanted to see into his world, and this is a start. If I use the word, he won't take me further than this. After a few minutes, I'm getting used to the amount of force and the pressure I need to use to make him groan with pleasure. He grips his hands into my hair, keeping his eyes fixed on me before thrusting into my mouth and stilling. He holds me there for a few seconds, and I have to concentrate hard on breathing through my nose. He grunts and his body trembles. As he pulls out of my mouth,

I taste his release on my tongue. He watches, waiting for me to swallow, smiling when I do.

He tucks himself back into his trousers and then takes a seat across from me. He smirks at my confusion. "We need to discuss this new arrangement."

"And I need to be tied up to do that?" I ask.

"What are we doing here, Liv?" he asks.

"I thought we were having some fun," I say with a shrug.

"Is it just fun to you?" he asks sceptically.

"Believe it or not, Vass, women can just have sex without falling crazy in love," I say sarcastically. He seems to ponder this for a moment and then he gives a satisfied nod and unties the belt.

Vass

"So, basically, you're like a real married couple," says Alex with a laugh.

"No, but it makes sense to make the most of our fake marriage," I say, and he raises his eyebrows doubtfully. I'm regretting telling my two best friends. Clarisse is staring at me, her mouth slightly open in surprise, and Alex just laughs at everything I'm saying.

I've been tying myself up in knots the last few days over Alivia. Since our kiss, all I've thought about is doing it over and over. And I had no idea how to be around her knowing I couldn't have her yet wanting her so badly. Hearing her tell me she's up for no-strings fun is the best solution to both our problems. This way, she doesn't need to date anyone else, and I get to quench this thirst I have for her. Once we've both had our fill of one another, I can go back to life before Liv, and she can go and work for my mother.

"And you don't think she's going to grow feelings?" asks Alex.

"She said not. I've made it very clear I'm not the marrying type and I don't want the whole white picket fence and kids. She seems to be on the same page. It's a win-win situation."

Clarisse sighs. "I think this will get messy."

"How?" I ask, frustration clear in my voice.

"Because, Vass, Alivia is a nice girl. She's doing a great thing for you and your grandmother, even if it is a little above and beyond. Now, the waters will just get muddy and hearts will get broken and it's just really not a good idea."

"Clarisse, you're overthinking it. It's just sex. It doesn't look like she's had lots of experience, and I'm the perfect man to help her out with that."

"Vass, I've always supported you in everything you've ever done, but this," Clarisse shakes her head, "this is not going to work out. I really like Alivia. She's becoming a good friend. She's the type of girl who falls in love and lives happily ever after despite what she's told you."

"Riss, she came on to me. You seem to have this impression that she's a good girl with a pure heart, but she got on her knees and came on to me."

She groans. "She's still a red-blooded female, Vass, of course, she fancies you. But you know at the end of this, you can turn your feelings off and walk away. You'll get over her by fucking your way through The Luxe, and she'll be left broken and forever scarred by you."

"Clarisse, you really know how to dampen the mood," I mutter. "We've talked about it and we're both happy to have some fun while we go through this bullshit to appease my grandmother. Don't ruin it for us." I stand, pulling my jacket on. "And don't go talking Liv out of this. It's done."

I decide to go and see Alivia. When I knock, there's no answer, so I use my spare key and let myself in. All the lights are out, so I head upstairs.

Alivia is sat on the bathroom floor with the door open and a blanket wrapped around her. "Liv," I say, and she jumps in fright. "Sorry, I didn't mean to scare you. Are you okay?"

"I'm not feeling great, actually," she says quietly.

"You're sick?" I ask, and she nods.

"I feel too shaky to get up, could you help me?" she asks. I hook an arm under her legs and the other around her back, and I lift her from the floor. She rests her head against my shoulder, and I take her into her bedroom, setting her lightly on her bed. "I'm so cold," she mutters. I pull her quilt back, and she gets under it.

"I'll get another blanket," I say, and I go to find one. When I return, she's visibly shaking. I lay the extra blanket on top and then go in search of a hot water bottle. When I return, she's asleep but still shaking. I tuck the hot bottle under her quilt and lay behind her, pulling her against me in the hope that it helps warm her up.

I'm awoken sometime later by the crashing and banging coming from outside Alivia's bedroom door. I glance down at Alivia, who has thankfully stopped shaking but is still tucked against me and peacefully sleeping. I get myself free and creep out of the room.

Clarisse is against the wall outside Alivia's room with Alex kissing her neck while pulling off his shirt. I raise my eyebrows and give a small cough to alert them that I'm here. They freeze, and Alex slowly looks in my direction. "Vass," he mutters, surprised.

"I thought you'd gone home," adds Clarisse, straightening her clothes out sheepishly.

"Clearly. Alivia isn't well, so I've been looking after her. Good night?" I ask with a smirk. They exchange a wary look, and Alex sighs.

"Look, man, we were gonna tell you, but we didn't know how we felt about it all," he explains. I put my hands up in surrender.

"Hey, I'm not judging. I love you both. Just go in with your eyes open. I don't want either of you getting hurt."

Clarisse kisses my cheek as she passes me to go to her room, and Alex pats my shoulder. I knew something was going on with them two. They had taken the banter up a gear and they were spending a lot more time together than usual.

Alivia is awake when I go back into her room. "Hey, how are you feeling?"

"Terrible," she groans. I pass her some paracetamol and a glass of water.

"We'll get the doctor to come and take a look at you in the morning. You feel a little warm." She lays back down, and I snuggle up beside her.

Chapter Sixteen

Alivia

Turns out that urinary infections can be the worst. I've spent the last four days holed up in my room resting, at Vass's insistence. His doctor came and ran some tests, and turns out I had quite a nasty infection, which accounted for my fever. I felt much better after two days of antibiotics, but Vass insisted I keep resting. Secretly, I think he's liked having me trapped here all to himself, not that he's laid a finger on me. He's been the perfect gentleman. We've watched film after film, caught up on comedy shows that I love to watch and he'd never heard of, and eaten pizza and fish and chips, mainly because Vass can't cook and he refused to let me up to do it. I can't deny that I've enjoyed it. It's nice to have someone take care of me. The most Daniel ever did was chuck a blanket over me as he left to see his 'friends'.

I'm in the kitchen washing the dishes when Vass comes in. He'd gone to a meeting earlier, and I've missed him, even though he was gone less than a couple of hours.

"Why are you out of bed?" he asks, placing a grocery bag on the worktop.

I smile. "I'm feeling so much better."

"I leave you alone for a few hours and you take full advantage," he says pulling various items from the bag. I pick them up as he places them down, examining each item and eyeing him suspiciously.

"Tomatoes. Onions. Garlic. What's going on?"

"I'm treating you to a meal. A good homecooked meal," he explains with a proud grin.

"You're going to actually cook? You said you've never even lit the oven," I remind him.

"I know, but have faith. I spoke to a very good friend of mine, and she gave me step-by-step instructions. You go and take a relaxing bath, and by the time you're done, it'll be ready."

I take a bath and my mind wanders to the usual thoughts. Mainly Vass and how I've seen a side to him that I never thought existed. He says he's not the settling down type, but he's really taken care of me these last few days, making me think up scenarios where things are different and he realises over time that it's me he wants forever. He hasn't made any promises. In fact, he's made it pretty clear this is a convenient thing for us both. And while we're faking a relationship, it'll stop us looking elsewhere and getting caught out by the press.

When I get back downstairs, Vass is plating up our food. I seat myself at the table, which he's set up with candles. There are roses in a vase and a glass of wine for me. He brings over two plates, placing one down in front of me. The smell of the food is amazing. "Chicken and pasta in a homemade tomato and garlic sauce."

"I love this dish. How did you know?" I ask. My mother makes this when I visit.

"That good friend I spoke to was your mother. She told me what you liked and gave me the recipe, followed by very precise instructions. She thought I was kidding when I said I'd never chopped an onion." I laugh. My mother wouldn't be able to comprehend that he'd never cooked, because as a child, she'd always spent time cooking with me.

I try a mouthful of the cheesy tomato dish. It's amazing, and I close my eyes in pleasure. "It tastes just like hers," I say with a smile.

Vass grins proudly and tries a mouthful. "Wow, this is good," he says. "Did Daniel ever cook for you?"

I laugh. "No, I haven't ever had a man cook me dinner. This is a first. Not bad for a pretend boyfriend."

"About that, would it be too soon to put this on?" he asks, handing me the box with the engagement ring that he'd previously presented me with. I open it, and it really is pretty. I take it out and try it on, holding my hand out in front of me, admiring how good it looks on my finger.

"I'll need to speak to my parents about it. It's clearly not going to be a secret like I'd wanted it to be, but this is just an engagement, right, so the wedding can still be a secret. When we call this all off, I can just say we called the engagement off," I confirm. Vass nods, snapping a photo of me on his mobile. "Vass, I've just had a bath. I look a mess." I laugh.

"I just felt the need to capture the moment." He shrugs. "You look beautiful." When he says things like that, it's easy to forget it's all a lie.

We finish the meal, and Vass orders me out the kitchen, telling me to go and choose a film in bed while he washes up. When he joins me, I press play on *P.S. I Love You*, another favourite of mine. Vass groans as he climbs onto the bed. "Another romance?" he asks.

"You love them really. I see you smile when you think I'm not looking."

It's been over a week since our agreement and Vass hasn't laid a finger on me, mainly because I've been ill, but I'm starting to wonder if he's forgotten about it. I snuggle up against him, and he places his arm around me. "I feel so much better," I say, hoping he'll take the hint.

"That's because I'm an excellent doctor."

"When are we going to continue with our deal?" I ask, jumping straight to the point. "Now I have the ring on, I thought maybe we could . . ." I trail off and look up at him. I like that he looks shocked. He wasn't expecting me to be so forward.

"Just so we're clear, you're talking sex here, right?" he clarifies.

"Yes, Vass." I huff. "You're terrible at taking hints."

He smiles and then, suddenly, I'm flipped on my back and he's crawling up my body with a dark look in his eyes. A thrill rushes through me. "You don't realise how long I've been waiting for this," he growls, nipping at my shoulder and moving his soft lips towards my neck. He pulls his T-Shirt over his head, and I run my hands over his hard muscles. His body alone turns me on.

I throw my arm over my eyes as Vass works his way down my body, torturing me with that experienced mouth of his. When he gets to my shorts, I feel his fingers hook in the waistband and then he slowly pulls them down my legs until my lower half is completely naked. He gives me a wicked smile. "Prop those pillows up higher. I want you to watch me." I follow his instructions because I've never in my life felt this turned on just from someone bossing me around. It makes me wonder exactly what he's like when he's in full Dominant mode.

When he's satisfied that we have eye contact, he lowers his mouth to my opening, dragging his tongue from the bottom upwards and groaning in appreciation, all the while keeping his eyes locked on mine. I hiss as his tongue presses hard against my clit and he begins to rub circles. The eye contact and the constant pressure of his mouth feels intense, and I begin to spiral. When he sees I'm on the edge, he ups the pace, lapping at me like I'm a damn feast. I close my eyes, dragged under by the pleasure, and he nips my inner thigh. "Eyes on me, Liv, or I'll stop."

He pushes a finger inside me, then two, hitting that sweet spot. It's all too much, and when I begin to tremble, he doesn't let up. I scream out as the orgasm rips through me and continues to roll wave after wave until I twist away slightly, easing up his pressure. "Fuck," I pant, my limbs suddenly heavy.

"You think that was good, just wait." He grins, moving his way up my body. He releases himself from his shorts and strokes his erection a few times. "Pill?" he asks, and I nod. "Are you happy to go without a condom? I get checked regular." I like that he's asked. I know I'm clean because I got checked after Daniel cheated. I nod again, and he moves forward, rubbing the head of his cock against my opening. He takes my hands and places them above my head, holding them there in one of his, and then without warning, he jerks forward, filling me. He pulls straight out and then moves forward again. It becomes a punishing pace, over and over, until he's fucking me so fast and hard that I'm moving up the bed.

After a few minutes, he stops and leans down to kiss me. "I need a different position," he pants. He guides me onto my stomach, then onto all fours. He pulls my hands behind my back and uses them as leverage to pull me against him as he slams into me. I feel the build-up of a second orgasm, but just as it's about to hit me, he withdraws, pushing my lower back until I'm lying on my stomach. He parts my legs and guides himself back inside me. At this angle, I feel fuller, and with the weight of his body over me, it's all-consuming.

He's like a damn machine, slamming into me and then changing position the second I begin to orgasm. I cry in frustration when he pulls me from the bed and places my hands against the wall. He lifts my left leg up, giving him better access. I feel his erection rubbing against that internal spot with each thrust, and this time, I can't hold back. I bite my lip, preventing any noise from escaping because he'll stop again, and I need this orgasm like I need air. I desperately clamp my mouth shut, and when I finally feel it hit, I cry out in relief, enjoying the tremble of my body as wave after wave hits me. Vass growls, squeezing my thigh as his own orgasm takes hold of him. He stills, resting his forehead against my shoulder and occasionally shuddering in pleasure.

He withdraws, gently slapping my arse. "I don't remember the last time I had vanilla sex," he pants, turning me and taking my face in his hands. "I forgot how good it can be." He places a kiss on my mouth and takes my hand, leading me to the bathroom.

"Vanilla?" I repeat, unable to hide my shock.

He gives me a lobsided grin. "Yeah, that was pretty vanilla."

"But we did it in about eight different positions," I say, watching as he turns on the shower.

"But I didn't tie you up," he points out, pulling me into the shower. "I didn't even wrap my hands around your neck," he adds, gently doing so. "Fuck, you'd look good in a collar," he whispers against my mouth. "Tied up in red rope." I feel his erection against my stomach. "Fuck, that's an image that'll haunt me," he mutters, picking me up and pressing me to the wall. "We gotta go again."

Vass

The following morning, I pour myself a coffee and take a seat at the breakfast bar. It's early, and Alivia looked so peaceful in bed, I didn't want to wake her. The back door opens and Clarisse comes in dressed in her running gear, red-faced and panting. "Hey," she gasps, grabbing a bottle of water. "Where's Liv?"

"In bed. You should have woken me for a run. I've been slacking," I say.

"I thought you might need a rest after the exercise you had last night," says Clarisse, giving me a pointed stare.

"Sorry, were we too loud?" I ask with a smirk.

"What the fuck are you doing, Vass?" She sighs. "This is so fucked up."

"I told you, we've come to an agreement."

"An agreement?" she repeats. "So, watching films together, eating out, sleeping in her bed every night . . . the cuddles, the kisses, the taking care of her when she's ill, that's all in this agreement, is it? Because to me, it looks like a damn relationship, and if that's the case, I'm so happy for you both. But I know you, and I know you're not seeing this how she will. You're gonna break that girl apart."

I'm annoyed by her tone and immediately bite back. "What's your problem, Clarisse?" I ask. "Jealous?"

Clarisse rears back, anger flashing in her eyes. "Are you fucking kidding me right now? I'm your best friend, Vass, and I care about you. It's me who'll pick up the pieces when it turns to shit. And believe it or not, I care for Alivia too. She won't be able to walk away from this."

"You're starting to sound like a nagging old wife. I love you, but you need to stop. It's our life, and at the moment, we're happy, so just back off."

The kitchen door opens and Liv stomps in holding her mobile phone out to me. "What the hell is this?" she growls, taking us by surprise. The screen shows today's gossip column. I don't bother to take it for a read because I already know what it says.

"And?" I ask, shrugging.

"And?" she screams. "You sent these pictures of me knowing the ring box was visible. My parents don't fucking know!"

"Actually, they kind of do," I reply, and her mouth falls open. "You said they were traditional, so I asked your father's permission."

"Sorry, you did what?" she whispers. Her voice sounds shaky, and she feels along the kitchen table until she finds a seat and lowers into it. I didn't expect her to look so upset. I thought it was a good move.

Clarisse takes the mobile from Liv and begins to read out loud.

"Hearts all over the nation will feel the pain today as we release the news that Vass Fraser is off the market. Photographs emerged late last night of Vass and his current beau, Alivia Caldwell, eating a romantic dinner for two. Vass posted the photographs on his social media account with the caption, 'She said yes.' Fans reacted in shock, and many took to social media themselves to show outrage for Vass's

ex-partner, Annalise Collinsworth. One fan wrote, 'Annalise's side of the bed isn't even cold yet,' while another wrote, 'What does he see in that lower class whore when he could be with his queen, Annalise?'

"It's clear that while some fans of 'Vannalise' were still rooting for the couple, some were showing signs of warming to the marketing guru, Alivia. One fan wrote, 'Congratulations, it's like a Cinderella story,' and another renamed the couple 'Aliviass'. Millions of females all over the world will be devastated at the news. But here at Gossip HQ, we're excited for the wedding, which we're certain will be a huge affair with many well-known faces. Watch this space for more."

"It had to be put out there, Liv. It was always gonna be the plan. And I get why you're pissed—they make it sound so much more dramatic in the news."

Alivia grabs a magazine lying nearby and throws it at me, letting out a frustrated yell. "Why would you do that, Vass? I told you it needed to be on the downlow. Why do you always rush into everything regardless of what I say?"

"You came to me, Alivia. You offered to do this," I remind her.

"Yes, to help you out, but this is out of hand." She groans. "I didn't think this through at all."

"Just ride with it," I say with a shrug, and she rolls her eyes.

"I feel like everything last night was a set-up, a stage for your little show," she mutters.

I frown in confusion. "What did you think it was, Alivia? A romantic meal for two?" I'm irritated and my tone shows it. She stares at me in silence for an uncomfortable minute before slowly rising to her feet and leaving the room.

Clarisse glares at me. "I told you," she snaps.

"Why would she think I was cooking a romantic meal for her when she knows this is a fake engagement?" I ask, baffled. Clarisse shakes her head in disappointment and follows after Alivia.

I leave it another twenty minutes before heading upstairs. Alivia is laying in her bed, her back to the door, and Clarisse is sitting by her side, flicking through her mobile phone. Clarisse looks up as I enter. "It got lots of coverage," she says sarcastically. "I think the message is out there. The great Vass is taken."

"Leave us," I say firmly, and she huffs angrily before storming from the room, shoulder charging me as she passes. "Childish," I say after her.

I lay on the bed behind Alivia and snuggle my face into her neck. "I apologise, okay. I should have been clear."

"You went to see my parents," she mutters, "like it was real. You asked my dad," she adds with a groan.

"Listen, this was going to get out, and it was always going to be big news. It's better I handle it my way. I should've told you that I was sending the pictures, and I'm sorry I didn't." Alivia turns over so that she's facing me.

"This is way bigger than I ever thought it'd be. The nation hates me, Vass. They want you to be with Annalise, and I can see why. Look at her," she says desperately.

I smile at her, tucking a loose piece of her hair behind her ear. "Liv, you're gorgeous, inside and out. Don't compare yourself to anyone else."

"It's hard not to when there's so much hate out there for me. Have you seen the comments online?" I shake my head. I never read the comments online. They're not important because none of those people know me. Sometimes

Clarisse will read them to me or tell me about them, but most of the time they aren't accurate, and I learned a long time ago not to let them affect me.

"I know it's hard, but you have to ignore it. It'll stop. They'll get bored. Now, get up, call your parents." Alivia whimpers and buries her head under the pillow.

"No, I'm staying in bed for the rest of my life," she mutters. I swat her on the backside, but she stays under the pillow. She looks sexy in her little pyjama shorts, and I feel myself wanting her again. I pull down the shorts, and she tries to wriggle away. "It won't work. I'm not coming out." She kicks out, and when she lifts her leg, I grip it, pushing it to one side and burying my face between her legs. The first lick stills her, and I smile to myself. I love having all the power. I don't let up until she's screaming and shuddering. She removes the pillow, her flushed face looking at me, and says, "Okay, you win."

I smirk and get up from the bed. "I thought I would."

I head for the shower to give Alivia some privacy to ring her parents. When I asked for their permission, her mother cried with happiness. I wasn't expecting them to be so on board having only met me once, but they surprised me, saying yes without hesitation. I've never had a girlfriend's parents like me. I've always been labelled the bad boy before they've truly gotten to know me.

By the time I go back to Alivia, she's finished on her call and is staring down at her phone. "Daniel called me," she mutters. I pull the towel from my waist and begin drying my arms. Her eyes fall to my semi-erect cock, and I arch an eyebrow in warning. "I'm meeting him for lunch today."

My hands still, a rage fills me, and it takes me off guard. Why should I care who Alivia is meeting? "No, absolutely not," I say firmly.

"He just wants to talk about things. He was shocked when he read the newspaper this morning."

"I said no, Alivia, it's not up for discussion." I continue to dry myself, ignoring the indignation on her face as she watches me.

"In case you'd forgotten, you aren't really my fiancé," she points out.

"Don't push me on this, Alivia. The answer is no." I glare at her sternly, pulling out my serious Dom face. I watch her shrink back slightly before she decides to fight back. Her chin juts out and she straightens her shoulders. It'd be cute if I wasn't so mad.

"There wasn't a question," she grits out.

"Alivia, if you go to see Daniel after I've said you can't, there will be consequences," I warn. There's hesitation in her expression, but I see the moment she decides to defy me because a steely look passes over her face and she stands.

"I have to get ready now. I'll see you at work tomorrow." I watch as she heads to the bathroom, a slight hurry in her walk. I grin to myself. Her defiance is going to be my new favourite thing.

Chapter Seventeen

Alivia

I glance around the restaurant nervously. I don't want to be spotted by any photographers, so I chose a quiet, little Italian place and purposely sat right at the back so I couldn't be seen through the windows. My mind wanders back to Vass and that heated look he gave me right before I left. He'd been sitting at the kitchen table with a coffee and his laptop when I'd walked in to say goodbye to Clarisse. He'd leant back in his chair, his full attention on me, and his eyes ran up and down my body like he was assessing my choice of jeans and vest before he gave me the most intense look.

A shiver runs down my spine as I picture it again. The man is hot. But then he'd gone back to his laptop like I wasn't even there and continued his work without a word.

Daniel heads towards me, a waiter leading the way. I stand, and he kisses my cheek. "Thanks for agreeing to meet me."

I smile and take my seat. "I'm sorry you had to read the papers for an update on my life. You could have called before, and I'd have told you myself."

"It took me by surprise, Livvy," he says. His pet name irritates me and I sigh aloud. "The thing is, I'm shocked. You've known the guy a few weeks and now you're engaged. It isn't you."

"Cut the bullshit, Daniel. Why'd you care?" I snap.

Daniel grabs my hands and holds them in his. "Of course, I care. I didn't want any of this. I love you. I always have and always will."

"Seriously?" I almost laugh. "You had an affair with my friend, with our employee."

"It was a weak moment that turned into something more. It's possible to love more than one person at the same time. I googled it."

I roll my eyes and shake my head, pulling my hands from his grip. "I thought I loved you, Daniel, but now, I look back and you're right. We weren't happy for a long time, and we stayed together because it was safe. We've both moved on."

"Just think about it, Livvy. He's the big time. What would he see in you?" He gives a small laugh.

My mouth falls open in surprise at his cruel words. "Wow, don't hold back."

"I don't mean that to sound harsh. You're gorgeous, but celebrity material? I don't think so."

"I haven't come here to be insulted. Why'd you ask to meet?"

"I'm worried. How'll this affect your parents? The press are eating you up right now," he begins to say, but I cut him off with a wave of my hand.

"You didn't help that when you went to them with a bullshit sob story and made me out to be the bad guy. How could you do that after everything?"

He looks ashamed. "I'm sorry, I was hurt. Look at the guy. I'll never win you back from someone like him."

I stand. "Daniel, you won't ever win me back because I hate you, because you broke my heart, and many other reasons. It has nothing to do with who I'm seeing." He grabs my hand again and pulls me to sit back down.

"Please don't go, I haven't finished."

The waiter places a bottle of wine on the table. "You ordered wine for dinner?" I query. Daniel was never a big drinker. I watch as he pours two glasses, already deciding that I won't be drinking mine.

"Just water for the lady, with a slice of lemon, and I'll take the same." We both look up in surprise as Vass pulls a chair over and takes a seat. My heart rate picks up as I glance nervously between both guys.

"Vass, what are you doing here?" I ask.

"I came to see what was so important that you decided to ignore me and meet with your cheating ex." My mouth opens and closes like a goldfish. "And didn't you learn your lesson last time we met?" he asks Daniel.

"Look, man, I just wanted to see her and talk through some shit," Daniel explains, looking positively pissed off.

"You had your time to talk when you were still together. Maybe you shouldn't have been screwing her friend and you'd have had more time," says Vass calmly.

"Please don't," I whisper-hiss at them both. Vass turns those steely eyes to me again, and I press my lips together to silence myself.

"You wanted to see my world, Liv," he says firmly, "so let's go." He holds out a hand for me to take, and I swallow hard before placing mine in it, a million thoughts racing through my mind. Is he saying what I think he is?

"You look angry," I whisper as he leads me through the restaurant.

"Positively livid," he grates out. He hands the waiter a fifty-pound note as we pass. "For the bill." I don't point out that we didn't eat anything, and that the wine was probably only a cheap bottle because Daniel has always been a scrooge with his money.

We roll to a stop outside The Luxe, and I realise Vass is serious about showing me into his world. A nervous excitement builds in my stomach. He hasn't spoken a word to me all the way here, and it felt like the longest drive ever. I watch as Vass marches to my side of the car and opens the door, then I climb out on shaky legs and follow him inside.

"Clear the main room, Maxim. I need privacy," he orders. Maxim gives a nod and rushes off. My mind is racing. The room is huge, so why is he taking me in there?

Maxim is asking guests to leave as Vass leads me towards the stage. I begin to pull back slightly, and he glances back, narrowing his eyes. I know he won't hurt me, and I'm excited to see what he's got in store, but a small part of me is going into panic mode. "You don't get to back out, Liv. You went against me, and this is the only way I know how to deal with it." He tugs me backstage behind the curtain. "Remove your clothes down to your underwear." When he sees how unsure I am, he gently pinches my chin in his fingers and forces me to look him in the eye. "Do you trust me, Liv?" I nod. "Then get undressed." He leaves me there alone.

I take a deep breath and look around at the clutter in the backstage room. There's makeup on a mirrored dressing table and an open wardrobe with all kinds of outfits falling out. There're shoes all along one wall, all different in height and colour. I begin to undress, thankful when I realise I've unintentionally put on matching white underwear today. It isn't my best, but at least it isn't my comfy period underwear.

Vass returns wearing dark denim jeans and a white shirt. It's a nice change from his usual suit and smart trousers. He points to some black stilettos and says, "Find your size." I go over to the row of heels, and when I spot my size, I go to push my foot in. "No," says Vass, causing me to jump in fright. "Bend over and get them, bring them to me." I frown but bend down to collect them. I hold the shoes out in front of me, and he points to the floor. "Put them down," he says. He clearly likes to see me bent over, so I make a show of slowly placing the shoes at his feet. He takes my hand. "Now, you can put them on," he instructs, holding me steady as I slip into the heels.

Vass leads me out onto the stage, and I suddenly feel conscious. Glancing around, I see that the tables are all empty and there's no one in here but us. Vass points to a painted cross on the stage. "That's where you kneel." I hesitate, and he turns his body so that he's standing in front of mine. "Didn't you understand what I said?" he growls. "I tell you once, and if you hesitate, it becomes a problem. I'm already way more pissed off than I should be when I'm in here, but you wanted my world, so here we are. Now, kneel." I go straight to the cross and lower to my knees. "Hands behind your back," he snaps, "and cross your legs at the ankles."

When he's satisfied that I'm exactly how he's requested, he pulls up a stool from the corner of the stage and sits directly in front of me. "I don't know why I'm so mad at you, Alivia, but I haven't felt this angry in a long time. You defied me with a glint in your eye. You wanted to push me to this," he says in a low tone.

"No, I just—"

"Don't answer me back and do not lift your head to look at me. I tell you when to speak and when to look up, is that clear?" he roars.

I nod, lowering my eyes. I wondered a few hours ago what Vass would be like as a Dom, and here I am finding out. "Yes, Sir, is all I want to hear from your mouth."

"Yes, Sir," I mutter.

"With less attitude," he snaps.

"Yes, Sir," I say calmly. I have conflicting feelings about this. I'm turned on, there's no doubt, and if he was to touch me now, he'd find me wet and desperate for him. But everything inside me is telling me to walk out of here and never look back.

Vass doesn't speak for some time. He stays on the chair and the most I can see is his bare feet. My knees begin to hurt, but I don't tell him. Instead, I remain exactly like he instructed, because if I stop all this, I won't get the reward. As that thought enters my head, I realise how fucked-up it is. "Your safe word is Luxe, Alivia. What is it?" he finally asks.

"Luxe, Sir," I repeat back.

Vass stands, moving the chair back to the corner. He holds out his hand for me to take, and I stand slowly. He leads me over to the centre of the stage where there's a wooden bench. "Have you ever been spanked, Alivia?" he asks.

"No, Sir," I murmur, the words sticking in my throat. Vass sits on the bench and orders me to lay on my stomach across his lap. I place my hands on the floor to balance myself. Some part of me knew spanking would be involved. When you think of this kind of thing, that's what comes to mind. But I never really *thought* about it. I never pictured myself bent over anyone's knee with my arse in the air, excited at the thought of pain being inflicted upon me and now, here I am, breathing fast, clenching my thighs together and waiting for his hand to touch me. I *need* his hand to touch me.

"How many do I give you for defying me today, Alivia?" he asks.

"One?" I suggest.

His hand crashes against my backside, and I yelp in surprise. "One what?" he yells.

"Sir, one, Sir," I rush to say.

He sniggers to himself. "Nice try, but we both know you deserve more than one." He runs a finger under the lace of my knickers and swipes his finger through my opening. He then holds it in front of my face, forcing me to look at the wetness there. "I think you'd like more than one, wouldn't you, Alivia?"

I swallow, clenching my thighs harder to get some kind of friction that'll ease the ache there. "Yes, Sir," I admit. I frown, realising that I do really want him to continue, because despite the initial shock, my backside is now tingling and my inner thighs are soaked.

"I'm going to start with five. If I feel happier after five, I'll stop, but if I don't," he pauses, rubbing his hand over my arse, "well, then we'll have a problem. Count out loud, Alivia, starting at one."

He brings his palm down hard for a second time. The skin burns and I flinch, inhaling before shakily saying "one" out loud. Vass rubs the spot gently, and I brace myself for the next one. The next two come in quick succession, both in the same spot as the first, which stings, but in a thrilling sort of way. The fourth and fifth are spread between each cheek, relieving the pressure slightly. I'm wet, like really wet, and I don't know whether I should feel shame or pleasure right now. *Is it wrong to enjoy being hit?*

Vass rubs his palm over my stinging backside. "I think five is enough for your first time," he says, continuing to rub the sore area. He pulls my underwear to one side, dipping his finger inside me, and I feel my face flush with embarrassment. "You enjoyed that," he states, sounding satisfied, and I can hear the smirk in his voice. He brings the finger around to my face to show me the glistening wetness again before pressing the finger to my mouth and wiping the stickiness across my lips. "Stand," he orders, pulling me between his spread legs. "I need to taste you. Kiss me."

I place my hands on either side of his head and lower my mouth to his. He doesn't move his lips at all and just lets me kiss him. When I pull back, he licks his lips. His eyes are full of heat as he murmurs, "You taste good."

Vass takes me to a large wooden frame fastened to the back wall of the stage. He pulls at two leather straps. "Stand here," he says, pointing to a spot. He fastens both of my wrists into the thick leather cuffs and then proceeds to do the same with my ankles. I'm spread open, unable to move. Vass goes backstage and returns with a pink vibrator. Opening the box, he takes out the large silicone object. Pressing a button, it buzzes to life, and he smiles. "You didn't have one of these in your drawer," he says. I've only used a vibrator once, with Dan, but I'm not about to tell Vass that, since he already thinks I'm a prude.

Vass runs the vibrating toy along my shoulder, goosebumps break out across my skin as he glides it along to my nipple. From his pocket, he produces a small bottle. He sprays the substance across my breasts and they glisten. The vibrator glides much easier across the lubricant, and he trails it to my other nipple before slowly pulling it down my stomach. "Eyes on me," he warns.

"Yes, Sir," I say, a quiver in my voice. He swipes the toy through my folds, it's slippery and combined with my wetness, it glides right over my sensitive clit, causing me to shudder hard. I surprised whimper leaves my mouth unexpectedly. He gently runs it over again; I jolt against the restraints and he gives a satisfied smirk. I feel the head of the toy prodding at my entrance. It's hard and the intrusion makes me gasp as he adds more pressure, forcing it to slide inside me.

"Vass," I pant for no reason. "Fuck, Vass, I'm . . ." I trail off and my head falls forward as I enjoy the warmth building quickly from my toes and rushing up my body. The vibrator is pulled from me and I let out a cry of protest. "Eyes," he repeats. I look into his bright blue eyes and hold his stare. He pushes the toy back inside me, and I whimper. Then he leans forward and sucks my nipple into his mouth, the warmth of his tongue circling the erect nub. I grip the straps until my fingers are numb. The warmth is too intense and the urge to squeeze my eyes closed so I can enjoy this moment alone, is overwhelming.

My body convulses and my legs begin to tremble. The warmth is rushing around me making parts shudder uncontrollably. It's so powerful, a scream escapes me and I feel tears leaking from the corners of my eyes. My breathing is laboured and I gasp for air, greedily sucking it into my lungs as the shudders turn to smaller jolts.

Vass breaks the eye contact and drops to his knees. I watch half with horror and half with a shameless need as he swipes his fingers through my wetness and sucks them into his mouth. He grins up at me and I almost melt with desire. He moves his face closer to my opening, and as his tongue pushes against my swollen clit, I groan in pleasure. He continues to sweep his tongue over the bud, lapping at my juices and occasionally sucking me hard enough to pull out more jolts of deliciousness, dragging out my previous orgasm until slow pulses have me rocking against him for more.

He stands, wiping his mouth on the back of his hand. He presses a gentle kiss to my forehead. "You're doing great, Liv," he praises. Then he disappears backstage, and I take the moment to breathe, closing my eyes and replaying what just happened, in my mind. My body feels alive yet exhausted and somehow, I know he isn't finished with me yet.

When he returns, he pinches something onto my nipple. I look down at the tiny metal clamp.

"Vass, I don't know if I can take much more," I whisper.

"It's all about pushing yourself, Alivia," he says, clipping the other clamp into place. He presses his hand against my pussy, his eyes boring into mine as he uses my wetness, dragging it to my ass. "Have you ever tried anal, Alivia?" he asks.

"No. And I don't want to, Vass," I say in panic, pulling at the restraints. It's not something that's ever appealed to me, despite Dan trying to push me into it many times.

"Shh, I'm not going to do anything you don't like," he whispers, placing a gentle kiss to the side of my mouth. He works his fingers between my legs, paying close attention to my clit. I relax against him, my head resting on his shoulder. I hear his zipper as he unfastens his jeans and pushes them to his hips. I glance down at his impressive erection. He grips it in his fist, pumping it until a bead of precum appears. I lick my lips, wishing my hands were free to roam his body. He lines his erection up with my opening and slowly pushes into me. Vass takes my chin between his fingers and forces me to look into his eyes again. I was embarrassed at first but now it's almost second nature. I want to see the need there, it's addictive.

He begins moving slowly, taking the chains that hold my wrist restraints and holding on to them for leverage. His thrusts are hard and fast, building another orgasm inside of me, but just as I'm about to fall off the edge, he pulls from me. I groan in protest and he smirks, moving behind me and gripping my hips as he relines himself back at my entrance. With a grunt, he pushes into me again, this time giving me no time to adjust before he's fucking me like something possessed.

Vass slows, pressing light kisses along my spine. "What's the safe word?" he asks.

I frown. Why is he asking about words right now when I'm so close to pleasure. "Huh?"

"Safe word, Alivia," he asks, more sternly this time.

"Luxe," I mumble.

"Good girl," he whispers. "Only use it if you're certain you need to."

I'm confused by his words but I soon forget them as he begins to move again and that warmth flutters around my body. I'm almost at the edge when I feel something prod at my other opening. Vass feels me tense because he buries his face into the crook of my neck and murmurs gentle words of encouragement. Something vibrates and begins to penetrate the tight hole, all the while, Vass fucks me slow, rocking back and forth to take my mind from whatever he's pushing into my backside. The sensation of the vibration, as his cock fills me, is mind blowing, and I cry out as the build-up to my orgasm rushes at me. I moan aloud, unable to control myself. "That's it, Liv, come hard," he whispers. And I do. Wave after wave hits me until I'm too exhausted to even hold my head up. And just as it begins to ebb away, Vass reaches for the nipple clamps, tugging them until they ping free. A moment of pain ripples through me followed by another intense orgasm. My throat is sore from screaming as Vass pounds into me with force.

I know the moment he comes because he roars so loud, I'm pretty sure everyone in the bar will have heard.

Vass

I've always been into kinky shit, ever since my father introduced me to a woman ten years older than me. I was fifteen at the time. Victoria taught me a lot about a woman's body. She spent three years teaching me, and I'll always be grateful to her for that. It shaped my future. I don't know where Victoria is now. She just stopped coming to The Luxe once I turned eighteen and that was that. By then, I'd taken to Dominating pretty well, and women were keen even back then to sub for me.

In all the scenarios I've ever been in, this one with Alivia was by far the best. I don't remember a time when I've felt such an intense need to come. And seeing her orgasm not once but three times was the highlight. I can already feel my addiction and it's to her—the need to be inside her, with her, next to her, a pure animal need.

I learnt at nineteen what addiction was. Drinking whisky became a part of the night—sex, whisky, more sex. The first time I really saw it as a problem, I was twenty-one and the press had splashed me all over the front of the newspapers. I'd been on a drink and drug fuelled weekend and never really came back from it. I spiralled out of control and kept spiralling up until my father died. Then something inside me clicked, and I realised I had responsibilities. My grandmother was heartbroken, and so was my mother, even though she'd never admit it after they divorced. The Luxe needed me to step up, and then Clarisse and Alex staged a friend-ta-vention. I went into rehab and straightened out. Occasionally, I've slipped once or twice, but Clarisse always manages to bring me back.

I rest my forehead against Alivia's damp back, our breaths coming in heavy bursts. I can still feel the pull of her, and it has my cock stirring again. I pull away from her quickly before I get too excited. I've already done way more than I should have for her first time.

I unfasten the restraints, resisting the urge to taste her while I'm crouched down at her ankles. She steps away from the structure and shakes her legs to get the blood flowing back. "How was that for you?" I ask.

She shrugs, but there's a tired smile playing on her lips. "Amazing. It was nothing like I expected."

"You were a natural," I tell her, and I mean it.

Once we're dressed, I take her hand and lead her from the room. The bar area is busy with people waiting to go into the main room, so as we walk through, people look in our direction. It's not unusual for me to close off the room, and I do it often if I'm training someone.

Carlos tries to get my attention, but as I decipher what he's saying, my attention is caught by a shrieking sound as Annalise barrels towards me yelling. She looks dishevelled and crazy. Her hand rears back and she slaps Alivia hard across the face. "You're a homewrecking whore," she screams, shoving at her.

"Whoa, stop," I shout, standing in front of Alivia as Annalise rains down blows against my chest. "Stop," I repeat in a stronger tone, and her hands fall to her sides. Tears are falling down her cheeks as she looks up at me through her wet lashes. "What's gotten into you?" I whisper.

Clients are all staring, and I'm so thankful there are rules in place to leave mobile phones at the reception desk because I'd hate to see any of this in the newspapers. "Let's go somewhere quiet," I say, taking Annalise by the hand and leading her towards the stairs. "Max, take care of Alivia. I'll be back shortly," I say, and he rushes off to the bar.

Once we're in my room, I turn on Annalise, fixing her with an angry glare. "What the hell was that?" I yell.

"Have you seen what they're saying, that she's the love of your life?"

"What the fuck has that got to do with you?"

"It was supposed to be me," she screams, stamping her foot in frustration.

"We've been through this, Annalise. I don't understand why you would come here like this and attack my fiancée—"

"Your fiancée?" she cuts in angrily. "Oh my god, they're right, she really is the love of your life, isn't she?" She turns her back to me, laughing. "What does she have that I don't? She's from a council estate. She isn't like you and me."

"What does that even mean? Are you forgetting you were only going to marry me for the money?" I remind her of the agreement we were going to put into place if my grandmother was to accept her, which thankfully she didn't. Annalise turns back to me and tears in her eyes begin to roll down her cheek.

"No, it wasn't just about the money. I love you, Vass. I really do love you," she whispers.

I take a step back, shaking my head. "No, you don't. It was an agreement between us. I didn't promise you anything."

She reaches for me, and I pull away. "I couldn't help it. I just started having these feelings, and I thought with time you'd feel the same as me." A knock on the door interrupts us, but it's a welcome break from the intense conversation that

I've found myself in. I open the door to find Maxim looking worried.

"Sorry to interrupt, Vass, but she's gone. I thought you'd want to know."

"Liv?" I ask, and he nods. "Gone where?"

"She was a little upset and she called a cab to take her." I mutter a string of curse words and look back to Annalise. "You need to go home."

"We have things to discuss," she snaps, folding her arms across her chest. "My father is threatening to go to the newspapers about our little deal." My patience is running out, and I close my eyes briefly to rein my temper in. I nod at Maxim and then close the door again, turning back to her.

"You signed the paperwork. If you break the confidentiality, then I'll bring your world down, Annalise. Don't think I won't."

"He's prepared to keep quiet," she says, "for a price."

"Really? And what does your father need money for?" He's a successful businessman and not short of money, but Annalise's face tells me different. "He's short of cash?"

"He wants to meet with you."

"Meeting or not, the NDA was clear. You will come off worse if he takes this to the newspapers. I have to go. See yourself out."

I run to my car, pushing the call button repeatedly on my mobile to ring Liv, but each time it goes to her voicemail. "Answer your phone, damn it," I yell into the recording.

I drive well over the legal speed limit to get to her place, desperate to check on her. After what we just shared, I'm terrified Annalise has messed it all up.

I arrive, getting out the car and pausing to take a calming breath. My heart is racing and my palms are sweating. I try the front door of Clarisse's, but it's locked. I knock and there's no answer.

"Liv, open the door, I know you're here," I shout, banging slightly louder. I pull out my key and push it in the lock, it won't go all the way in, indicating there's a key in the other side. "Damn it, Liv, come on, let me in."

The window from Liv's bedroom opens and she pops her head out. "What do you want, Vass?"

"Why did you leave?" I ask. "I said I was coming back."

"You were busy," she snaps, "checking that your ex was okay."

"Hey, aren't you Vass Fraser?" asks a passing guy, stopping.

Of all the times to get spotted, this isn't the best, but he clearly isn't reading the signs, so I force a polite smile and nod. "Yeah, that's me," I mutter.

"Any chance I can have a photo? You're a legend," he says with a wide grin, pulling out his mobile phone.

Liv sighs. "See, always other business to attend to."

"Come on, Liv, don't be stupid," I shout, pausing for a photo with the guy. "Look, let me up, so we can talk like adults. This is ridiculous," I reason. The man slaps me on the back, thanking me before continuing on his journey.

"Your ex hit me in the face, Vass, and you took off with her, leaving me with your damn security," she yells, slamming the window.

I take a few deep breaths. It's a perfectly good night, ruined by drama and I don't have any tolerance for drama. I march back to the car and get in, slamming the door. I take one last look up at her window, she isn't there, so I start the engine and speed off. If she can't talk about it like a damn adult, then I'm not going to stand in the street begging.

Chapter Eighteen

Alivia

I peek through the blinds, watching as Vass drives away. Reality hit me around the same time Annalise slapped me. I'd been tied up and fucked, and I enjoyed it. What does that say about me? Am I his submissive now? And how do we work together or even look one another in the eye after what we just did? I get into bed and bury myself under the blankets, shame enveloping me.

The next morning, I arrive at the office late. I slept through my alarm and traffic was a nightmare. I already feel like the day is going to go wrong, and I've not seen Vass yet. I get straight to work, replying to various emails and setting up meetings in our main room for some large customers. It's almost midday when the conjoining door between mine and Vass's office opens and he enters. His steely expression tells me he isn't planning on apologising. A female follows him out. She's dressed well and reminds me of Annalise. Her blonde hair is styled to perfection and her makeup is flawless. Her bright red lipstick is a little much for this time of the day, but it suits her.

"Melody, this is Alivia Caldwell. She works for me in marketing," introduces Vass, then he turns to me. "Melody is taking Bianca's place as my personal assistant."

I fake a smile. "Fantastic, that will free me up a bit."

"It certainly will." I watch his eyes check out Melody's backside as she moves to Bianca's desk to place her belongings down. He catches my eye and grins, but it's not his usual playful smirk. This one tells me he's pissed with me. And that's just fine because I'm pissed at him too, so I force a bright smile.

"Maybe we can get that offer moving from your mother? I'm dying to get my teeth into something more." He arches a brow, waiting for me to explain. "At her offices," I remind him. "The original job offer."

Before he gets a chance to reply, Melody strides back towards him. "Thank you so much for this. I'm so excited about being your personal assistant." She places her hand against his chest and stands on her tiptoes, placing a brief kiss on his cheek. She laughs at the lipstick mark she's left on his skin, wiping it gently with her thumb. For a second, he looks uncomfortable, almost like he wants to back away from her, and I smirk, I've never seen him look awkward because of a woman before.

"No problem," he replies. Then he moves closer to my desk, leaning down so we're almost at eye level. "You're not going anywhere, Liv. I haven't finished with you." There's promise in his words as he backs away and returns to his office.

"Oh my god, he is so gorgeous," Melody announces excitedly.

"Some people seem to think so," I mutter, pulling my diary from my bag and flicking through it like I'm too busy to chat.

"I have to say, he's the best sex I've ever had. What that man can't do with his wicked tongue." She sighs, taking her seat, and I slam the diary closed.

"Well, I don't advise you go there again because he usually fires the staff he fucks."

Melody glances at me. "Well, I was told he usually only fucks and chucks, but he's been back to me several times." I bite back the snide comment on the tip of my tongue. "Although, I hear he's engaged now to some poor Cinderella. What a waste of a good man."

I stand abruptly. I know I'm being oversensitive, but I can't stop the jealousy I feel. I grab my handbag, as I have to meet Vass's grandmother for lunch. She had someone call me this morning to arrange it, and I felt I couldn't say no even though it's the last thing I want to do right now.

※

I drive into the car park of the huge hotel. It's an expensive place to stay, so I'm already panicking that the lunch will blow my measly budget.

I report to the check-in desk and the receptionist points me in the direction of the restaurant. I take a breath to steady my nerves and head towards the sound of clinking glasses and flowing conversation. The smell of food makes my stomach growl, adding to my anxiety.

The waiter shows me to the table where Vass's grandmother is already seated. She's chatting across the aisle to a lady at another table. As I approach, she stands and kisses both my cheeks in greeting. "Thank you so much for meeting me at such short notice, Alivia." She looks genuinely pleased to see me.

"It's not a problem at all, Ms. Fraser," I say with a nervous smile, taking a seat opposite her. I have no idea why she'd want to meet me without Vass and there was no way I was going to ask him when he's clearly being a dick.

She laughs. "Please, call me Angela. If you're going to marry my grandson, then you should at least call me by my name." I inwardly groan, having forgotten about that minor detail. I don't know what Vass has even said to her, and I didn't tell him this morning because I'm still mad. "I'm annoyed at Vass, truth be told," she continues, pouring water from a jug on the table into her glass and then filling mine. *Me and you both, lady*, I think to myself. "He didn't tell me about the engagement."

I breathe a sigh of relief, at least I won't trip on his lies. "It was a surprise to me, actually. I wasn't expecting it, but I'm sorry he didn't tell you. The weekend was a whirlwind."

"You weren't expecting him to propose?" she queries, and I shake my head. I'm not good at telling lies, and I can feel my heart beating out of my chest. She eyes me for a second, assessing me, and I shift uncomfortably. "I might be an old dyeing lady, Alivia, but I can promise you that I'm not stupid." I take a gulp of my water, noticing that my hand is shaking with nerves. "I know all Vass's tricks, and his mother's. They think they can fool me when actually he's the fool all along."

"He is?" I ask, chewing on my lower lip. *Fuck, I should have told Vass about this meeting.* The waiter comes over, and I haven't even looked at the menu properly, so I glance quickly while Angela places her order. My eyes scan for the cheapest item, a crab cake with salad, and I hand the menu back to the waiter as he takes my order. Once he's gone, she clasps her hands together and smiles tightly.

"I like you, Alivia. I get a good feeling from you."

"Thank you," I squeak out.

"Vass doesn't realise it yet, but he does love you, or at least he will in time."

"Mrs. Fraser, I mean, Angela," I say, hearing the nervousness in my voice, "I'll be honest with you. I feel a little uncomfortable, and I think we should perhaps invite Vass along."

"Don't be. I have his best interests at heart, I promise," she says with a smile. "The thing is, The Luxe ruined the men in my family. My husband, my son, and now, my grandson. Men are weak around that place, and if I could, I'd burn it to the ground, but Vass loves it. It's all he's ever known. However, it almost ruined him once, and I don't want that to happen again. The deal I made with him was that he needed to find love before I would sign over my half. He only has a short amount of time left, so you can imagine why he's rushing to get you up the aisle. I've since updated my terms; Vass has been too busy to meet with me to discuss them. There is a clause that states how long he must stay married for." My heart slams hard in my chest. "And you should know the terms before you accept his deal. Because whatever he's promised you, you should have all the facts so you can weigh up the worth."

"How long?" I almost whisper.

"As long as you need."

"I don't understand what's going on," I mutter.

"I wanted Vass to find a real woman, one who will change him for the better, and you are that woman. You're so far from what he usually goes for that he's falling for you, and he doesn't realise it. Tying him to you will prevent him from running, which he always does when things get tough."

I take a moment to process what she's saying. "So, you want me to give you a time? Weeks, months?"

"Whatever you think it'll take for him to realise that love is not as scary as he believes."

I sigh, rubbing my brow. "Can't you see he's happy as he is?"

"Vass thought the women with the flashy cars and expensive perfumes were the ones for him. I knew he'd fall hard for a girl who came from a lower-class background." When I raise my eyebrows, she presses her hand over mine and smiles kindly. "That sounded cruel, but I don't mean anything by it. The fact that you just chose the cheapest thing on the menu tells me that you don't expect anything, you didn't come here thinking I was going to buy you lunch just because I have money. I like that quality in you. The fact that you also refused to stay at The Luxe when you needed to leave your apartment shows you have pride. Vass needs a woman who will stand up to him, who will challenge him, and above all else, will love him for him and not his net worth. He's got that in you. The mistakes the past men in my family made were choosing women who wanted it all, money, fame, and I'm including myself in that. I'd give anything to do it differently."

"What's to say Vass won't cheat on me and ruin our entire marriage because he actually craves the lifestyle he's currently living?"

"Real love will stop him messing it up."

I give a small, sad laugh. "You really believe that, don't you?" Our food arrives, giving me a chance to gather my thoughts.

"I believe you're the one for him. I want to go to my final resting place knowing he's settled and happy."

"And what about me?" I ask. "I just wanted a job so I could pay my smarmy landlord the rent, and since walking into Glamour Cosmetics, my life's been chaos. And I know it's my own fault because Vass never asked me to do this. I met you and felt sad that you might die not knowing Vass's future, but actually, it was none of my business. I should never have gotten involved because I'm falling in love, Angela. I'm the one with my heart hanging out my chest, just waiting for him to throw a scrap of attention my way. It's tearing me apart. Yah know, we're now trying to score points against each other. That's how messy things are getting, and we're not even a real thing. I'm getting hurt for something that doesn't exist." It feels good to get things off my chest, and she listens with a sad expression.

"So, I get why you wanted a fairy tale ending for your grandson. And I should be grateful for this amazing offer, it's like a Cinderella story. But what you and Vass failed to think about in all this, was me. I'm stuck in the middle of your two's games. It's not okay." I stand, leaving my salad untouched, and place a twenty on the table to cover the cost. As I pull my coat on, I smile. "Yah know, he's happy, Angela. He's got his head screwed on, and he's got an amazing group of friends who'll catch him before he falls back into drinking. You should know he's doing great."

"I'll pay for lunch. It's the least I can do," says Angela, but I make no move to take my money back. "You're right, I've behaved appallingly. But please don't make any rash decisions. He loves you, Alivia, he just needs time to see it."

I shake my head. "I should go. I need to walk away from this whole situation. It was nice to see you again, and I hope you make peace with Vass's life choices. Don't waste these last few months trying to change him. He's perfect as he is."

I step outside and lean against the wall, burying my head in my hands and trying desperately not to cry in the street. I can't go back to Vass just yet, I feel too overwhelmed, so I call the one person I know will make this better.

She answers after one ring, and I smile at the happiness in her voice. "Liv, I was just thinking about you."

"Mum, can I come home for a while?" My voice cracks.

"Of course, you don't even need to ask. Is everything okay?"

"Not really. I'm ending things with Vass."

Vass

"Did Alivia say where she was going for lunch?" I ask Melody. She shakes her head, tapping away on the keyboard of her computer. I glance at my watch and see it's been two hours, and I'm starting to worry. I go back into my office and try to call her again, but it goes straight to voicemail. I leave her another message asking her to call me.

I hear a commotion from outside my office and the door bursts open. David Collinsworth barges past Clarisse, who tries desperately to stop him.

"It's fine, Riss," I say, nodding for her to leave us alone. "Please, take a seat."

He ignores me and paces in front of my desk. "I want the million that you promised my daughter," he grates out.

"I didn't promise Annalise anything. In fact, the paperwork I gave her states that the marriage will only go ahead with my grandmother's approval. It also had a very clear clause that either of us can pull out at any time and that would result in the payment not being made."

"Bullshit. I can take your contract to the newspapers and get paid that way. Fuck your gag order."

"Then I'll take Annalise to court, and she can explain to the judge why you've broken the agreement."

"And I'll tell the damn judge what a bastard you are. How you like to fuck girls who are weak and at your mercy. She was brainwashed by you."

I laugh. His theory wouldn't stand up in court and he knows it. "Is your business in financial difficulties, David?" I ask and his face turns red with anger. "Because if you need a loan, I can sort that for you, you only have to ask."

"How dare you. I'll get that money from you one way or another," he yells, storming out the office and slamming the door.

It opens immediately and I'm surprised when my grandmother walks in. "Another visitor, I'm so popular today," I say with a wry smile. I kiss her on the cheek and pull out a chair for her. "To what do I owe this pleasure?"

"I remember your grandfather sitting in that chair," she says with a wistful smile. "He thought he was Peter bloody Stringfellow." She laughs. "Have you heard from Alivia?"

My smile fades at the mention of Alivia's name. "No, we aren't exactly on speaking terms, but she went for lunch and hasn't returned yet." She gives me a guilty nod, and I scowl, "What have you done?" I ask.

"We met for lunch. She's a lovely girl, I really like her."

"I know, it's why I'm marrying her," I say suspiciously, wondering where this conversation is leading and why the hell Liv didn't mention this lunch date.

"Or not, as the case may be," she mutters, watching me for a reaction.

I let the words sink in. "What do you mean?"

"I know it's a fake wedding," she begins, and I curse Alivia for spilling. "She didn't tell me," she adds, like she's read my mind. "I'm not stupid, Vass. I knew you and your mother would come up with a plan. I offered Alivia time to win you around. I thought by adding a year or so into the deal, you'd naturally fall in love and I'd get my wish. Alivia didn't take it well."

I close my eyes and take a deep breath. "What did she say?" I ask through clenched teeth.

"That she couldn't go through with any of it."

I push my chair back abruptly, standing. "Where the hell did she go?" I yell.

"She didn't say. Vass, I'm so sorry."

"You have no idea what you've done," I hiss, grabbing my mobile phone and my jacket and heading for the door.

I drive straight to Clarisse's. Relief floods me when I see her car parked up outside. I knock on the door and wait for a minute but she doesn't answer so I try my key, relaxing more when it slides in the lock, at least she isn't blocking me out again. Once inside, I rush through the house looking for her. She's not in the kitchen or living room so I take the stairs two at a time, bursting into her bedroom. "Liv?" There's no reply and I stare at her empty bed. The only thing on it is a note addressed to Clarisse. I pick it up, my heart hammers wildly in my chest as I look around for a sign that she's still here. My eyes fall on the wardrobe door slightly ajar. I open it to discover it's empty. She's taken her clothes.

I drop onto her bed, crumpling the note for Clarisse and hanging my head in my hands. Fuck. I don't know how to put this right, it's out of my control. The door opens and Clarisse comes in looking concerned. "Your new PA said Liv didn't come back from lunch and you rushed out to find her. What's going on? Why's her car outside if she's not here?"

"Alivia's gone," I mutter. "My grandmother scared her away with her damn contract."

"She wouldn't just disappear," she snaps. "Did she tell you where she was going?"

I hand her the note with her name on the front. "She left you a note. Not me. Just you." My heart feels heavy, and I struggle to breathe right as Clarisse takes it.

"Maybe I can call her, speak to her?" she suggests gently.

I shake my head. "Don't worry about it. She's gone. It's for the best."

I leave her to read her note in peace and head back to The Luxe. I always thought I'd feel free once this whole thing was over, but I don't, not even a little bit.

By the time I get back, there's only one person I need to see. I enter her room without knocking and Ella spins around with a whip in her hand and a man at her feet. "Vass," she gasps, "what's happened?" She whispers something to the man, and he nods, getting up and leaving. "Vass?" she repeats.

"It needs to be a lot. The urge is overwhelming," I mutter, falling to my knees in front of her and bowing my head.

"Vass, are you sure this is—" she begins warily.

"Just do it, Ella," I yell, and she jumps at my tone.

I pull my shirt over my head and then rest my hands on my knees, bracing myself for the first slice. The buzzing in my head is so loud, I welcome the heat that burns with the first strike. I inhale slowly, letting it wash over me like a cleansing balm before exhaling. The next hit's harsher and

I almost smile. With each slice of the cane, I zone out, allowing it to take me away from it all.

The cane drops to the floor beside me, and I stare at it blankly. Ella falls to her knees in front of me, grabbing my face in her hands. Her lips are moving, but I can't hear over the loud buzzing.

Eventually, I push myself to stand, and Ella's hands fall to her sides. Her eyes look sad, and I hate that she's sad for me. How dare she be sad for me? I pull on my shirt, feeling it stick to my back, and then make my way out of Ella's room, stumbling once or twice. I can't work out if I'm dizzy from the pain on my back or my heart, but it's overwhelming, making sickness bubble in my stomach.

I practically fall into my office, then I steady myself and take a few deep breaths. Making my way to my desk, I drop in the chair and hiss as my back presses against the leather. I pull open my bottom drawer, one I never go into.

Occasionally, I look in to remind myself how far I've come and how I don't need it. It's a test of my resilience. But right now, it's all I can think about, and even the pain burning into my skin hasn't taken that away. My hands shake as I take out the five-hundred-pound bottle of whisky. I flip it over a couple times from one hand to the other, deliberating what I'm about to do.

Within seconds, the cap is off and the bottle is pressed to my lips. As I take my first gulp, I tell myself it's just to ease the pain of my back. Nothing more and no big deal. Tomorrow is a new day, and I'll laugh about this.

It helps the pain. In fact, I can't feel a thing, I muse, standing on shaky legs. My vision is slightly off, but the good news is that my hearing seems fine now. I laugh to myself and make my way from the office to the bar. Maxim looks at me suspiciously as I stagger past him. Everyone is so judgemental around here, no wonder I keep my circle tight. I bang my hand on the bar to get Carlos's attention. He goes to get my usual water, and I shake my head.

"Not this time, Carlos . . . Carluss . . . Carlossss. Am I saying it right? It doesn't sound right," I slur. "Carlos . . . it's Carlos, isn't it . . . I'll take a double shot of your finest whisky, hold the rocks." Carlos hesitates, glancing behind me like he's waiting for permission. "Now, Carlos," I snap. He grabs a crystal tumbler and pours the double shot, handing it to me. "In fact, just give me that." I sigh, taking the bottle from his hand. I want to pour my own damn measures without permission or judgy looks.

I go to the main room. It's lively in here tonight and I need my mind occupied. I notice Ava sitting by Mr. Bennett, a boring arse banker. When she notices me staring, her head drops and she walks towards me just like I've taught her. I pull a silk collar from my pocket and clip it around her neck. Tonight, she's mine.

I take a seat in front of the empty stage. Ava kneels by my chair, her eyes cast down to the floor. I find myself staring at the large wooden structure. Snapshots pass through my mind of Liv screaming my name and I feel my cock harden instantly. I narrow my eyes, *Fuck that bitch*. She left at the first chance she got.

I wrap my hand into Ava's hair and pull her head to my lap. "You may as well get busy," I slur. I relax back into the chair as she makes quick work of opening my trousers and pulling out my cock. I drop my empty glass on the table and drink from the bottle. It's easier. Ava sucks me into her mouth. I forgot how good she is at this, and I press down on the back of her head, forcing her to take me in deeper.

NICOLA JANE

Pulling out my phone, I snap a quick picture of her, checking it with one eye because two makes it blurry. I feel zero guilt as I click the send button to Liv. I want her to know that I'm over it, that she was nothing special and I've moved on already. *She was too fucking weak for me anyway.*

Chapter Nineteen

Alivia

I stretch out my legs on the fresh green grass and tip my head back so that my face warms in the glow of the sun. It's been a week since I left London and arrived at my parents'. I had no plans when I stepped off that train. I wasn't sure if I was ever going to return to my job, or to the house I share with Clarisse, but that same night I'd left, I received a picture from Vass with his cock choking some poor girl and I realised there and then that my life in London was done.

I'd tried hard to scrape it back together after Daniel broke my heart, and meeting Vass was a turning point for me. It pains me to admit just how much I'd fallen for him, and had he not sent the picture, maybe I'd have gone back to London, even if it was just to say goodbye. But he did, and it fucking hurt me way more than I thought it would.

The click of a camera makes me open one eye. I sigh at the sight of another photographer snapping my picture. The reporters haven't been as full-on as they were in London, so I'm thankful for that, but still, you'd think they'd be bored now. "How are you, Alivia?" he asks casually as he snaps another picture. It's a loaded question, and he'll pick apart my answer and print something completely different.

I force a bright smile. "I'm good, thank you for asking."

"How do you feel about the headlines this week?"

"I haven't read them. I'm moving on and whatever is printed in those papers isn't of interest to me," I say firmly.

I push myself to stand and brush my arse to make sure there's no grass stuck to me. I was enjoying the sunshine in this beautiful park before this prick turned up. "So, you don't know about Vass falling back into old habits?" he asks with surprise.

My step faulters, but I recover quickly and walk away. *What does he mean by that?* Has Vass gone back to Annalise? It wouldn't surprise me, and that desperate cow would probably take him back.

I take a slow walk back to my parents' house, trying to convince myself that I don't care what Vass is up to, and thinking up better names than the fans had for the pair. Cunt-alise-ass is my favourite, but it's hard to mash two names with a curse word, so I doubt it'll catch on.

My parents fall quiet as I enter the kitchen. With all the rooms in this house, the kitchen is where we always end up gathering, though I've never understood why. "What?" I ask, pouring myself an orange juice.

"Nothing," says Dad far too quickly. I give him a pointed stare and raise an eyebrow.

"Tell me," I push because they're hiding something.

"Clarisse called. She's here, in town, and she rang to get the address. She'll be here any minute."

"Okay, well, that's not so bad. Why the guilty looks?" They exchange another, but before I can probe further, there's a knock at the door and I go to answer it. I'm excited to see Clarisse. We've texted a few times, but I made it clear I didn't want to discuss Vass at all.

I swing the door open and the smile freezes on my face at the sight of Clarisse and Vass standing before me. Vass is holding on to Clarisse with his eyes closed, and she looks like she's struggling to support his weight. "I'm so sorry, but I need your help," she says with a pleading look in her eyes. I sigh and step forward, taking Vass's other arm and throwing it around my shoulder. He groans like he's in pain. "I didn't know where else to go."

"He's drunk," I state as we lower him onto the sofa. He falls face down, groaning into a cushion.

Clarisse nods sadly. "He hasn't stopped since you left. The press are having a field day. He's making a show of himself every night in The Luxe, and I just needed to get him out of there. Help me to help him, Liv. Please."

"I don't think he'll want my help, Riss. He's a big boy, he can do what he wants."

"He's heartbroken," she whispers.

I scoff. "Vass Fraser only loves himself. He's not like this because of me—he's like this because he's going to lose his precious Luxe."

"That's not true. He loves you, Liv. I know he does. And you love him. He's been to Ella every night," she adds, lifting his shirt slightly. I gasp at the sight of the red, angry welts scarring his back. "He does it to curb the urge to drink."

"Well, someone should tell him it isn't working," I mutter. "Jesus Christ, we need to clean that mess up."

I go back to the kitchen, where my parents sit looking sheepish. "Thanks for the warning," I hiss, grabbing a bowl and filling it with warm water and Dettol antiseptic.

"We know you miss him, Liv," says Dad. "Stop being stubborn." I roll my eyes. I didn't tell them the truth about our sham relationship, so they wouldn't understand.

Vass is sleeping when I return, and I take great pleasure in grabbing his shirt and running scissors up the centre to remove it. I'm sure it would have cost him a small fortune. I drop some cotton wool into the bowl and turn to Riss. "Go and see my parents, have a cup of coffee. I'll take care of this." She smiles gratefully, and I wonder if Alex has bothered to help her this last week.

I begin to dab the open wounds, and Vass stirs, letting out a groan. "Stay still, I'm trying to help," I mutter.

He opens one eye and blinks a few times. "Liv?" he whispers, his voice croaky.

"Uh-huh," I sigh, "the one and only."

"What are you doing here? You left me," he mutters, trying to push himself up.

I force him back down by putting pressure on his shoulder. "That's how you would see it," I mumble, dabbing harder and causing him to hiss.

"I need a drink," he murmurs.

"That's the last thing you need. Now, sleep it off." He doesn't need much convincing and closes his eyes while I tend to his wounds.

I return to the kitchen and empty the red-stained water down the drain. Dad hands me a coffee, and I take it gratefully. "Thank you," says Clarisse sincerely, "I didn't know what else to do."

"Maybe try rehab?" I suggest.

"I promised I'd never take him back there. It's a last resort."

"I don't know what you expect me to do. I'm not a doctor, I don't know how to fix this," I say, and my mum smiles.

"Yes, you do, Liv. Of course, you do. Just be you. You told me that when you were ill, he looked after you, stayed with you. It's your turn now to look after him."

"It's not that easy, Mum," I hiss. "I can't be around him right now, I'm not strong enough."

"Why are you fighting it?" she asks. "If you love him, then stop fighting against him and fight for him."

"You don't get it," I mumble.

"You're sad without him. That's all I need to know."

Vass sleeps for most of the day. I begin to wonder if he really is asleep or he's avoiding me and the awkward conversation we'll inevitably need to have.

I'm sitting out on my parents' front porch when he appears with a blanket wrapped around himself. I've never seen him looking so vulnerable and weak. He shuffles and sits down next to me, wincing with each movement. The silence hangs between us, and I'm not sure what he expects me to say. "I'm sorry," he mutters. "For all of this. I'll ask Clarisse to take me home in the morning."

I sigh. "Whatever you want, Vass."

"What I want is to rewind to last week, when we were happy together," he says quietly.

"Happy? Were we, Vass? Because I felt like the whole thing was one big stageshow for you. Looking back, was any of it real, our friendship even?"

He looks at me with anger. "How can you ask me that?"

"I'm not mad at you, Vass. I'm mad at myself. You didn't make me any promises, and I fell for you anyway. I didn't think I would, but after speaking to your grandmother, I realised the whole thing was a toxic mess and I was the only one who'd get hurt. I had to walk away. And then you sent me that picture . . ." I trail off when he looks at me with confusion. "You remember the picture?" I ask, and he shakes his head. I give a cold, empty laugh and pull out my phone. I don't know why I kept it, maybe to remind me of why I wasn't ever going back to see him.

He groans, closing his eyes in exasperation. "Fuck, Liv, I'm so sorry. I do stupid shit when I'm drunk."

"You're free and single, Vass, you don't need to explain anything."

"I do. I shouldn't have done that. I just... it was a shock when you left without explaining."

"I needed to get away."

"I wasn't ready for that."

I smile sadly. "Me either, but here we are. It was for the best. A clean break."

"But you live in London. You have a job and—"

"I'm not coming back, Vass. I'm going to stay here until my head's straight. You should go back to London with Clarisse and sort yourself out. It's not fair on her to have to look after you."

"If that's what you want," he mutters. I stand, nodding before heading inside and leaving him on the porch.

I get into bed and pull out my mobile. Since I saw the reporter earlier, his comment has played on my mind, and with Vass turning up, I need to arm myself with protection. Reading his downfall might help me with that.

Most of the pictures are of Vass falling out of bars and clubs. There are ones of him alone and others where there's a woman on his arm. There's even one of him kissing someone else.

A headline from yesterday catches my eye. *'Vass falls back into old habits after heartbreak.'* I sigh and scroll down to the story.

'Vass Fraser is back to his old tricks this week, after his messy split from Alivia Caldwell. Sources close to Fraser have revealed his two-thousand-pound bar bill after he went on a bar crawl Wednesday evening. Vass, named as one of Britain's hottest men, was not shy as he got up close and personal with several different

women throughout the evening in front of our cameras and even posed for a picture with an unknown blonde that was too X-rated for us to print. It's safe to say that while Fraser is living his best life in London, his ex-fiancée, Ms. Caldwell, is hiding away at her childhood home in Brighton, where this week she was spotted out and about lunching with her mother, fifty-four-year-old Caroline Caldwell. The pair were spotted looking amazing in Brighton's town centre, and the question on everyone's lips is who will snap up this single beauty.'

I scoff. So, now, all of a sudden, the press like me? What a joke. I turn off my phone and pull the sheets over my body. I can't sleep, too annoyed by that stupid story. I shouldn't have read it.

There's a light tap on my door, and I sit, pulling a sheet around me. Vass pops his head around the frame and whispers, "You awake?"

"If my dad catches you, he'll kick you out," I whisper-hiss.

Vass comes in quickly and closes the door. "Sorry, I can't sleep."

"What do you want me to do about that, Vass?" I snap. He stands by my bed looking confused and lost. It pulls at my heart, but I hold my resolve strong and glare at him.

"Just stop." He sighs. "Stop being like this."

"Like what? Angry, pissed off, jealous that you've spent the week fucking your way around London?"

"I didn't do any of that," he growls, clenching his fists by his sides. "They make up what they want." I'm pushing his buttons and it sends a thrill through me. "Stop," he snaps. "Stop looking like that."

"Like what?" I ask innocently.

"That look right there got us into this mess in the first place," he snaps, pacing the floor. "Those defiant eyes of yours call to me and I can't stop it. I lose control." I glance at him through my eyelashes. I know the look he means, and I can't help it. He stirs a fire in me that I can't hold inside.

"I thought you controlled yourself pretty well actually," I mutter, and he spins to face me, pointing his finger at me.

"Stop it, I mean it," he warns.

"How are you so sure that you didn't screw all those women?" I ask, "You couldn't even remember the picture you sent me. I bet you have no memory of the last few days," I sneer.

"Because," he growls, "if my balls were empty, I wouldn't be so fucking hard," he snaps, and I glance at his obvious erection and press my lips together to hide the laugh that wants to burst out.

"I need a drink," he says suddenly, and that wipes the smile from my lips.

"You can't have a drink, Vass."

"You don't understand the pain I'm in, Liv. I *need* it," he says, sighing heavy. "This pain will get worse if I don't have at least one drink. I can't just stop. It needs to be gradual." I shake my head. Clarisse warned me that he'd try this.

Vass leans in close to me, anger on his face. "Then give me some money so I can get myself a damn drink," he growls. I shake my head again, not breaking eye contact, making sure that defiant look is clear on my face. Clarisse took Vass's money and bank cards while he slept. Vass takes a few deep breaths, trying to calm the beast that so badly wants to come at me.

"Alivia, this isn't a game," he snaps, "and stop looking at me like that. Fucking you won't stop my pain," he growls.

My mouth suddenly feels dry. I feel like the devil is inside me as I begin to unfasten my silk pyjama shirt. He freezes, watching my fingers unfasten each button. I slide it from my shoulders and drop it to the floor. I lay back and run a hand up along my stomach. His eyes run over my black lace underwear, and I can see my plan's working. His mind is on me, not the drink.

I slip my hand inside my panties and breathe out a sigh, closing my eyes briefly as pleasure ripples through me. I pull out my hand and place my wet finger in my mouth, sucking it clean. Vass's eyes burn into my own as hunger overtakes him. It's not a sensible decision but it's the only way I knew I'd distract him. Besides, my hearts already shattered, it can't get any more painful.

"I need to feel you here, Sir," I whisper, tugging down the lace bra so that my breasts are free. Vass kneels at the side of my bed, still just staring as I place my hand back into my knickers. I keep the eye contact, showing him that I remember his rules. He needs to feel in control of me right now, so I give it to him willingly. Vass lowers his mouth to my breast. I feel his breath as he gets close, and then his warm tongue circles my nipple.

"I know what you're trying to do, Liv," he growls, nipping at my erect nipple.

"I'm just trying to help you, Sir," I say with a wicked smile. Vass climbs onto the bed, his large body towering over me. His hands wrap around my throat, and he leans down, kissing me hard and hungrily. When he pulls away, I'm gasping for breath, and he loosens his grip slightly. He moves down my body, settling himself between my legs. I watch him fiddle with his jeans, shoving them down to his thighs. Then his hands go back to my neck and he thrusts himself inside me, putting pressure on my neck at the same time. I gasp in shock, the sensation surprisingly exciting, and my body hums to life as Vass begins to move. He kisses me with such passion, I'm lost under his spell once again.

"Do you like this, Alivia?" He pants, his face twisted with desperation and pain as he thrusts harder.

"Vass, I need to come," I tell him, desperately trying to hold back.

"You're not, Alivia. Don't come yet, hold it in," he orders. I grip the sheet tight, trying hard to control myself. Vass squeezes tighter and my breath gets stuck. Right before I begin to panic, he leans close to my ear, "Come for me, baby. Come over my cock."

I let go, pressing my hand to my mouth to stop the scream that wants to rip out of me. I shake so hard, I'm pretty sure I pass out for a second. Vass begins to slow his pace, and I wonder how the hell he controls himself so well. "If you won't get me a drink, then I'm going to spend all night buried in your pussy," he whispers. He pushes himself up onto his hands so his arms are straight, and he looks down between us, watching our connection as he pushes himself in and withdraws slowly. "I can see your cum on my cock," he whispers.

He eventually pulls from me, "I want to feel your mouth around me," he instructs, kneeling back and stroking his erection.

I kneel in front of him, staying up on my knees with my backside in the air. I press my tongue against the head of his cock, licking the bead of precum from the tip. I look up at him as I take him into my mouth, relaxing my throat so I can take him in farther. He hisses and grips the mattress. I continue the slow torture of deep throating Vass's cock until I feel it swell. He suddenly pulls me away and takes a few deep breaths. "Not yet," he says, regaining control of himself.

I sit on his lap facing him. I want to ride him until I make him so lost in me, he won't think about drinking. I take his face in my hands and rain kisses over his stubble, along his jaw, and over his cheek. He lines himself up, and I slide down his cock. Our lips lock together, and I keep the kiss gentle as I fuck him, rocking back and forth in a slow rhythm. I run my hands through his hair, my long nails scraping softly against his scalp. For the first time, I feel so connected to him that I want to cry, and as I continue to rock, I feel him stiffen. He groans quietly in my ear as he releases his orgasm inside me. His cock is still semi-hard as I continue to move while my fingers rub fast at my clit. Vass takes my nipple in his mouth and it's enough to send me over the edge, panting as I come for a second time. He snatches up my hand and sucks my fingers into his mouth, his tongue moving around each one as he tastes our combined juices.

Vass keeps us connected, even though he's only semi-hard, and he pulls me on top of him as he lays down. "Rest," he orders, closing his eyes.

"Like this?" I ask with a laugh.

"I told you, I'm staying inside you all night."

Vass

I must've fallen into a pretty deep sleep, but I'm awoken when my cock stirs to life inside Alivia. I turn her over so that I'm on top, fucking her like I can't get inside her deep enough, each thrust harder than the last. The night continues like this, sleeping for half an hour or so and then being woken by Alivia twitching in her sleep, which makes me hard and so I fuck her again. By six a.m., I feel so exhausted but the need to drink is still on my mind.

I reach for her again, but she moves away. "No more," she groans, clamping her legs closed. As if that'll stop me.

"Yes, more," I grit out, flipping her over and pushing a pillow under her stomach so that her perfect rounded arse is raised. I rub some lubricant against her tight hole, and she flinches, reaching back and batting me away from that area. I put pressure against her with my thumb, until it slips inside, causing Alivia to wince. "Vass," she hisses. I press my hand to the middle of her back, holding her there while I play with her tight arse. She gives up trying to stop me, and I reward her by pushing a finger into her pussy. She hisses, and I know she's sore, but I continue, spreading her juices over her arse.

I kneel behind her, and she begins to object again, moving forward to get away from me. I grip her waist. "Alivia, keep still," I order, and her movements stop. Pressing the head of my cock against her arse, I ease it through the tight hole. Liv grips the pillow and buries her face into it to muffle the scream that escapes. Once I'm fully in, I stop, giving myself a chance to compose.

"The least you owe me is your virgin arse," I whisper, wrapping her hair around my fist and tugging her head back. I begin to move, and she whimpers as the pain becomes more intense. I feel her relax as her moans are replaced with grunts of pleasure. "Do you like it?" I pant into her ear. Alivia nods, pulling her hair tighter in my grip. I slap her thigh hard, and she jumps.

"Yes, Sir," she groans.

Her hand slips under her stomach and she presses it against her pussy, then she begins to shudder, gripping my cock tighter as she climaxes. The pressure is enough to drag another orgasm from me, and I fall over her as I spill inside her arse. A wave of sickness passes through me and sweat drips down my back. I flop down beside her, throwing my shaky arm over my eyes. I've been inside her for most of the night and all I can think of is getting a fucking drink. I turn away from her and wrap the sheet over me. I feel her eyes burn into my back, and then I feel the mattress lift as she stands. Once she's left the room, I release an unsteady breath. I'm glad she didn't force a conversation from me, sex is one thing but talking, I'm just not ready for it.

Chapter Twenty

Alivia

I read a quote once, 'Never give up on something that you can't go a day without thinking about.' I thought it was sweet when I saw it in some woman's magazine, and at the time, I was dating Daniel. This past week, watching Vass fall apart, makes me see that quote is a pile of crap. Vass can't go a day without thinking about alcohol, but he has to give it up before it takes him completely. Clarisse assures me that it'll pass, that the worst is over.

My days have been spent watching him sleep. He shakes and shivers the whole time, occasionally groaning like he's in physical pain. I change the bed sheets twice daily because he sweats continuously. My nights are spent comforting him, keeping his mind focussed on my body and not his next drink.

I speak to his mother and grandmother every day with updates. They're worried, and his mother keeps talking about sending him back to rehab, but I'm with Clarisse on this one. I'd rather we try first, instead of making him more miserable.

❧

I sit on the toilet, the seat closed, and peer at the little white stick. I know it said to wait two minutes, but seriously, does that really change the outcome? I stare and stare, then the first blue line appears. According to the instructions, that means that the test is working. I look at my watch. It's only been thirty seconds, but, Jesus, this seems like a lifetime. I look back to the stick and freeze. *No, no, no, no, this can't be happening.*

"Are you okay in there?" shouts Vass, sounding amused. I stuff the test in my waistband, dropping my shirt over it to hide it. I go into the bedroom and Vass is sitting up in my bed watching television. He smiles and holds a hand out to me. I notice that he isn't shaking anymore. He's looking so much better.

"Did I tell you how grateful I am?" he asks for the tenth time. I smile and head to my drawer. With my back to him, I take out the stick and hide it under my underwear, checking one last time to confirm the two blue lines, half of me hoping that I'd imagined them.

"You seem better today. Would you like to try some dinner?" I ask, and Vass nods.

"Yeah, I do feel hungry actually." He hasn't eaten a thing at all since he arrived, preferring just to drink water. I go downstairs and make Vass a cheese sandwich.

When I get back upstairs, I halt mid-step. Vass is holding the white stick, staring down at it intently. I take a breath. I wasn't ready to tell him yet, as my biggest fear is this will tip him over the edge again and I can't repeat the last week. I gently place the sandwich down on my dressing table while my mind races to find words that'll make this feel better in some way.

"Vass, listen . . ." I begin.

His eyes finally meet mine, but I wasn't prepared for the anger I see there and I close my mouth immediately. "You're fucking pregnant?" he spits, venom in his words. "I wondered what you were hiding behind your back. I wish I hadn't looked." He shakes his head angrily. "You think I can be a father? Look at the state of me."

"Vass, I know it's a huge shock, it is for me too," I say calmly.

"I bet it is," he mutters, his tone laced with disgust. I frown, not sure what he means, but he continues to rant. "It's more than shock, Alivia. It's the worst news I've ever had . . . EVER!" he yells, turning away from me and throwing the plastic stick across the room.

"It's not great news—"

"You've got that right."

I take another calming breath. "But you don't need to be so rude. I'm still processing it myself, so maybe we should talk about this later when we've both had a little time."

He turns to face me, a cruel grin on his face. "There is nothing to talk about. I thought you were different, but it turns out you were just like the rest," he spits out.

"You're angry, I get it."

"You think this will pin me down, Liv?" he asks, his tone now mocking. "You think I'll change for you and be a family man?"

I cross my arms and stare at the floor, determined not to get upset in front of him. "Nope, that's not what I think at all."

"Because let me tell you something, it won't, so save yourself the heartache," he says angrily. "Save us both from it."

"You should leave," I begin, "before you say something you might later regret."

"We're not having this fucking kid, Alivia. Get rid of it. I don't care what it costs, just get fucking rid." His words hit me like punches and I flinch, blinking away the tears that balance carelessly on my lashes.

Vass's mobile lets out a shrill ring, and we both glance to the table where it vibrates. He reaches for it and answers the call. "Yeah?" He falls silent and presses his lips together. "Right, okay, I'm on my way." He drops his mobile on the bed and then begins to pull on his clothes.

I watch silently, reeling from his vicious outburst. "My grandmother's in hospital," he mutters.

I only spoke to her this morning, and she sounded fine. "Oh, god, is she okay?" I ask in a panic, suddenly forgetting our current drama. I go to my wardrobe and rummage through.

"What are you doing?" he asks.

"Coming with you," I say. We have to put our problems aside for a moment and deal with his grandmother.

"No," he says sharply, as I pull out a shirt. "Clarisse will come. I'm fine from here," he says, looking away.

I don't know how I feel about his sudden reluctance to involve me in his family. I've spoken to her every day, and I've grown fond of her. "Vass, I want to see her."

"I don't want you there," he mutters, gathering some of his belongings.

"I spend a week not sleeping and comforting you, letting you use my body to distract you from drinking yourself stupid, and now, I can fuck off?"

"I hate it when you curse like that," he mutters, shaking his head.

"Well, apparently, I'm not what you're looking for anyway, so I'm not too worried about that," I snap, slamming the wardrobe closed.

Vass sighs and buries his head in his hands. "It's a clusterfuck, Liv. We've messed it all up."

I hate him in this moment. I let anger take over, grabbing his arm and tugging him towards the door. "Just go. Leave. I want you to leave," I yell, shoving him through the doorway. I slam the door in his surprised face and slide down it until my arse hits the floor. I rest my head on my knees and let silent tears fall freely. The week's been so brutal, and I'm exhausted. Once again, I let Vass Fraser use me and hurt me and I feel foolish.

Vass

I wink at the pretty nurse as she hands me the pot of pills for my grandmother. "Please make sure she takes them as soon as she wakes up. Maybe she'll shout at you a little less," she instructs.

"I doubt that very much, but I'd much rather she yells at me than at you." I watch the sway of her arse as she leaves.

Three days I've been here, only going home to shower and change before returning to sit with my dying grandmother. The doctors tell me she won't get out of here, but there's a lot of fight left in her. I can tell every time she's asked to take her medication and she causes a fuss.

"Stop flirting with the nurses," she grits out, opening her eyes.

"Were you pretending to sleep so you couldn't take your meds?" I ask suspiciously.

"There is no point, they don't help," she tells me again.

"Just do as you're told for once." I sigh, grabbing her frail hand and emptying the tablets into her palm. She begrudgingly throws them into her mouth and sits while I hold the glass for her to swallow the water. The door opens slightly, and I turn just in time to see the back of a female's head as she leaves.

I frown at my grandmother, and she gives me a guilty smile. I place the glass down and head towards the door just in time to catch a glimpse of Alivia rounding the corner. I run to catch her up. "Alivia?"

She turns to me slowly, looking unsure, so I smile to show her I'm not about to scream at her again. "Sorry, I was just here to see your grandmother," she mutters.

"I didn't know you were in London," I say, surprised at the relief I feel at seeing her.

"I'm just visiting Clarisse and thought that I'd come and see Angela while I'm here." I can't help but look down at her stomach, but of course, it's flat.

"Clarisse didn't say," I mutter.

"I asked her not to," she admits, and I nod in understanding. It's the least I deserve.

"She's awake if you want to see her now," I offer.

"It's fine, I'll come back later when you've gone."

She turns to walk away, and my heart skips a beat. I realise I don't want her to leave. "Wait, can we talk?"

She shakes her head sadly. "It's not a good idea, Vass. Give your grandmother my love."

That feeling of loss begins to overwhelm me again and I take a few deep breaths before running after her. I grab hold of her wrist, and she spins to face me angrily, ready to fight. I release her and hold up my hands in apology. "We have to talk, Liv. We can't leave it like this."

"You said all you need to. I'm okay with it, Vass. Let's just call it a day and go our separate ways."

"No," I snap, and she arches a brow. "We'll talk now, Alivia."

She shakes her head in annoyance. "Fine, let's talk, Vass. I know I have plenty to say." She marches off in front, and I hesitate before following. Somehow, I feel I might regret forcing this conversation.

Alivia sits on a wooden bench, staring straight ahead. I lower beside her. It's clear she doesn't want to even look at me right now, and I don't blame her. "I was in shock. I didn't expect it," I begin to say, and she laughs sarcastically, shaking her head again in disappointment. "You told me you were on the pill, so I was blindsided."

"I was on the pill," she growls. "I didn't lie to you."

"Then how the hell did it happen?" I ask.

"I don't know, I'm not a doctor," she snaps.

"Maybe I jumped to conclusions," I admit, and she scoffs, "but I made it very clear I don't want children. There's no room in my future for kids."

"You think I want this?" she snaps, looking at me like I've lost my mind. "With you, of all people?" That hurts, but I keep quiet. "I live with my parents, Vass. I'm not set up to have a kid on my own, and for you to accuse me of trying to trap you, of doing this on purpose . . ." she trails off, glaring ahead again.

"I shouldn't have gone off at you like I did. I have no excuse apart from being completely scared shitless. I panicked and my mouth ran away with me."

"What about the part where you told me to get rid of it?" she asks. I hesitate, and she laughs coldly. "I didn't think so," she says, standing. "You meant it all, so don't sit here and feed me any more of your bullshit. I'm done with it, and I'm done with you."

"Alivia, we've got to be grown up here and talk—"

"Grown up?" she repeats looking astounded. "You're living your life as a playboy and I'm the one who needs to grow up? Newsflash, I didn't tantrum when I discovered I was pregnant, that was all you. And just so you know, I don't have to do anything I don't want to, and that includes getting rid of my child." She begins to walk away but thinks better of it, spinning to face me. "I wish I'd never met you. Going for that interview at Glamour was supposed to be my fresh start, and somehow, I ended up here with my heart in tatters as a single parent. I think I hate you," she whispers. I hang my head to avoid seeing the tears in her eyes as the guilt overwhelms me. "I was going to pass these to your grandmother to forward on, but as you're here, I forgot to give you these," she adds, reaching into her handbag and pulling out a plastic bag. I open it and peer inside, finding the car keys to her company car and her engagement ring inside.

"Alivia, you can keep these," I say.

She shakes her head. "Thanks, but like I said, I don't want anything from you. I never have."

My mobile rings and I pull it from my pocket, frustration clear in my voice as I answer. "Mr. Fraser, it's the hospital. Your grandmother's taken a turn."

"Christ, okay, I'm on my way back," I mutter.

Alivia is already walking away, and this time, I let her.

I go back to my grandmother's room to find two doctors and a nurse standing by her bed with their faces solemn. A doctor approaches me. "I'm so sorry, Mr. Fraser, there was nothing else we could do," he says. "She passed peacefully."

They begin to exit the room, leaving me alone with her. I take her hand, and it still feels warm. I must sit there for some time before a nurse comes in with a clear plastic bag. "These are her possessions," she says quietly, placing them on the bed. I give a slight smile, taking it. "Is there anyone we can call for you?" I shake my head. The one person I want to speak to hates me right now. "Well, take your time."

"I'm done," I mutter, standing and kissing my grandmother one last time on the head. "Thanks for everything. You've all been amazing. I know she was difficult but she would have been grateful too."

When I get back to The Luxe, I head straight for my office and empty the plastic bag onto my desk. Inside is her jewellery—she always loved her jewellery—and it suddenly hits me that I have no one to pass any of this to. There're two envelopes inside the bag, one addressed to me, and one addressed to Liv. I frown. Why would she leave a letter for Alivia?

I rip open the one addressed to me, scanning over it and realise exactly why Liv has a letter. I laugh to myself. The sneaky old girl just had to give it one last shot.

Clarisse comes in and stops when she sees me. "Oh, I didn't expect you in. How's your grandmother?" she asks.

"She's passed," I say, and Clarisse looks horrified.

She gasps. "Oh god, Vass, I'm so sorry. I didn't realise. Are you okay?"

I shrug. "I think it's still sinking in. She was ready. Her pain was too much, so I'm pleased it's come to an end for her sake, but I'm going to miss her so much." Clarisse takes a seat.

"And you're not feeling the need to reach for the bottle?" she asks cautiously.

I shake my head. "I've thought about it, but I'm controlling it well. You didn't tell me Liv was in London." She looks away, guilt all over her face. "It's fine. I know you were protecting her. I get it. She came to the hospital."

Clarisse winces. "How did it go?"

"Terrible. It's what I deserve. I've handled the whole thing badly. When is she leaving?"

"This evening. I think she was meeting her ex, something about getting the last of her stuff."

"I need to see her. My grandmother left her something," I explain.

"You didn't hear it from me, but I'm meeting her at my place in half an hour. I promised her dinner."

Chapter Twenty-One

Alivia

One thing I won't miss about London is the traffic. I pull my suitcase up the garden path to Clarisse's, thankful that I'm finally done. Getting my last few clothes from Daniel's place was unbelievably awkward, but once I'd made the decision to move back home to Brighton, there was no point in leaving anything here in London. It's not like I'll be coming back anytime soon.

I let myself in to Clarisse's place, dumping my case in the hall. I decide to make a start on dinner. Since being pregnant, I'm hungry all the time. I managed to get an early scan in Brighton which confirmed I'm eight weeks already. That pinpoints the pregnancy to when I got sick and Vass came to look after me, explaining why the pill failed. It never even crossed my mind at the time.

"You took your time saying your goodbyes?" Vass stands as I enter the kitchen, taking me by surprise.

My heart immediately speeds up. "Why are you here?"

"My grandmother passed earlier today," he mutters, and I lower onto the nearest stool. I feel sad I didn't get to say goodbye.

"I'm sorry for your loss."

"I came to give you this," he says, sliding a white envelope towards me with my name scrawled across the front.

"What is it?" I ask, picking it up.

"It was with her belongings. I got one too."

"Do you want me to open it now in front of you?" I ask, and he nods. I guess we're both wondering why his grandmother left me a letter. I fold out a pretty piece of writing paper and glance over the handwritten note. As the words penetrate my brain, I gasp, slapping a hand over my mouth. "Well, what's it say?" Vass probes.

I shake my head, tears filling my eyes. "I'm so sorry, Vass. I didn't ask her to do this. Please don't hate me." I hand him the letter. "I'll sign it straight over to you, I promise."

Vass smiles and takes the letter, placing it on the countertop. "I know what it says, Alivia." He rounds the table and takes my hands. "I don't want you to sign it over to me. My grandmother wanted you to have it, so I want you to have it."

"I'm moving back to Brighton. I've made plans to move into an apartment," I say, my brain racing at a hundred miles an hour.

"Stay," he says. "Stay in London. Live in my grandmother's . . ." he laughs, "*your* mansion."

I feel sick as I shake my head in protest. It's too much to take in. "I need my parents, Vass. They'll help me with this baby."

"Liv, you're the owner of a million-pound stately home. Move your parents in. They can live in the west wing. I'd really like it if you stuck around."

"Why?"

"Maybe I was a little harsh before, Liv. A lot harsh, actually."

"What are you talking about?" I ask, confused.

"Us . . . the baby . . . I don't know exactly." He gives a nervous laugh. "I was wrong. I don't want you to terminate the baby. It took a while to process, but now I have, I think I'd like to try."

"I'm not an experiment," I mutter, trying to pull away, but he holds me tighter.

"It's all coming out wrong," he says. "It always does when I'm around you. All I know is when I'm not with you, Liv, I can't breathe. It's like all the things that made me so fucking happy before do nothing for me now. And all I can think about is you. I crave you, Liv, and only you. I don't know what sort of father I'll be, but I know I want this baby. I want you both."

His words pull at my heart, and I blink the tears away. "It's not that easy, Vass. You've hurt me so much."

He takes my face in his hands and raises my head to look at him. "I know. I've been a dick. But I'll spend every day making it up to you. I swear. Just give me one chance to make it all right."

"I need time," I whisper.

He nods eagerly. "Of course. Whatever you need, it's yours."

"This is a complete one-eighty from what you've been saying for weeks," I remind him. "You confuse me."

"It's not an excuse, but my grandmother being sick consumed me for the last week. Now she's gone, I realise what I wanted all along. When you left before, I tried to block you out. I convinced myself I didn't need you or love you, but I was so fucking wrong. I was hurting because you'd left, and I just didn't know how that felt, so I drank. And despite everything, you still helped me. I've never met anyone who cares so fucking much that they'd hurt themselves to save the other."

"I've always been a mug," I mutter.

"No," he whispers desperately. "No, you're not a mug, Liv. You're fucking perfect. And I'm an idiot to think I could be touched by you and walk away unscathed. You're like nothing I've ever known, and I want to spend forever with you. I'm nothing without you, Liv. Nothing." He takes a breath before adding, "If you can tell me right now that you hate me, that you don't feel anything towards me, I'll walk away. I'll leave you alone." I don't reply because I know I can't say those words out loud. If I did, they'd be a lie. "Do you love me, Alivia?" he pushes.

Tears slip down my cheeks and he wipes them with his thumbs. "You're not playing fair," I whisper. "It's not as simple as that."

"I just need to know how you feel. Am I fighting a losing battle?" I shake my head once. "So, you love me?" he repeats. I nod, and he releases a shaky breath. "I love you so much, Liv. I promise, I'll make up for everything."

He places kisses across my face, and I don't have the strength to stop him. My heart hurts, but at the same time, it feels hopeful. Maybe his grandmother was right—maybe Vass does love me. All I know for certain is I love him with my whole heart, and I'm not strong enough to walk away again.

One month later...
Vass

I place the iPad in front of me, moving my coffee to the side. I never read the gossip columns, but today, I'm happy, and I want to see what the world is saying. I smile as the headline appears.

'A Fairy Tale ending for Vassivia. Vass Fraser finally married the love of his life, Alivia Caldwell, yesterday in a beautiful ceremony in their London mansion. The happy couple opted for a small gathering, inviting only close friends and family members. However, the couple posted a snapshot of their wedding bands on their social media accounts before jetting off to an undisclosed location for their honeymoon. The pair haven't had a smooth ride, but it's clear to see their troubles seem to be firmly behind them. Caldwell was spotted out in London earlier this week sporting a very small bump, and Fraser later confirmed the pair are expecting their first child. In a short

statement released by the pair's press office, Fraser said, "I am very happy and excited to announce that Alivia and I are expecting our first child. We're very much in love, and we're excited to see where our future will take us together as three." Here at The London Enquiry, we'd like to wish the couple all the best and a very heartfelt congratulations on their wedding.'

A note from me to you

For those that already know my work, Lying to Love You is completely different to anything else I've written. It was nice to break out of my comfort zone and write something other than MC and Mafia. Vass and Alivia have consumed me for the last few months, even though I originally released it back in 2019. To dive back into their story and re-edit as well as make some small changes, has been a journey. It's one of my favourite books and I plan on a second book to catch up with how their lives are working out, so watch this space...

I'm a UK author, based in Nottinghamshire. I live with my husband of many years, our two teenage boys and our four little dogs. I write MC and Mafia romance with plenty of drama and chaos. I also love to read similar books. Before I became a full-time author, I was a teaching assistant working in a primary school.

If you'd like to follow my writing journey, join my readers group on Facebook. You'll find the link at the beginning of this book under Social Media.

Popular books by Nicola Jane

The Kings Reapers MC

Riggs' Ruin https://mybook.to/RiggsRuin
Capturing Cree https://mybook.to/CapturingCree
Wrapped in Chains https://mybook.to/WrappedinChains
Saving Blu https://mybook.to/SavingBlu
Riggs' Saviour https://mybook.to/RiggsSaviour
Taming Blade https://mybook.to/TamingBlade
Misleading Lake https://mybook.to/MisleadingLake

Surviving Storm
https://mybook.to/SurvivingStorm
Ravens Place https://mybook.to/RavensPlace
Playing Vinn https://mybook.to/PlayingVinn

The Perished Riders MC
Maverick https://mybook.to/Maverick-Perished
Scar https://mybook.to/Scar-Perished
Grim https://mybook.to/Grim-Perished
Ghost https://mybook.to/GhostBk4
Dice https://mybook.to/DiceBk5
Arthur https://mybook.to/ArthurNJ

The Hammers MC (Splintered Hearts Series)
Cooper https://mybook.to/CooperSHS
Kain https://mybook.to/Kain
Tanner https://mybook.to/TannerSH

Printed in Great Britain
by Amazon